"WHAT IS IT ABOUT YOU, MR. LOWELL, THAT OTHER WOMEN FIND SO ENCHANTING?"

Taking a step closer to Julia, Jamie gazed deeply into her eyes, making it impossible for her to look away.

"Well, first of all," he began, "I start by telling the lady how beautiful she is. How the black of her eyes is like the rarest of pearls lying safe and warm beneath the azure blue of the sea."

Julia listened, knowing all the while that he had fined and honed his craft until every wooing word slipped like poetry from his lips. And yet she couldn't help feeling affected by them.

He reached for the glass behind him and dipped his the wine. Mesmerized, Juli Jamie bring his hand to her ever so softly rub a sprinkle along her lower lip.

"May I?" Jamie didn't bot for the refusal they both kne incapable of offering, befor forward and, with his tong the wine from Julia's mouth.

The Fictitious Marquis

ALINA ADAMS

AVON BOOKS ◆ NEW YORK

THE FICTITIOUS MARQUIS is an original publication of Avon Books. This work has never before appeared in book form. This work is a novel. Any similarity to actual persons or events is purely coincidental.

AVON BOOKS
A division of
The Hearst Corporation
1350 Avenue of the Americas
New York, New York 10019

Copyright © 1995 by Alina Sivorinovsky
Published by arrangement with the author
Library of Congress Catalog Card Number: 94-96559
ISBN: 0-380-77811-4

First Avon Books Printing: June 1995

AVON TRADEMARK REG. U.S. PAT. OFF. AND IN OTHER COUNTRIES, MARCA REGISTRADA, HECHO EN U.S.A.

Printed in the U.S.A.

RA 10 9 8 7 6 5 4 3 2 1

1

When the hangman's noose was finally slipped over Jamie Lowell's neck, he'd already imagined the act so many times that it almost felt familiar.

Tightly braided rope sliced into his skin, scraping Jamie's neck as raw as both the wrists bound behind his back. A nail protruded from the center plank of the gallows platform, piercing his right foot. Jamie tried shifting his weight to the left, but succeeded merely in slicing the sharpened tip across the most sensitive part of his sole. His toes curled, the entire leg jerking reflexively, then slammed back down on the nail with an even greater force than before.

Jamie gave up. He reasoned that, in a few moments, that minor aggravation would be the least of his troubles. Instead, Jamie attempted to count his blessings, which granted, at this dark moment in time, appeared rather sparse. The best he could think of was that, at least, he had been spared the indignity of a public execution. During the past months spent shackled at Newgate, Jamie had seen enough such spectacles through the bars of his cell to understand that escaping a similar fate was indeed a great fortune.

On days when a public hanging was expected, every window overlooking the prison was booked in advance by young bloods seeking a sensation, and by the occasional sober looking tradesman come to enjoy the sight of justice catching up with his less fortunate brethren. The mob gathered overnight and pressed up against the barrier in front of the scaffold. In the hours before an open execution, prison inmates struggled to snatch a wink of sleep, squeezing both palms against their ears in a futile attempt to block out the constant, blood-hungry roaring of the crowd. As time grew nearer to the appointed hour, the throng grew more excited, more ferocious, more ribald. As if the entire procedure were a holiday spectacle staged especially for their amusement.

By dawn, thousands of faces breathed as one, eyes tied to the back door of the prison, necks twisted from the effort of craning up, always in search of the better view. They cheered as the hangman appeared, dragged his chained victim to the noose, and solemnly cut through the bindings—only to entangle the poor soul in a much deadlier trap moments later.

It truly was no small blessing that some peculiar quirk of fate had placed Jamie's hanging hour at such a time when a faster and thus less public death served the interests of all involved.

He felt strangely calm, considering his executioner was already climbing down the platform, ready to spring a latch beneath the trap door and send Jamie swinging.

He heard the latch being pulled, and wondered if he should close his eyes. But there was no time to deeply contemplate the quandary as Jamie's feet slipped out from under him, and he dropped downwards. A burning sensation seized his throat, strangely similar to the one he got from drinking liquor too fast. Jamie's Adam's apple crushed into his windpipe and he instinctively opened his mouth, trying to lap in a gulp or two of air, but he accomplished nothing save biting his tongue.

His heart pounded madly, seemingly bent on exploding out of his chest. His eyes crossed, blurring his vision to the point where all colors faded into a distorted gray. He flailed madly, finally understanding at this late date in life why it was that every fish he'd ever caught always did the same, and tried to free his arms, his legs, anything to make the pain lessen.

And then he was falling, the ground flying up to meet Jamie's face at a speed he never would have guessed possible for such a previously settled object.

He hit the dirt on his stomach, feeling the last bits of air still left in his lungs being smacked outward. The rope about his neck loosened just a little, but it was enough for Jamie to gratefully gulp in as much sweet air as he could. Dirt coated his mouth and nostrils. He breathed in air and coughed out mud. His head still spun from the unexpected plunge downwards.

Eyes only barely starting to focus, Jamie painfully rolled over on his back. If he remembered correctly, the magistrate at his sentencing had pronounced that Jeremy Lowell was to be hanged by his neck until dead. He did not think he was dead. But, then again, maybe the professionals knew best.

Jamie squinted upwards. The trap door of the platform still swung back and forth, squeaking horribly in each direction. Immediately above it stood the hangman, knife in one hand, severed end of Jamie's tattered noose in the other.

"Jamie Lowell?" The first odd thing about the voice was that it came not from above, but from beside him. The second oddity was that, unless Jamie had truly taken leave of his senses in all this excitement, the voice most certainly belonged to a female.

Agonizingly, he forced his head to the side for a better look.

He saw skirts. Many, many of them, one on top of the other, as was the style of the day. In this case, the outermost skirt, a pale cream of pink, was curved away from the front and caught up on either side at the back, so that it fell in three large loops, showing a petticoat intricately embroidered with roses and lilies. This same pattern was repeated further upwards, on the puffed sleeves, and on the long apron of sheer, embroidered linen that accessorized the open-front gown.

So taken was Jamie by the grandness of the material—

and, after prison, anything not made of gray burlap probably would have struck him as exquisite—that it took him a while to finish glancing upward and actually acknowledge the young lady inside of the gown. She could not have been more than a year past twenty, with ebony black hair that, no matter the efforts of pins and bonnets, still gave the impression of being wildly uncontrollable and spilling onto a face dominated by a pair of eyes so equally black that they appeared out of place, gleaming as they did above the sun kissed spatter of freckles across her nose and cheeks.

She stared down critically at Jamie, studying him in the same manner his late mum had once judged a piece of day-old meat that the butcher held out for her inspection.

Finally, the young woman sighed, snapping open her parasol, and fanning it dismissively in Jamie's direction. "Very well, then," she told the hangman. "I suppose he shall have to do."

It took the strength of two Charlies to drag Jamie Lowell to his feet and into the single room of Newgate Prison reserved for conversation. The young lady stood waiting for him, a look of disgust on her face serving as instantaneous explanation for why she'd declined taking a seat on the sole mold-covered chair in the room. Her parasol continued bobbing at a most frantic pace, stirring up a wind that caused the lace fichu framing her throat to flap like the sail of a fishing boat lost in a storm, yet succeeding little in keeping the general stench of the room from the lady's delicate nostrils.

She said, "My name, Mr. Lowell, is Julia Highsmith."

Not known about St. Giles's Rookery for his ability to keep a civil tongue, whether he were bosky on Madame Geneva, Strip-me-Naked, Blue Ruin, or merely on the intoxication of hearing his own tongue wag, Jamie blurted the first thought that came to his head, "Was I mistaken then in my hearing about town that fine ladies of the *ton* such as yourself, Miss Highsmith, dare never to speak to a male stranger lest previously introduced?"

"Considering the uniqueness of our meeting site, Mr.

Lowell, I daresay we may consider our introduction to have been performed by no less than a servant of His Majesty the hangman, and pray let us proceed to the issue at hand."

Jamie turned sideways, so that she might look at his still shackled hands, and replied, "I am humbly at your service, m'lady."

She paused for only a moment, seemingly gathering strength for the delicate task ahead, then abruptly jerked up her chin, forcing the words in a hurried torrent, lest she give herself a chance to reconsider. "I come to you, Mr. Lowell, with a proposition of business. In exchange for my securing your freedom from the gallows, and indeed, from Newgate Prison altogether, you are to render me a single favor, the terms of which I will further outline to you, upon your agreeing to accept the bargain."

"I continue to listen humbly, m'lady."

"Upon my father's death three years ago, he entrusted the capital of my inheritance, some one hundred thousand pounds, to his younger brother, my uncle Collin, the duke of Alamain, under the terms that not a farthing of it were to come my way until the day that I should marry a man my uncle deems agreeable. Presently, any expense, ranging from the running of my household to my purchasing a single fruit ice from Gunther's, must first be submitted for my uncle's approval. I am sure you would agree, Mr. Lowell, that it is a most uncomfortable manner in which to live."

Without a trace of gaiety in his expression, Jamie commiserated, "Aye, surely myself and each of my mates at the gallows do sympathize with your dire and tragic predicament."

She bristled at his thinly disguised rebuke. "I assure you, Mr. Lowell, that I desire the sympathy of neither you nor your mates, nor do I deserve to feel the object of your contempt."

"On what grounds could a ruffian of my stature and situation ever show any cause for lavishing contempt upon a lady of your obvious high breeding and manner? Pray tell me, Miss Highsmith, in honor of what occasion have you deigned to visit our humble lodgings at Newgate? Could it be that the fashionable sport of the upper classes has progressed from fox hunts to hangings?"

"For a man with his life still only moments from the noose, your tongue does run to the glib, Mr. Lowell."

He took no umbrage at her saucy attempt to plant him a verbal facer, explaining, "One hour ago, Miss Highsmith, I did not imagine myself to be still breathing upon this minute of the clock. So you see, all that transpires after is mere folly."

She sighed, stealing a glance at the door in regret over ever having initiated this conversation, but, nevertheless, resolved to continue. "In order that I may claim my inheritance, it is necessary that I make a good marriage and bring it on a platter for my uncle to devour. In the past, I have lived most comfortably off an allowance he grants me monthly, and had no cause to trouble myself with the provision of my father's will. However, recently, it has become imperative that I acquire a sum of money that can only be realized with the bequest from my father's estate. To that result, I am compelled to acquire a husband as soon as possible."

Jamie felt certain that Miss Highsmith could not possibly be waltzing about the subject he thought she was.

Yet, although she focused her eyes on every corner in the room except for Jamie's face, Julia kept talking. "In exchange for escaping the gallows, you are to marry me and accompany me on a honeymoon to France—during which time you are not to question any of the actions I undertake there, nor are you ever to repeat them to another living soul. You will then remain my husband for the period of one calendar year. Should, during the course of that year, you perform any deed which might cause the *ton,* but most importantly my uncle, to doubt the legitimate state of our marriage, I will personally see you returned to prison and hung up for all to cheer. However, if you acquiesce to your part of the bargain, at the end of one year, you will receive one thousand pounds to disappear from England and be presumed dead. Agreed?"

Jamie only wished all those who'd known him before

could be present to spy Jeremy Lowell without a word in his head.

Finally, he stammered, "But surely, I am not the sort of fiancé your esteemed uncle would recognize fit to be presented upon his silver platter."

"I did not choose you at random, Mr. Lowell, amongst the remaining refuse in this institution, but with a purpose. The magistrate tells me you are by far the cleverest, quickest of tongue scoundrel ever to stand in his court. Your crime is separating maidens from their life savings with such charm and sweetness, that, rather than feeling in the hips, they come instead to speak in your defense before the bench. Truly a rake in possession of such talents can cajole one elderly duke into doing his bidding. Furthermore, I surely do not intend to present you to my uncle dressed as you are today. We have three months in which I am to see you washed, deloused, outfitted, and tutored in the finer graces, until you truly can masquerade as a titled gentleman for the space of the necessary year."

"One more question, m'lady? Would it not be simpler indeed, for your ladyship to engage a gentleman of her born class for such an endeavor?"

"It would not," Julia lectured as if he were a particularly soft-in-the-head schoolboy. "For, if I were to marry a gentleman of my own class, he inevitably would wish to stay married for a period longer than the necessary year."

"Are you truly that irresistible, Miss Highsmith?"

She disregarded his barb. "I do not wish, at this time, to marry, and, were it not for the money I need, would have chosen not to."

"And may I inquire as to the nature of business—in France, did you say?—that forces your ladyship into such a devious arrangement?"

"You may inquire, but be forewarned of all such queries going unanswered." For the first time since he'd come in, Julia actually raised her eyes to meet Jamie's. "Well, then, what shall it be? I must be going. I have no intention of damaging my reputation by being spotted driving through London so well after sunset."

He thought about it during the time it took the clock on

St. Sepulchre's Church to chime three in the afternoon. Julia crossed her arms and waited, face set in an expression of impatience. She tapped her foot against the dirt-covered floor, shaking it lightly after each tap, lest the filth settle permanently, and drummed five fingers along the rim of her parasol.

Jamie cleared his throat, feeling the nerves that deserted him at the gallows finally make their appearance, and asked, not solely in jest, "Would it be too-late now to return to the noose?"

As secrecy about Jamie's true origin was the most important aspect to making Julia's plan a success, no sooner had he agreed to trade a hanging for matrimony, when Jamie found himself being rather unceremoniously wrapped in a moth-chewn carpet by Miss Highsmith's coachman. The man in the three-cornered hat and French gloves then proceeded to hoist the awkwardly rolled bundle upon his shoulder, walk silently down the halls and through the back gate of Newgate Prison, and, sniffing distastefully, stuff Jamie into the rear of Miss Highsmith's carriage.

Over the whinnying of her four chestnuts, Jamie distinctively thought he heard a woman struggling to control her laughter.

His intended, no doubt.

Mouth choked with carpeting, Jamie nevertheless managed to spit out, "I daresay, Miss Highsmith, I was rather hoping for a smaller, sportier curricle. Or a phaeton, perhaps?"

"Oh, the devil with you." Julia shoved the carpet that was Jamie deeper into her carriage.

Face completely covered, he focused his efforts on avoiding suffocation. Eventually, the painful bouncing about made Jamie think that they had left the pavement of London, and were progressing somewhere into the countryside.

Robbed of both his sense of sight and hearing, he was forced to rely solely on smell. And, as the air no longer reeked of week-old fish heads and dishwater, he felt safe in presuming that they had abandoned the slums and alleys of Clare Market, St. Giles's Rookery, Clerkenwell, and, indeed, all of the East End. Although, without aid of the sun and moon, he couldn't discern whether they were heading north, south, east, or west. Wherever it was, he reassured himself, it could only be an improvement over standing chained to the moldy wall of a prison cell. They would probably have food. Of course, Miss Highsmith had offered nary a word in the bargain about meals being included. Which was a shame, since, anticipating being dead by three, Jamie had not eaten for hours.

Finally, after what had seemed like a fortnight of struggling to draw breath and only inhaling a mouthful of attic dust, Jamie felt the carriage draw to a stop. He heard the horses' reins being tightened about the carriage brake, and Miss Highsmith disembarking. Jamie, unsure of what the role called for him to do next, mutely sat and waited for his orders. Besides the carpet dust, Jamie's nostrils sucked in a whiff of freshly cut greenery, as well as a cornucopia of wildflowers and recently chopped wood. Now that the carriage had stopped, he could also hear chirping birds, accompanied by the rustle of squirrels as they darted through the trees.

"Go on with you, then." A French glove yanking the carpet away from Jamie's face identified the speaker as the formerly silent coachman. "I am not meaning to carry your meat and bones a second time. Go on. Moses will show you."

Moses, he peered into the darkness and guessed, would be the sour-faced butler waiting beside the carriage.

Jamie untangled himself from the carpet, stepped outside, and, mindful of the pristine splendor of Moses' uniform, rather self-consciously dusted himself off. After two months of starvation rations, the prison-gray shirt and pants that once had been only a single size too large, now necessitated Jamie's holding his trousers up by the waist, lest they slip down. He wasn't wearing any shoes, and his feet were covered with sewage and filth.

Moses, clearly, was far from impressed.

It was too dark now for Jamie to make out every detail

of his new residence. He did notice a splendid arch of
sweet-smelling ivy growing over the front door, past the
iron balconies that decorated every window of the house.
Each window was constructed out of a dozen individual
panes of glass.

And for Jamie, who'd made do for seven and twenty
years with oiled paper to keep out the wind and cold, it
were those many panes of glass that finally obligated him
stop and think about exactly what sort of bargain he had
agreed to.

Miss Highsmith may have only driven him a few miles
from Jamie's old home in St. Giles, but she might as well
have flapped her arms and carried him to the wilds of Af-
rica, for all of Jamie's familiarity with her way of life.

And now he had three months in which to learn it well
enough to fool a duke. Or else return to London.

And the noose.

2

Julia Highsmith waited until she had locked the bedroom door behind her, removed her capote and demicornette, and splashed her face with two handfuls of cold water from the basin before she allowed herself the luxury of shaking so violently that she needed to clutch onto the table or risk collapsing. The cold water stung her face, dripping down Julia's cheeks and chin to form minuscule damp circles upon her chemisette. Her heart pounded against her rib cage, sending the lace and silk rose flounces of her bodice bouncing in rhythm. She squeezed both hands into fists. The intense trembling painfully forced her fingernails into her palms.

She had never bought a man before.

And not just any man. A convict.

Truly, such was not the manner in which Julia had, at sunup, intended to spend her day.

Over breakfast of pineapple in cream with Aunt Salome, the most strenuous topic of conversation had revolved about the Philharmonic Society's finally allowing vocal items to be performed at their concerts, and the shocking rumors of Princess Caroline locking Her Royal Highness Princess Charlotte into a bedroom with Captain Hesse— "The duke of York's illegitimate son, that chap is, you mark my words," Salome swore—and telling her young daughter to amuse herself.

Miriam's letter arrived midway through their meal, carried not by mail coach, but by an out-of-breath French courier who apparently knew no English beyond "pence, quid, shilling," and obviously assumed standing about expectantly with one palm facing upwards to be a universal hint of remuneration.

Salome handed the boy a few coins, and ordered Cook to fix him a plate in the kitchen. She slit the top of Miriam's envelope with a silver and pearl opener, carefully unfolding the much-wrinkled pages and smoothing them out against the dining room table's edge before preparing to read out loud. Julia, always interested in her cousin's letters, filled as they inevitably were with the latest gossip and fashions sweeping France, eagerly pushed away her plate and leaned forwards, elbows resting on the table, her ebony eyes sparkling in anticipation.

Equally as interested in hearing what her daughter had to say, Salome began reading Miriam's letter in her usual, buoyant tones, rushing through the perfunctory salutations and inquiries about the household's health, to reach the far more interesting middle. Only this time, instead of pressing the letter to her chest and smiling mischievously at Julia over the top of the paper, keeping her in delicious suspense before revealing just what sort of new French intrigue Miriam had disclosed, Salome stopped short, head jerking still as if coming in contact with an actual, physical barrier.

She knitted her brows, reading the paragraph again for confirmation, and then a third time in disbelief. Her eyes grew wide. She inhaled sharply, forgetting momentarily to exhale.

"What is it, Salome?" Julia half rose from the chair, reaching for her aunt. "Are you ill?"

Ever since her doctor had diagnosed Salome's heart condition a few years earlier, Julia lived in constant fear that her aunt's every gasp was a symptom requiring immediate medical attention.

Salome shook her head, wordlessly sliding Miriam's letter across the sleekly polished table for Julia to read.

She snatched it up instantly, skimming the cream stationery, searching for the sentence or phrase that had so devastated Salome.

She located it quickly enough. How could anyone help but miss it, when the entire letter proved no more than a desperate cry for rescue. Stunned, Julia sat back down in her chair, swallowing hard and looking up at Salome. She said, "We must help her."

"Yes. Yes, I will go immediately to France. Perhaps—"

"You will do no such thing." Julia caught the harshness in her tone, and guiltily tempered it, remembering that she was, after all, the younger of the two, and possessed no business lecturing her aunt as if she were a child. Salome Weiss was as aware as anyone, of her doctor's edict, restricting traveling time to absolutely no more than an hour at a stretch. It was for that reason alone that, in the last few years, Miriam and her child had been the ones making the annual visit from France to England, and not the other way around. Softening, Julia explained, "You know you would never survive such a long journey, Salome. And what good could it do Miriam to have you fall ill on the way?"

They both knew the truth of Julia's words, although it took nearly an hour more for Salome to feel fully persuaded.

Finally, in an uncharacteristic burst of anger, she told Julia, "What a curse old age is. In my mind, I feel no older than when Miriam was still a child. And yet here I sit, useless."

"You are not useless. You may not be able to physically rescue Miriam. But you can help me think of an alternate plan."

Her aunt, shoulders slumped, forehead resting upon the palm of one hand, did not even bother to look up when she answered tonelessly, "There is nothing we can do."

"There must be." Julia drummed her fingernails on the table's edge, pecking out an obscure Rossini march, and insisted, "There simply must be some way. We are her only chance."

For over an hour, while the tea in their cups grew first lukewarm, then cold, then thoroughly undrinkable, Julia and Salome twisted their brains, attempting to squeeze any viable plot for saving Miriam and her little daughter, Alexia, from the fates promised them. Unfortunately, even as the maids were entering to clear the table, giving up any hope of Julia and Salome finishing their breakfasts, the best plan either one could imagine was the one least likely to be carried out. Because in order to see it through, they would need a great deal of money.

Julia pounded her fist in frustration against the table, feeling for all the world like a knight ready to ride out and do battle, only to realize he had no knowledge which way lay the front. "If only I might somehow convince Uncle Collin to part with the inheritance Papa left me."

"Not until you are married, and that's a fact."

"Then I shall go out and get married." Julia crossed her arms against her chest, digging both elbows into her stomach, the perfect picture of unstoppable determination. "He shall have to pass on my money then."

Despite the gravity of their situation, Salome could not help a brief smile at the child's impetuousness. Gently, she reminded, "It calls for a groom, as well as a bride, to make a wedding."

"London is crawling with basket scramblers and gazetted fortune hunters in Dun territory who would leap at a chance for a well-breeched life, in exchange for marriage to me, and a moratorium against asking too many questions."

Salome shook her head. "I would pray you to remember the most important provision of your father's testament. Not only must you marry in order to receive the monies promised, but you must marry a man your uncle deems suitable. The duke of Alamain would never agree to a rolled-up suitor who hasn't a feather to fly with, and, on that count, at least, I must wholeheartedly agree with him. I will not allow you to step into a lifetime of misery with a pink of fancy, *point-non-plus* Cyprian who cares not a bit for your happiness. It would be too dangerous. For all of us."

Grasping her aunt's unspoken meaning, Julia swore, "I

could keep it a secret from him. As Mama did from me all those years."

"And, in the end, the lying killed your mother, the same way that it might now kill my Miriam."

"No," Julia said. "I will not let that happen. Somehow, I will find a man to marry, and I will claim my inheritance. And I will do so in the three months' time that Miriam has left."

"It would necessitate a man of immense charm and wit to convince your uncle that he is worthy of your hand in marriage, and that a swift and speedy wedding is indeed for the best. The duke is no fool. I have not yet met a gentleman in the *beau monde* capable of charming a Banbury tale past Collin Highsmith."

Nevertheless, Julia insisted on drilling her aunt about every available—and needy—gentleman of the *ton* she had ever come in contact with, seriously considering every possibility, only to eventually come to the same realization about each of them. Those who might prove willing to enter into a sham marriage under such circumstances would never appear worthy enough for the duke, and those who might pass his stringent inspection had no reason for tying themselves down to a wife they barely knew.

Exasperated, Julia exclaimed, "If only we were in a fairy story where I might sketch the perfect candidate and watch him come to life off a piece of paper."

Salome soothingly stroked her niece's hair, assuring Julia that she had done all she could, and that Miriam and Alexia now lay in God's hands. But Julia refused to be appeased so easily.

Pleading multiple household obligations, Salome excused herself, rising from the table, and leaving the dining room. She clutched Miriam's letter to her bosom as if the folded sheets of paper were the absent girl herself, petting them gently with one hand, and sighing painfully.

Yet, because she knew her niece ever so well, as upset as she was, Salome took the time to pause at the door and warn, "Promise me that you will not, the minute I disappear from sight, rush off and commit some impetuous atrocity that we shall both regret in the more lucid light of day."

Sincerely, Julia replied, "I cannot think of a single atrocity to commit at this moment."

"Good. Let us hope that it remains so."

Julia watched her aunt go, convinced that somewhere, somehow, there was an exit to their dilemma. Hoping that a change of topic might prod her thoughts into a more productive direction, Julia reached for the newspaper Moses had long ago lain beside the now absolutely frigid teapot, and unenthusiastically began to read.

She knew, of course, that the *Examiner* was not exactly the sort of newspaper a young lady of her ilk should be reading. But she found its crusading editorials, with their unapologetically liberal slant, a great deal more entertaining than the repetitive drivel to be found in the *Morning Post*, or the *Entertaining Companion for the Fair Sex*.

Making the newspaper an even more illicit, and consequently exciting, read, was the knowledge that its publisher, Leigh Hunt, had, for the past two years, served a prison sentence for the crime of writing ill against the regent. Julia wondered if it were that experience that now prompted Mr. Hunt to join Mr. Jeremy Bentham in his quest for English prison reform, and she read their successive article on the topic with a great deal of curiosity.

While the initial paragraph was interesting enough, asserting that in no other European country were there so many offenses on the statute book, including stealing five shillings from a shop, that demanded the death penalty, it were the remainder of the piece that captured Julia's attention.

In a self-righteous fervor, Leigh Hunt expounded at length on the basic unfairness of the English class system, bringing as example a young, unnamed convict he'd met and gotten to know during the brief time when their jail sentences overlapped.

For nearly a full page of newspaper, Leigh Hunt went on and on, raving of the fellow's native intelligence, charm, and innate goodness, insisting that, had the poor soul been born of a different class, he might have been prime minister, rather than a convict. Surely, a young man capable of wooing nearly one hundred young ladies out of their admittedly meager dowries was a young man of talent and promise. Surely, he deserved more than the noose that now awaited him at Newgate prison?

It proved not at all difficult for Julia to pry the anonymous charmer's Christian name out of Leigh Hunt. As soon as Julia confessed a similar interest in prison reform—as well as a passionate fondness for the *Examiner* and the writings of Leigh Hunt in particular—the gentleman was more than happy to provide Miss Highsmith with further information. Almost as happy as the magistrate who'd sentenced Jeremy Lowell was to accept Julia's bribe in exchange for setting Jamie free.

The entire exercise took less than a day.

Julia barely had time to think about what she was doing, so preoccupied was she with actually doing it. And, if truth be confessed, she rather feared granting any thought to her actions, reluctant to come face-to-face with the audacity and multiple hazards of her endeavor.

She'd never even taken a thorough look at the man until the moment he crawled out of her carriage and stared up at Julia's home as if she'd delivered him to heaven.

Jamie Lowell must have stood twice her height, with each arm and thigh the size of a small cannon. Granted, he was dreadfully thin. Julia had been able to count every rib through the tatters of his prison uniform. But put some food in his stomach, and what was to stop Mr. Lowell from murdering them all in their beds and absconding with the family silver?

He certainly looked as if he harbored a temper. Julia supposed it was the red hair. And the jutting features that so reminded her of a hungry bird of prey.

The magistrate had told her Jamie was seven and twenty years of age. But there was something in his eyes, an exhaustion, that made him appear nearly a decade older.

She needed to handle him very carefully. Tell him too

little, and he wouldn't know enough to carry out his purpose. Tell him too much, and she risked losing control of the situation all together.

But the decision over when and how much to tell Jamie Lowell would necessarily come later.

Currently, Julia stood wrestling with the much more immediate dilemma of what exactly she might tell her Aunt Salome.

Much to her credit, Salome neither swooned, nor screamed, nor emitted any other sound she would have been perfectly justified to emit upon learning what Julia had done.

Instead, the older woman merely cocked her head and told her niece, "You know, of course, my darling, that this is not quite the same as those stray cats you so liked to bring home as a child."

An image of Jamie Lowell at the back door mewing for a saucer of milk made Julia smile, but she suppressed it. "Yes, Salome."

"This, I suppose, is what comes of letting an impressionable girl read the *Examiner*. My dear, what were you thinking?"

Truthfully, Julia replied, "I was thinking of Miriam. A man who charmed over one hundred ladies and Mr. Leigh Hunt and Mr. Jeremy Bentham, surely such a man should be able to do the same with my Uncle Collin. He already has all the tools necessary. And I can quickly teach him the finer points of acting a gentleman."

"Regardless of the esteemed Mr. Hunt's opinion on the matter, it will certainly take a great deal more time than a few hours to turn braff and scaff of Mr. Lowell's kind into a gentleman. Just where do you plan to accomplish this changing of a sow's ear into a silk purse, Julia?"

"Why, here, of course. Where else could I set him?"

Salome stared at her niece as if Julia had, on the spot, gone all about in the head. "Have you run mad, my dear? What if someone were to drop by for a visit or for tea during the day? What would we tell them? Why, the gossip alone would scandalize us beyond all repair. As your chaperon, I simply cannot allow such a thing."

"We can keep him in his room."

"Like a rabid animal? Now, that's simply cruel, Julia." Salome brought her palms together, tapping the thumbs thoughtfully against her lips, and softly asked, "How much of our situation do you intend to reveal for this man?"

"As little as he needs to know in order to serve his purpose."

"And have you given any thought to what might happen if, somehow, he were to learn more than he should?"

"How can he? You and I are certainly not going to tell him. And no one else knows of it, except for Moses and some staff."

The older woman pursed her lips, dropping her shoulders and sighing deeply. "I have lived with a fear of discovery for most of my life, Julia. I would have given anything to spare you a similar existence. This man is a danger to us. We simply may not take such a risk. You can understand that, can't you?"

She put out an arm to pat her niece on the shoulder, but the girl petulantly pulled away, glaring at her aunt with a combination of stubborn anger and little-girl pleading.

Julia did seem ever so proud of her plot, so pleased that she might help Miriam and Alexia. Salome shook her head, recognizing in Julia the same loyalty and doggedness that had checkered her late mother. Whenever either one painted that look of utter determination upon her features, the opposing party might as well pack up their objections and give in. The battle was already lost.

Reasoning that perhaps a more agreeable approach might quickly show Julia the impracticality of her actions, Salome swallowed her misgivings and, instead, reasonably pointed out, "He'll need new clothes, of course. Or is Newgate releasing prisoners with a full wardrobe these days?"

Julia beamed, certain the worst of their squabble were finally over. "We can order some from town."

"Oh, that I shall like to see. You and I marching into the

beau's favorite outfitters and requesting a wardrobe of men's clothes. Why, of course, Julia, how could I have been so foolish? You are absolutely right. That, most certainly, will not inspire a syllable of gossip."

Feeling very much like the mistress who purchased a horse in town, asked for it to be delivered, and now headed to the stables for a closer look at what exactly she had bought, Julia changed clothes, replacing the pink and white gown of that afternoon with a simpler, light blue satin summer frock, and headed towards the guest room Moses had set up for Mr. Lowell.

Julia bit her lip, and, ever so slightly, inched the door forward a hairline crack, so that she might be able to peek in without being noticed.

True to his word, Moses had seen to it that Jamie were washed and clothed appropriately. His skin, minus the layer of brownish grime that earlier had appeared part of his natural complexion, now glowed a freshly scrubbed, almost newborn pink, and the previously tangled shock of ruddy bangs that fell across his face lay sunset red and neatly combed above a pair of robin's-egg-blue eyes. He had discarded—and hopefully burned—his prison rags, trading them for a pair of faded breeches and a one-size-too-large white shirt, previously in the possession of one of Moses's sons. It could hardly be deemed the current fashion, but the too wide, flowing sleeves did give Jamie the appearance of a rather dapper gypsy. Or a pirate. Unfortunately, neither image was quite what Julia's plans required for him to be.

Still unobserved, she watched Jamie move cautiously about the room, briefly running his fingers along the mahogany veneer, the walnut writing desk, and the brass inlay marquetry on the bed, before guiltily pulling back his arm, as if in fear of breaking something. Odd, Julia thought, how at the prison, he'd seemed so much older than she was, while now he reminded her more of a small child under strict orders never to touch his aunt's valuable Minton plates. As if to reinforce her mind's picture, Jamie snapped both arms behind his back, one hand holding the other, clearly terrified of touching the wrong object and inadvertently breaking it.

Starting to feel more and more like a voyeur, Julia took a deep breath, squared her shoulders, and, knocking loudly, pushed his door open the rest of the way.

Jamie jumped, every muscle visibly tightening, and spun about. Stunned by the extremity of his reaction, Julia gasped and froze in her place, momentarily unsure of what to do or say.

Recognizing that it were only she, Jamie dropped his arms and exhaled, brushing the once again loose bangs from his forehead. Noting Julia's disorientation, a faint, mocking smile bubbled to his features, and Jamie asked with mock formality, "Does protocol demand my bowing in your presence, Miss Highsmith?"

Thankfully, his sarcasm was more than enough to shock Julia back into loquaciousness. Leaving the door open for the sake of a propriety she had certainly long surrendered after that afternoon's little excursion to Newgate Prison, Julia set her hands on hips, and coolly told Jamie, "A mere falling to your knees will do."

He obeyed instantly. "Your wish is my command."

But the smirk never for a moment left his eyes.

"Oh, do get up, Mr. Lowell, you look positively corkbrained."

"And how would you have me look, then? I assure you, I am capable of assuming any pose or dramatic temperament."

"I know. That is precisely why, at this very moment, you are here, enjoying my hospitality, as opposed to listening for your neck to snap on the gallows."

A shadow of fear passed across Jamie's face. Julia could almost hear him recalling that final moment of a hanging, when the executioner reached through the trap door to jerk the condemned man by his legs, thus breaking his neck.

Jamie looked so sincerely green from the prospect that Julia felt a twinge of guilt at torturing him so.

However, in a moment, he was springing to his feet and

booming theatrically, "So what shall it be, m'lady? Whom shall I become? A hussar? A dragoon, perhaps?"

Jamie stretched himself to full height, back military straight, eyes straight ahead, imaginary riding crop tucked under his arm, and proceeded to mock-march across the room in a manner identical to those of the beplumed and gold-laced officers Julia often saw fraternizing with the merchants of St. James Street.

"Or would Miss Highsmith prefer a gentleman of leisure?"

Instantly, the soldier of a moment before became a gambler at one of the many men's clubs—White's, Boodle's, Brooks'—that Julia had only heard about. Face set in immobile concentration, Jamie pantomimed tilting his hat over his eyes, and stooping in near exhaustion over the green baize tables for yet another game of whist, faro, or hazard.

"How about a dandy, then?"

Jamie stuck his nose up in the air and turned dramatically towards the mirror, making a great show of pretending to brush each hair on his head until it lay just right, then creasing down his starched cravat until every fold stood impeccable.

The characterization was so perfect that Julia could not contain her merriment any longer, and burst out laughing in sincere appreciation of his talents.

Encouraged, Jamie next offered, "The Jew moneylender on Clarges Street."

Julia's heart skipped a beat in her chest.

"Stop that." She had meant to shout the command, but, instead, it come out only as a whisper.

Unable to hear her, he shriveled up, both hands turning into grotesque claws that reached out and snatched at the silver platters and diamond necklaces brought to him by well-to-do gamblers, eager for the loan of extra cash so that they might return to the tables.

Only Julia was no longer laughing.

Without a word of explanation, she seized Jamie by the shirt collar, yanking him upright.

He stared at her queerly, unsure of the exact offense

he'd committed, but, regardless, ready to loudly defend
himself.

Unfortunately, she had no intention of granting him such
an opportunity. Refusing to even acknowledge Jamie's
confusion, Julia shoved him aside, wiping her palm distastefully on the bodice of her dress, and, turning sharply,
stormed out of his room.

3

She flew the length of the west wing hallway in a rage so blinding, Julia barely avoided barreling into the upstairs maid while rounding a corner.

It took her two flights of stairs, and the length of one dining room, one ballroom, and the parlor, before Julia felt some confidence in getting her temper under control.

Walking past the kitchen, she heard the faint murmur of Moses in conversation with Cook. The sole words clearly audible were "Gavin" and "Lady Emma." But even they stopped the moment Julia entered. Both Moses and Cook simultaneously tightened their lips, suddenly engrossed in chopping vegetables, a task that, on an average day, Moses would deem far below his station.

Julia sighed.

It was growing so tiresome, the way all conversation about Gavin and his new bride ceased the instant Julia strolled into hearing range. The habit might even have been amusing, if the mere thought of the young lord didn't still send a pain so searing through Julia's heart that she sometimes feared cracking in two.

Julia forced her tone to sound light, determined never to show her true feelings, and risk being pitied. "Have Lord Gavin and Lady Emma returned from their . . . trip, then?" She wasn't yet feeling up to mouthing the word "honeymoon."

Moses cleared his throat and avoided Julia's gaze. "Aye, that they have. This morning."

Now it was Julia's turn to feign interest in the plate of scones resting by the stove. "I must remember to pay Gavin and his wife a proper visit in the near future. Welcome them home."

"Of course, Miss Julia." Cook refused to so much as glance in her mistress's direction, choosing instead to spoon a serving of parslied potatoes in cream sauce from her pot into a pair of plates, and follow that up with an equally generous portion of garden peas. She inquired, "I am ready to serve, miss. Will Mr. Lowell be joining you?"

"You cannot be serious," Salome announced to Julia upon entering the dining room and seeing their dinner table set for three. "He is to eat with us?"

Julia shrugged, "If I am to marry him, I suppose he shall have to, at some time."

"I had hoped an hour of private contemplation might force you to reassess your rash decision of this morning. Really, Julia, this is most bizarre. The game is over, my pet, what say we hand the wretch a few pounds for his trouble and send him on his way?"

"Then where does that leave Miriam and Alexia?"

"You cannot be expected to sacrifice your life for theirs."

"Miriam would do the same for me, I know it."

Salome threw her hands up in the air, at last acknowledging the hopelessness of turning Julia from this silly plan, and now simply hoping that she might curb at least a bit of the damage this child seemed so set on inflicting upon her reputation.

Wishing that the entire problem might somehow disappear, Salome reflected, "If only you had accepted Lord Neff's proposal. How much simpler everything would be."

"Do you truly think so?" Julia plucked a rose petal from their table's centerpiece, and rubbed it between two fingers until pink juice soiled her hand. "After all, I could never have confessed to Gavin what it were I was rescuing Miriam from. If I married him, the situation might only have been more complicated. I don't think I could have borne lying to him." Julia turned to Salome. "Is that why you never married the marquis of Martyn? Mama told me how ever so much in love with you he was."

Stiffly, Salome replied, "The marquis of Martyn is an old, dear friend, nothing more, nothing less."

"But he did propose to you, did he not?"

"As Lord Neff did to you."

"And you turned him away. As I turned Gavin away." Julia paused before gently prying, "Was it for the very same reason?"

Salome hesitated, unwilling to delve too deeply into the topic. For both their sakes. "A similar reason, yes."

Seeing her aunt's discomfort, Julia tactfully attempted to back out of the awkwardness. Projecting a cheerfulness she truly could not feel, Julia enthused, "Well, I, for one, am happy that you did. From what I hear talked about, he is a horrid, bitter old man who rarely leaves his home. No wonder he never married."

Softly, Salome reminisced, "But the marquis was not always the way he appears now. A long time ago, a very long time ago, before you were born, he was quite a different sort of fellow all together. Rather dashing, I'd say. And most charming."

"Well, then," Julia exclaimed. "If the marquis of Martyn can go from charming to horrid, why are you so certain that I cannot tame Mr. Lowell from convict to gentleman?"

"Because, my darling," Salome told her, knowing full well that anything she said most likely would float in one young ear and out the other, "as in all things, it is much simpler to slip-slide downwards, than it is to claw one's way back uphill."

Unsure of what wisdom she were obligated to gather from such a cryptic statement, Julia requested an explanation. But Salome, worn out by the developments of the day, pleaded a headache, and, before retiring, only warned Julia to count the silverware both before and after sharing a meal with their houseguest.

* * *

"Mr. Lowell, you are using," Julia corrected, "the inappropriate fork. That is a dessert fork. You are eating your chicken à la russe with a fork designated for the apricot tart."

"Begging your pardon, Miss Highsmith. But we did not have many dessert forks in prison."

Julia wanted to strangle him with her napkin. Already, she had twice explained to him what each utensil was for. But, from the moment they entered the dining room, Julia had felt forced to compete with the crystal chandelier and handcarved paneling for Jamie's attention. His head swiveled like a newborn bird's as he drank in the furnishings, the mahogany table built to seat thirty, the bronze figures in imitation of Greek marble, the hanging red damask, the vases of fresh flowers in every corner. Watching him gape so openly at objects which, to Julia, were as familiar as the back of her hand, unnerved her.

What had she been thinking, boasting that, in the scant space of a few months, she could turn a street rodent into a gentleman so fine, he would withstand the eagle eye of her fastidious uncle?

This wretch could barely differentiate among his silverware!

Frustrated, Julia nevertheless refused to allow herself the pleasure of imagining how different her present circumstances might have been if she had accepted Gavin's proposal of six months past. Granted, such a match was impossible, Uncle Collin had made that point and the reason behind it perfectly clear. Still, since she could never confess the true reason behind her refusal, the pained look on Gavin's face when she rejected him without just cause often floated to the surface of Julia's mind at the most unexpected moments, scraping a fresh dagger into her already aching heart.

And it was that pain that prompted Julia to tear into Jamie with an intensity that surprised even her. "The following, Mr. Lowell, are further conditions to our arrangement. I do suggest that you listen closely, for I have no intention of repeating myself into infinity."

He blinked in sincere surprise at her outburst, and

slowly lowered his fork. It clanked loudly against the plate, echoing from wall to wall.

"Condition one. You are not to leave your room unless given permission by either myself or Moses. And you are certainly not to wander outside of the house, or onto the grounds."

"Indeed, warden, I understand perfectly."

"I will not compromise my reputation by your being seen. Who knows what the people would think, my housing a strange gentleman."

"I suspect m'lady knows exactly what the people would think."

Julia blushed furiously. Never in her life, had a man spoken to her in such a fashion. Obviously, this barbarian's lack of manners stretched from table etiquette to simple conversation.

"I am not one of your Drury Lane whores, Mr. Lowell. I daresay you had best refrain from addressing me as such."

She had hoped that the sternness in her voice might chasten him. Instead, it seemed only to amuse Jamie further. He leaned back in the chair, crossed his arms, and calmly proceeded to assess Julia from head to toe. "Now, then, Miss Highsmith, how does a fine lady such as yourself know of The Lane?"

She could not understand how this kept happening to her. No matter how well Julia felt she had the situation in hand, somehow, Jamie would succeed in snatching it away from her. And the cockiness in his eyes as he deliberately tossed each baiting syllable in her direction made Julia want to personally return him to the gallows and open the trap door.

"I do not know of it," Julia stammered, trying to make him understand. London was a man's world. No lady of good parentage who valued her reputation would ever allow herself to be seen walking down Bond or St. James unless accompanied by her maid or footman. The clubs, shops, and smart hotels that prospered in such areas were all dedicated to serving the men of the aristocracy. For ladies, the high life was restricted to weekly Wednesday night balls at Almack's Assembly Rooms on King Street. Julia's only knowledge of events taking place outside of those rooms came from eavesdropping on the conversations of oblivious gentlemen.

But how would a man like Jamie Lowell, a man who, to all appearances had gone about doing what he wanted, when he wanted, until the law caught up with him, ever understand just how structured and sternly dictated her world truly was. And thus how intriguing every crumb from the outside seemed.

Julia's mother, familiar with her child's penchant for hiding around corners hoping to overhear things, had warned the girl that such a trait could only get her into trouble. One day, she would inevitably blurt out something she had no business knowing, and then be forced to explain herself.

Thankfully, Julia was spared continuing to verbally extricate herself by Moses's entering the dining room and announcing that Miss Highsmith had visitors.

She turned to Jamie, meaning to dismiss him, but instead found that it was he who had decided to do the honors.

Waving one arm in her direction, he urged, "Go on, then. We shall continue our discussion at a later time."

Even Moses, known far and wide for his unchanging facial expression, was forced to raise an eyebrow at such impertinence.

Julia stood up and pushed her chair in, smoothing down her hair, and the muslin of her dress. "Who is it, Moses?"

He hesitated before revealing, once again with no expression, "Lord Gavin, miss. And Lady Emma."

She swallowed hard and instinctively turned her back to Jamie, lest he see the rainbow of emotions streaking across her face. Julia forced her voice to remain neutral, but succeeded only in sounding stilted. "Show them to the parlor, Moses."

"Very good, miss."

"And as for you," Julia pivoted. "Kindly take the back stairs to your room and stay there until I say that you may leave."

In an uncannily perfect imitation of Moses, he intoned, "Very good, miss."

Proper young ladies, Julia had been lectured often enough, did not dash down hallways, skirts hiked up above their ankles, hair flying every which way. So she forced herself to take small, measured, ladylike steps all the way to the parlor.

Gavin stood when she entered, and moved to take both her hands in his, smiling broadly. His presence filled the room like a blinding ray of morning sunshine in that first moment after drawing back the nighttime drapes.

Was it Julia's imagination, or did Gavin grow more handsome every time they encountered each other? When he was still an unbreeched boy of three, clutching his nurse's hand and sucking on a sticky piece of bullseye candy, she had already considered him perfection itself. But now, the man Lord Gavin Neff grew up to be quite simply took Julia's breath away.

He stood only a head taller than she, as sturdy and muscular as Jamie Lowell was gaunt, and with golden blond hair that, in childhood, had billowed in glorious curls past his shoulders, but now lay smartly cut to the base of the neck.

"How truly wonderful it is to see you again, Julia." Both of Gavin's thumbs gently rubbed the backs of her fingers as he clutched her hands in greeting.

She hadn't the strength to respond. Julia's tongue stuck to the roof of her mouth, blocking any words from escaping her lips.

Were it up to her, she might have felt content in their merely continuing to stand as is for all of eternity, but Gavin, gentleman that he was raised, politely turned aside, loosening his grip on one of Julia's hands so that he might gesture with his free arm. "Surely, you remember my bride."

Miss Emma Trent—no, Julia corrected herself, she was Lady Emma Neff, now—greeted her with a display that, while certainly conforming to every rule of *ton* etiquette, could hardly have been described as overflowing with sincerity or warmth. She said all the right things. She smiled. But the expression never quite reached her eyes. And, despite being a good two inches shorter than Julia, the new Lady Neff nevertheless conveyed the impression of surveying Julia from some lofty mountaintop only she were allowed on.

"So, then." Realizing that neither woman was about to help make polite conversation, Gavin took the responsibility upon himself. "Julia, tell us of all that is new since our absence."

As a gesture of his familiarity with the household, Gavin settled on the same windowsill where he and Julia, in the years before he'd gone off to school, had often sat reading. Immediately, Lady Emma rose from where she'd been critically examining the spinet, and moved to perch beside Gavin, so that there might be no more room on the sill.

To Julia's judgement, the act was thoroughly unnecessary. Not to mention deliberately provoking. Lady Emma's obvious show of possession might have been warranted if she were in any danger whatsoever of losing Gavin to another woman. But she most certainly was not. She was Gavin's wife now, and no one could change that fact even if they wanted to. Which, all in all, convinced Julia that Lady Emma's leap from spinet to windowsill was prompted by nothing more than her malicious need to remind Julia just who it was that had finally won Gavin.

Furious, both at Lady Emma and at Gavin for marrying such a chit, Julia recovered her tongue long enough to blurt out the one answer to Gavin's polite inquiry sure to make them both take notice. Casually, she informed the man she loved, "Oh, Gavin, have you not heard? I am to be married."

Perhaps if Jamie had been better at doing as he was told, he might have managed to circumvent his most recent holiday at Newgate Prison. However, seeing as how obedience had never made up a particularly prominent chunk of his character, Jamie waited a good three and one half seconds after Julia left the dining room before completely disregarding her orders.

Instead of sneaking off to his room as she had demanded, Jamie instead snuck down the hallways in silent pursuit. Luckily, Julia was so preoccupied with hurrying to greet her visitors that she did not notice him following behind at thirty paces.

But, then again, maybe she did. Because the moment Julia stepped into the parlor, she closed the door soundly behind her.

Now Jamie was faced with a pair of options. He could shrug his shoulders and utter *"C'est la vie."* Or he could continue with his quest to discover just what sort of unexpected guest was capable of throwing Miss Julia Highsmith, a lady courageous enough to brave a solo journey into London's East End, into such a tizzy. In the end, the decision over what to do was an easy enough one for Jamie to make. To start with, he did not speak any French.

Ignoring queer glances from the pair of maids walking down the hall, carrying armfuls of bed linens, Jamie attempted pressing his ear against the door.

Nothing.

The hand-carved wood, with its intricate crest of lions bearing crowns on their heads and knights charging into battle, must have been a good five inches thick. The only sounds Jamie could hear were the scratches of his own fingernails on the fine sanding.

He squatted down on all fours, inhaling enough floor shellack to insure his lungs gleaming just as brightly as the finely polished floor, and proceeded to peer through the crack below the door. All he could spy was a pair of men's Hessian boots, a tassel dangling from the V-shaped front. It reminded him of the silken cord dangling discreetly in the dining room, for the summoning of staff. Fleetingly, Jamie wondered what he might summon if he mischievously decided to tug on this gentleman's boot tassel.

But there was no time for further pondering of the matter when, in the next instant, Jamie distinctively heard Julia's voice from inside the parlor. "Oh, Gavin, have you not heard? I am to be married."

"Why, Julia, how wonderful!" The fellow with the boots, the one she had called Gavin, exclaimed, "Do tell us all about him."

"Oh, yes," Jamie whispered, "Do, Julia."

"He is very handsome." He heard Julia stand up and pace the room as she continued to extol Jamie's alleged virtues. "And such a wit. I daresay you will find him no equal in all of England."

"And what of his family, Miss Highsmith?" As far as Jamie could discern, the third voice inside the room belonged to a woman who didn't so much speak, as languidly purr every word. "Surely, you are marrying a man of peerage. A baron, at the very least. Or perhaps a duke? A count? An earl?"

"Why, my dear Lady Neff, it is very kind of you to worry about my future position. But, fear not, I shall be very well provided for." Julia paused for a moment, drawing out the tension to its highest possible peek, before lowering her voice and cautioning, "Of course, you must both swear to keep this in the greatest of confidences until I am ready to make the official announcement."

"Of course, of course," Lord Gavin sounded in a most peculiar hurry to hear her news. Almost as if he held some sort of personal stake in the matter. "You have my word as a gentleman, Julia."

"I appreciate that, Gavin." She paused for a second time, and Jamie could practically hear Julia smiling—or was she merely reconsidering the impetuousness of her actions?—as she revealed, "My betrothed, you see, is a marquis."

4

"Truly, Julia, I believe that you have taken leave of your last senses." Salome sat before her mirror, attempting to roll hair as wild and curly as Julia's into a tight widow's bun.

Her niece stood, back pressed to the door, guilt wrestling for control of her expression with the equally powerful forces of mischief and self-defense. "It was the first title I could think of. After all, we had spoken of the marquis of Martyn only a few hours past. I suppose the memory of it stayed in my head."

Salome said, "Perhaps it occupied the place where your common sense once used to reside."

"Are you very cross with me, Aunt Salome?" The hand behind Julia's back nervously twisted the doorknob this way and that, so that their conversation was counterpointed by a rhythmic clicking.

"Cross? Cross? My darling niece, I have passed cross so long ago, that I no longer even see it from where I am standing. For what I am feeling at present, there exists no word to describe."

"I had to tell Gavin something. You should have heard the way Lady Emma spoke to me." Julia took a step forward, releasing the knob, and bringing both hands in front of her, anxiously rubbing one palm against the other while, in a small voice, she said, "I have been thinking, Aunt Salome."

"No, my dear, I truly don't believe that you have."

"You said that the marquis of Martyn were a dear friend of yours, did you not? And that he never married?"

"No, Julia." Salome stood up, snapping her jar of powder closed with such force, it raised a minor snowstorm on her bureau.

"But you did not yet even hear what I intended to ask."

"No." Salome repeated, turning to face her niece. "I will not use my twenty-year acquaintance with the marquis of Martyn to bully him into adopting that criminal you dragged home from the gallows."

"But he does not have to adopt him. He just needs to pretend for a bit. The marquis rarely goes out in society, so it isn't as if he will be asked many questions. All he has to do is agree—no, actually, even less, all he has to do is not deny it when we present Jamie as his ... his cousin, or nephew, or something of that sort. He does not need to honestly make Jamie his heir. He just needs to go along with our pretense for a very little while. And I can even pay him for it. Anything he likes."

Julia took it as a positive sign when, finally, Salome didn't immediately deny her request. "You must give me some time to think about this, Julia."

"As much time as you like. Only, I really did plan to take Jamie riding in Hyde Park next week. So that I might start introducing him around as my fiancé."

"Next week, did you say?" Salome looked at her reflection in the mirror, ripping out each hair pin one by one, needing to start all over again. "I suppose I should be grateful that you did not say this morning."

"Good morning, Mr. Lowell."

Jamie rubbed the sleep out of his eyes just in time to see Moses drop a dozen pounds of clothing across his chest, then announce, "Miss Highsmith wishes you to try these on for size."

But Jamie was reluctant to move. He had spent his first night at Julia's home marveling at the sheer softness of the

linen-covered pillow under his head, and at the way his blanket smelled so sweetly of lilac and powder. Only at dawn had he finally allowed himself to sink into sleep, still fearful that a new day might prove the previous one a most horrible sort of nightmare—the sort that initially masquerades as a dream.

"If it does not disturb your beauty rest too greatly, Mr. Lowell, I would ask that you proceed to do as bade. Today."

He blinked to clear his vision, and focused on the image of Julia leaning against the far wall of his room. She wore a green muslin frock with pale lace along the hem, bodice, and sleeves. Her ebony hair lay plaited back off her face, and fastened with a matching spring ribbon, the shade of which brought out a pinkish tinge to her cheeks, and made her eyes seem so black that they appeared almost blue.

On any other woman, Jamie would have conceded the package to be attractive. But, in the case of Julia Highsmith, he was willing to make an exception to the favorable estimate. Because, in the case of Julia Highsmith, every pleasant feature was permanently overshadowed by her mouth, which never ceased moving.

Still, Jamie reminded himself wryly, when it came to this young woman, his task were to continue acting pleasant, as if his life depended on it.

She said, "The clothes belonged to my late father, so I doubt that they might prove exactly your size. We shall need to see about acquiring some more appropriate attire at a later date. Do get on with the business of wearing them, Mr. Lowell. We have quite a lot of ground to cover today."

Back home, the accepted response to such a cheeky, high-handed order would be—with all due respect, of course—to stand up and elegantly spit at the silly chit. The only factor that presently prevented Jamie from starting off his morning in that particular manner was the minor fact that, if she so wished it, the chit in question could happily send Jamie back to prison.

And that would be a very bad thing indeed.

From the moment he'd looked up through the swinging

trap door at his hangman, Jamie vowed never again to make a return trip up the platform. In that instant, he hadn't yet known how such a goal might be accomplished. But now he did. All Jamie had to do to avoid the noose forever was please Miss Highsmith.

And, luckily, pleasing women just happened to be what Jamie did best.

Only there was a slight wrinkle. Despite her seemingly honest demeanor, Jamie possessed no guarantee that, once he'd fulfilled her purpose, Julia Highsmith might not get it in her head to send him right back to the gallows, if only to insure Jamie's mouth staying permanently shut regarding their deception.

He had no intention of allowing that to happen. Jamie was prepared to do, or say, anything to prevent it. And, at the moment, only a single, obvious plan of defense was coming to mind.

Still refusing to budge, Jamie pawed through the mass dumped across his lap, pulling out a pair of black pantaloons and a deep green, many-caped driving coat with golden buttons. He remarked in all apparent innocence, "Gor, these certainly are fine clothes, m'lady. Why, I daresay, they're fair bang up the marker fine enough for a marquis."

At least his observation proved enough to close that pair of strawberry-red lips for a good ten seconds. Julia stifled a gasp, blushing and pursing her brow as she wondered if Jamie knew . . . How could he know? And, finally, how much did he know?

Flustered, she exclaimed, "For goodness sake, Mr. Lowell, do confess to what purpose it is that you delight in taunting me so?"

Actually, Jamie was wondering the exact same thing right about now. He wished he could answer that question, not only for her sake, but for his own as well. A reasonable man might think that, for the sake of self-preservation if nothing else, Jamie should be trying to stay on Miss Highsmith's good side, not needlessly aggravating her. And yet, from the moment they'd met, Julia Highsmith had provoked a most violent reaction in Jamie. But it was one he felt hard-pressed to apply a verb or even an adjective to. The fact of the matter was, he felt incapable of remaining indifferent to her presence.

"I was merely making polite conversation, Miss Highsmith."

"Or you overheard my exchange with Lord Gavin and his wife, and are now attempting to embarrass me with my own false boasting."

"Or that."

Julia raised her palms to shoulder level. "So. You heard. But I simply could not stand the manner in which Lady Emma posed her questions. She goaded me into the lie."

"But you provoked it, by offering news of your marriage."

"That was the Lord's truth."

"Your marriage to a marquis?"

She tossed her hair lightly over one shoulder. "I knew that I would eventually need to conjure up some sort of title for you, in order to satisfy my uncle. In this manner, the decision was made for me. All's well that ends well."

"Except for one minuscule detail, Miss Highsmith."

"Well, yes. But I intend to worry about that snag at another time. Presently, I am more interested in seeing how you fit those clothes. We must have you looking like a gentleman, before I begin the Herculean task of teaching you to sound and act like one."

"Very well, then." Still modeling a face innocent enough to twin an angel's, Jamie threw off his blankets, setting one bare foot upon the hardwood floor.

"Good gracious, Mr. Lowell," Moses snatched at the covers and tossed them back over Jamie's legs. "There is a lady present."

Jamie turned to Julia. "The lady told me to dress. Today, I believe the command was."

He didn't dare look to see how his attempt at appropriating some sort of upper hand with Miss Julia Highsmith was faring. Dressed only in his nightshirt, Jamie rose from the bed, stretching languidly. He pretended to yawn, thus necessitating closing his eyes, and avoiding Julia's gaze for a few more moments. It gave her more time to look.

And to realize that it wasn't only Jamie's silver tongue that had so charmed the ladies of his past.

Finally, he turned his head sideways, no longer able to bear the suspense, and snuck a peek at Julia. She still stood against the wall, not even bothering to turn her head in propriety. But her sable eyes remained stubbornly blank. She might as well have been staring at nothing.

Jamie bit down on his lower lip, and exhaled in frustration with such force, it made the bangs on his forehead fly up.

That's it, he decided to himself. *The lady is pure icicle, straight down to the core.*

"Well?" Jamie entered the drawing room without knocking, and turned sideways, offering Julia a thorough view of his new clothes. "How do I look?"

He only asked to be polite. Because, after admiring himself in an upstairs mirror, Jamie felt that he really didn't need Julia's assessment. He knew how he looked. Even in clothes half a size too small, he looked good.

In point of fact, he'd never looked better in his life.

Despite Jamie's general disdain for the fashions of the aristocracy, he had to admit that they made up in attractiveness what they lacked in practicality. The tight-fitting pantaloons emphasized his muscular figure, while the glossy black waistcoat and top hat made him appear taller. And smarter. The clothes, Jamie thought, made him look like Somebody.

And that, after all, was all Jamie had ever wanted to be. Because it was the one thing everyone predicted would never happen.

His father used to tell the neighbors that his no-good wrong-un of a son would be in prison before he made it into long pants. He insisted to anyone who would listen that the boy was daft, and a fool to boot. Sometimes, Jamie wondered if the reason he'd finally turned to thieving and swindling was because that was exactly what everyone expected him to do.

With one expertly pointed finger, Julia bade for Jamie to stand in the center of the room while she walked all

around him, studying Jamie from every possible angle.
She clicked her tongue against her teeth, cocking her head
first to one side, then another, and pursing her lips.

"Well, then?" Jamie demanded. He could feel the confidence of only a moment earlier withering away under her
gaze.

"Presentable," she conceded. "You appear presentable."

"Only appear, m'lady?"

"There's more to being a gentleman, Mr. Lowell, than
merely pulling on a pair of Wellington boots."

Julia lectured, "You must always wait to be introduced
to a lady, before you may speak to her . . ."

"Even if she is about to be run down by a phaeton?"

". . . At a formal dinner, it is imperative that you make
equally polite and animated conversation with both the
lady on your right, as well as on your left . . ."

"Now would that be with, or without, my mouth full?"

". . . Stand up when a lady enters or leaves the
room . . ."

"What if a pair decide to do so simultaneously? Do I
bob up and down, or merely hop in place?"

". . . It would not harm you to learn up a bit on fox
hunting, so that you may make conversation with the other
gentlemen . . ."

"Gentlemen foxes, m'lady?"

Jamie wondered exactly how Julia expected him to remember all her instructions. So far, she had passed the day
drilling Jamie on every piece of cutlery in the house, until
he felt as intimately acquainted with the blasted salad and
dessert forks as he did with the back of his own hand.
They reviewed the differences in properly addressing the
daughter of a baronet versus the wife of an earl versus the
mother-in-law of the prince regent.

Jamie asked, "Do tell me, Miss Highsmith, when exactly the circumstances would require me to make the lady's acquaintance. I am fairly certain that her circle of
friends only very rarely intersects mine."

Yet, because Julia took every fine point of etiquette so

seriously, Jamie felt compelled to at least put on a show of feeling the same. After all, the eventual death date inscribed on his tombstone in Pauper's Field was up to this lady's discretion.

She drilled him, "And the Princess Charlotte is married to Prince Leopold, third son of—"

"Third son of Prince Francis of Saxe-Coburg. Yes, I know. In point of fact, I draw my inspiration from that impoverished German principality whose chief industry, at least as far as I can see, appears to be marrying into much wealthier royal families."

They spent the remainder of the afternoon going over likely topics of fine society conversation, and even Julia was impressed by how much Jamie appeared to know of recent European politics.

"I am literate, Miss Highsmith." He recognized how much the fact surprised her. "I taught myself to read as a boy, and since then, not a week has passed when I didn't follow world and local events with the aid of a newspaper."

Jamie saw no reason to add that, more often than not, the said newspaper ended the day serving not only as his tutor, but as his blanket as well.

For seemingly the first time since they'd met, Julia turned to truly look at Jamie. Not assess him like a new addition to her stable or wardrobe, but truly look at him, like a human being.

Like a man.

"Why, Mr. Lowell," she said, not unkindly, "you are not nearly as primitive as I thought you were."

"Thank you, m'lady." He bowed from the waist.

She slipped one thumbnail into her mouth, before guiltily realizing what she had done, and snatched it away. Yet she continued watching Jamie with a great deal more interest than ever before. Finally, Julia said, "What is it about you, Mr. Lowell, that those other women found so enchanting?"

Sensing an opportunity brewing, Jamie took a step closer to Julia, standing close enough to touch her if he so desired.

She continued. "You must have been dreadfully charming, convincing them not only to part with their savings, but to defend you in front of the magistrate, as well. How in the world did you do it? Tell me. I've always dreamed of possessing such a power over people. Why, it's almost like being a wizard, isn't it?"

Jamie thought, *Or like holding a return trip to the gallows over someone's head.* But he didn't dare verbalize the opinion.

Instead, Jamie said, "It, charming a body, I mean, it is a rather difficult process to explain, Miss Highsmith."

"Oh." Julia's eyes clouded over in disappointment. "I was so hoping you might teach me."

Jamie wondered if it might be the married fellow with the tasseled boots that Julia was so interested in learning to charm. He said, "I could show you how I did it. Would that be of help?"

"Certainly," Julia offered him the first sincere smile of their acquaintance. "I might even be able to use it on my uncle when soliciting his blessing for our marriage."

Wryly, Jamie remarked, "I sincerely doubt it."

"Very well, then. Go on."

He'd never performed under such pressure before. It added a pleasant drop of excitement to an act that, after a while, had become merely a boring routine. And it certainly gave Jamie a wonderful opportunity to finish up what he'd attempted that morning. Hopefully with a tad more success this time around.

Taking a second step closer to Julia, he gazed deeply into her eyes, making it impossible for her to look away without risking embarrassment. On one level, it was almost like the staring game played by children.

"Made you blink."

5

Julia prayed that Jamie couldn't see just how much his intimate presence affected her.

It had proven difficult enough that morning to feign indifference, all the while feeling unable to tear her eyes away from the handsome figure outlined beneath his nightshirt. Undressed, Jamie's legs appeared even longer and more muscular than she might previously have assumed, the contours of his thighs radiating a strength and athletic virility that overwhelmed Julia's senses until she had to snatch at the wall for support. She couldn't stop herself from wondering what a body that taut might feel like pressed against her own.

But it weren't only the physical pleasures of such indecent musings that made Julia dizzy. Confusion played a large part in it all, as well. For, despite her eternal love for Gavin, Julia had never once felt similar mental pictures racing so uncontrollably through her mind.

She didn't know what had possessed her to ask Jamie Lowell for a lesson in persuasion. Or was it seduction?

Surely, the way he now towered above her, eyes boring so deeply into her, Julia feared Jamie could see right through to her soul, surely such a pose could only mean one thing.

And the worst part of it was, Julia no longer even felt

confident in her ability to refuse him, no matter what course of action Jamie decided to pursue.

But no, that wasn't true, either. The worst part of it was that, as he stood close enough for her to smell the sweet cologne she'd ordered delivered to him that morning, every fiber in Julia's body was rooting for Jamie to choose the less honorable rout.

Yet he certainly was taking his time in the matter.

For what seemed like the longest of eternities, he only stood before her, beaming a smile that was certainly nothing like the roguish, mocking grin Jamie usually flashed in her direction. This was a softer, kinder expression. Almost dreamlike.

Finally, Jamie slipped one arm about Julia's waist, his fingers brushing ever so gently beneath the curve of her breast.

"Well, first of all," he began, "I would start by telling the lady how beautiful she was. How the black of her eyes was like the rarest of pearls lying safe and warm beneath the azure blue of the sea. How her skin was the color of rose petals just waiting for a touch of sunshine to send them blossoming."

Julia listened, knowing all the while that he was just offering examples, that he had fined and honed his craft until every wooing word slipped like poetry from his lips. And yet she couldn't help feeling affected by them. Jamie's warm breath caressed her face, until she wanted nothing more than to close her eyes and swoon against his chest.

Effortlessly, and all the while continuing to whisper endearments into her ear, Jamie reached behind him for the bottle of sherry on the table. He splashed a drop into a glass, then, still moving with the quiet grace of a cougar, dipped his finger into the wine. Mesmerized, Julia watched Jamie bring his hand to her mouth, and ever so softly rub a sprinkle of sherry along her lower lip.

"May I?" Jamie didn't bother to wait for the refusal they both knew Julia incapable of offering, before leaning forward and, with his tongue, licking the wine from Julia's mouth.

The sheer softness of his lips surprised her. She would

have never expected a body as hard as Jamie's to be capable of such softness. Or of the gentleness with which he pulled her to him. The part of her mind still capable of reasonable thought understood that everything, even this tenderness, was part of Jamie's well-rehearsed seduction act. Only a rake and actor of the finest caliber could be capable of making what was clearly his coercion feel so much like a consensual act on both their parts.

But, at that moment, it wasn't her mind that Julia felt like listening to. Her heart hammered against Julia's chest, spreading the sweet warmth deeper and deeper throughout her body, until even Julia's fingertips tingled with pleasure. She leaned into Jamie, letting him support her own weight along with his, reveling not only in the purely physical sensations he stirred in her.

Yet, in spite of everything, Julia understood that she had no business acting in such a manner. Not out of some obscure fear for her reputation, or of being irreparably compromised. But because she feared that, if Jamie chose this moment to question her reasons behind the intrigue that bound them together, Julia would no longer possess the strength to continue lying.

And once Jamie knew the truth, well, even a sewer rat probably harbored some standards. He might refuse to help her. Worse, he might even choose to reveal her secret to anyone advancing the right price. Julia could think of several people willing to make him an offer. Then where would she be?

Worse, where would Miriam and Alexia be?

Digging her palms into his chest, Julia used more mental strength than physical to break Jamie's embrace. She pulled away to arm's length, barely stopping to catch her breath before smacking one of Jamie's cheeks with her open hand. "How dare you?"

But Julia was no longer sure whom she was angry at—Jamie, for taking such liberties with her person, or herself, for wishing he'd done it earlier.

He barely flinched from the blow, absently rubbing his smarting face, and remarking, "Funny. I've never had any complaints before."

"Then let this be your first unfavorable review." Julia's cheeks burned crimson. She hoped he would assume that was from fury, rather than passion.

"Ah, well, I suppose I am a bit rusty. Prison and all. Even a stellar athlete needs regular practice."

"So you consider it sport then, do you, Mr. Lowell?" Julia tried not to let her interest in his reply show on her face.

"Life, my dear Miss Highsmith, is all sport. A fox hunt, or a horse race, perhaps? And I'm afraid I've fallen out of practice. Would you care to assume the task of helping ease me back into the saddle, as it were?"

Now he was simply teasing her. Probably in retribution for her rejection of a moment earlier.

Julia squared her shoulders, feeling strangely buoyant for the first time since they'd started this duel. Truly, she felt a great deal more confident in her ability to come out on top in a verbal sparring match than in a situation of the more intimate nature.

She told Jamie, "Sadly, I must decline your request, Mr. Lowell. You see, I ride so quickly, I am afraid that you and your mount would merely get lost in my dust."

"Come along."

Julia barely waited for Jamie to finish chewing his breakfast the next morning before announcing, "My carriage is waiting outside. You can either, once again, hide out of view, or instead borrow Isaac's uniform and travel as my footman."

"Are we traveling far?" Jamie asked.

"A few dozen miles. It should not take us more than half a day or so."

"And is there a reason for this journey, save another opportunity to wrap me in your floor coverings?"

"As a matter of fact there is," Julia told Jamie. "We are off to make you a marquis."

"Will the prince regent be knighting me at the Brighton Pavilion?" Jamie craned his neck to look up at Julia, from where he was sitting at her feet, in back of the carriage. "Or perhaps beside a favorite tree stump in the woods?"

Salome, across from Julia, despite sitting in excruciatingly close proximity of Jamie, continued to silently stare out the window, ignoring Jamie's presence as if his words were no more than the buzzing of an annoying fly. Despite Julia's plea that even a half-day carriage ride could prove too much for her, Salome had insisted on accompanying them. She was, quite possibly, the only person in England capable of reasoning with the marquis of Martyn, and Julia knew that, without her, their plan had not the faintest chance of succeeding.

Julia said, "Do hush up, Mr Lowell. Someone may hear us."

Or at the very least wonder why Miss Julia Highsmith were holding such an intense conversation with her stockings.

"We have yet to meet a second carriage on this road. Furthermore, as the future marquis of Someplace, I can say whatever I want, however loud that I want. In case you were not aware of it, m'lady, such is the privilege of rank and title."

The same inner strength Julia had once employed to resist his advances, she now summoned to quiet her urge to smack him upon the head with her parasol. Patiently, she explained, "You are not the marquis of Somepl—the marquis of Martyn quite yet. It will take a great deal of verbal persuasion to convince the current holder of that title to declare you his heir."

"Verbal persuasion," Jamie said, "I can do that."

"And a great deal of money."

"That, you may do."

The butler who greeted them at the door smiled broadly at Salome, instantly beckoning her inside and sending a maid to hurry up and tell His Grace he had visitor.

When Julia and Jamie tried following her upstairs in anticipation of meeting the Marquis, Salome raised her hand, palm up, preventing them from coming any closer, and said, "Let me speak to him first alone. I daresay, the three of us may prove a bit much to spring on a man about to acquire a host of new relatives."

As ordered, Julia and Jamie waited in the drawing room for Salome to return with the marquis.

Careful not to upset the precariously balanced bust of Emperor Vespasion teetering on the top level, Julia slipped a volume of poetry from one of the bookshelves framing the fireplace, and settled on the yellow-brown, nankeen covered divan facing the door. She opened her book, pretending to be engrossed in its contents, while, at the same time, keeping her eyes fastened firmly on Jamie.

He stood appraising the marquis's drawing room in much the same hands-behind-back manner that Jamie once employed for the guest room in Julia's home. Fascinated by a silver gilt-covered tankard standing upon a kingwood sofa table, Jamie crouched down for a better view. Tentatively, he ran one finger along the vessel's meticulously engraved exterior, marveling at the dozen trumpeting angels that made up the handle, and the intricate grape vines snaking up its sides. He looked, for all the world, like a man coming face to face with God. Or a commoner making his first acquaintance with the playthings of the peerage.

Julia snapped her book shut. "Now, see here, Mr. Lowell. I am afraid that such things simply will not do. You must remember the part you are playing. How am I to take you out in public if you intend to gawk at every piece of finery we encounter?"

With mock seriousness, Jamie intoned, "I do promise to control myself in the future, Miss Highsmith."

Expecting an argument, Julia felt most discombobulated by his seeming acquiescence. Somehow, she preferred it when Jamie put up a fuss. It made things easier. Although, if pressed, Julia most certainly would find it hard to articulate just what those ambiguous "things" might be.

Instead, she told him, "I spent all last night planning your debut into society."

"Aren't I a bit old to be presented at Carlton House?"

"Don't be daft," Julia said. But she could not help smiling. "Listen. See what you think. We will begin with a

ride about in Hyde Park, to introduce you to my friends
and such. Then perhaps an evening at the theater. Mr.
Edmund Kean is performing at the Drury Lane all this
month. And, of course, Almack's. We shall have to put in
at least one Wednesday night appearance. I will ask Aunt
Salome to speak to Lady Cowper about acquiring some
vouchers. She really is the kindest of the patronesses. I
would never dare approach Lady Castlereagh for anything.
Or the Countess Lieven. Remind me to order you knee
breeches for the occasion. Almack's once refused admit-
tance to the duke of Wellington himself, simply because he
came wearing trousers. Isn't that terribly wicked of them?
Oh, and I received the most interesting invitation this past
week. Alderman Goodbehere is to lay the first stone for
the new Coberg Theater. They're calling it after Prince
Leopold, so who knows what sort of fine people may attend the ground-breaking."

Watching Julia count off their social calendar on her fingers, Jamie was reminded of an eager child making a list
of gifts she expects to receive on her birthday. A very naive child, lacking the vaguest idea of how matters actually
got accomplished in the real world. Julia Highsmith would
have never survived trying to make her living as a con.
She was too impetuous. A truly fine scam required a great
deal more careful thought than her attention span seemed
capable of.

He said, "Perhaps then you are the appropriate person
for me to ask, as I have been puzzling over the issue for
many a year. When your fine ladies and gentlemen of the
ton go for a ride about in Hyde Park, where, exactly, are
they headed?"

Julia slowly lowered her hands in her lap, brow furrow-
ing in puzzlement. "I beg your pardon?"

"Where are they headed? After all, without a destination
in mind, the entire act becomes nothing more than going
around in circles, don't you think? Like a dog chasing its
own tail."

Never having heard one of her favorite activities catego-
rized in just such a fashion, Julia felt hard-pressed to provide Jamie with an adequate answer.

He inquired, "Surely, they don't just ride from one end of the park to the other and then back again?"

"Why, no," Julia said, "Of course not. Sometimes we . . . we stop. And we talk. And we visit. And on Sundays, I like to watch the rowing matches and the boat races on the Thames. You know, above the Westminster Bridge."

"Oh. Well, then." As surprised by her reply as Julia was by her inability to make it sound more intelligent, Jamie pretended to understand, nodding his head vigorously. "I suppose that makes all the difference."

Nearly an hour after she disappeared past the blue silk and stitched gold fleur-de-lys wall hangings, Salome finally returned, telling Julia and Jamie that the marquis of Martyn were waiting for them in the parlor.

"He has agreed to listen to your offer. That was the best I could do. And even then," Salome added cryptically, "it came at the cost of a most intriguing promise."

The present marquis of Martyn proved to be a reed-thin gentleman of six and eighty years, barely capable of maneuvering across the width of his drawing room without the aid of a footman and a golden-tipped cane. Yet, when he spoke, it was with a bark loud enough to be heard in London.

He waited silently for Julia to make her offer, proposing a fair trade of thirty thousand pounds in exchange for the marquis agreeing to let her parade Jamie about London as the estate's legal heir. Seemingly unimpressed, the marquis coughed and hacked into a white linen handkerchief, pausing only to unwrap it and examine the contents within all the while Julia spoke.

It was only when she paused to take a breath that the seemingly frail gentleman snatched up his cane, swinging it so wildly that he barely missed smacking Jamie.

"What use have I for thirty thousand pounds? Will I purchase women with them? A dandy's wardrobe? A meal so rich that its juice drips down my chin for days after? Poppycock! I have no need for money."

Julia stammered, "It is only, Your Lordship, that I

learned of your lack of heir, and I thought, due to, to your nearness—"

"Go on then, miss, out with it. Due to my nearness to the where? The tomb? The grave? The great beyond? Let us make a game of it, shall we?" He poked his long-suffering footman with the ubiquitous cane. "Hitch, you keep score, now. Which one among us can conceive of the most synonyms for where it is I am ever so close to. Go on, young man, hop to it."

Realizing that he was being addressed, Jamie jumped, and gamely offered, "The flesh-eating worms."

Julia gasped in horror, but the marquis seemed to find Jamie's contribution most amusing.

He told the footman, as the latter stood rubbing his shin from the blow, "I like this lad, Hitch. Shows some gumption, he does."

"Aye, Your Lordship, indeed."

"Almost wish I could make him my heir."

"You still can," Julia pointed out. "In a fashion."

The marquis's head bobbed up and down like a puppet on a stick, saliva of delight dripping from one corner of his mouth. Another instant, and Julia expected him to start bouncing in his chair like a fidgety child. Seizing the stick yet again—this time both Jamie and the footman ducked instinctively—the marquis of Martyn held it up like a conductor's baton and announced, "I've got it. Are you a betting man, Mr. Lowell?"

Lest Jamie answer incorrectly, Julia rushed to reassure, "Of course, he is, Your Grace."

"Is that true?" He stared at Jamie through a pair of slits for eyes. "I, myself, could never trust a man who lets a lady speak in his stead. Or," he indicated Salome with a toss of a head, "ask for favors in his absence."

Solemnly, Jamie replied, "I am whoever Miss Highsmith says I am. No more, no less."

"Then would you care to make a wee bit of a wager?" The marquis beckoned Jamie forward with a hand so bony it appeared to possess more than its adequate share of fingers.

"What sort of wager?" Jamie snuck an unsure peek over

his shoulder, as Julia gestured him to do whatever the old man wanted.

"A duel," the marquis of Martyn said. "Winner gets to take my family name in vain."

"A duel, Your Grace?" Jamie wrinkled his brows in confusion.

"A duel, boy, a duel." The marquis wasn't quick enough to catch Jamie with the cane, but it weren't for lack of trying. "Pistols at dawn, or perhaps some more appropriate hour. I so rarely rise before noon."

"Be careful, my lord," the footman warned. "I fear you becoming overly excited."

"Blast it, Hitch, I want to become overexcited. I yearn to become overexcited. I daresay, on several occasions, I even ache to become overexcited." The marquis took a deep breath, feebly tapping his chest as he coughed out, "I told the young lady I have no use for money. But I do have use for some excitement. For some variety. Nay, for some ribaldry, even. Now be a good servant, and fetch my pair of pistols. You spend enough hours in the day polishing them. Might as well see some good come of it all."

"Now, see here, Your Grace." Jamie stared helplessly at Hitch's swiftly disappearing back. "I have yet to agree—"

Julia grabbed Jamie by the arm and pulled him back towards her, whispering, "Humor the man. He is old and frail. I don't doubt that just this mere shouting will wear him out."

He wriggled out of Julia's grasp, chewing nervously on his lower lip and mumbling, "I certainly hope it's important, this cause that you so badly need your inheritance to fund."

"It is important. It is worth dying for."

"You mean," he corrected bitterly, "it is worth *my* dying for."

Hitch, bearing the silver carved box with the pair of pistols inside, escorted the marquis past the house and onto the estate grounds. Julia, Jamie, and Salome followed along behind.

Indicating the elderly peer ambling ahead of them,

Jamie told Julia, "I have yet to see any signs of his growing weary."

"He will. Soon." Although even Julia could no longer feel certain of it.

"By the by," Jamie added, as Hitch handed him the dueling weapon, "did I neglect to mention that I never learned to shoot?"

Stunned by his confession, Julia could only stare blankly at Jamie, finally managing to suggest, "Well. He is old. How fine of a shot could he be?"

"Oh, no," the marquis sounded as enthusiastic as a school boy. Even his previously sallow cheeks had acquired just a touch of color. "You will not be dueling me, Mr. Lowell. My eyesight is hardly what it used to be."

"Then whom shall I shoot at?"

"Why, Hitch, of course."

Jamie and Julia both pivoted to stare at the footman. He returned their curious gaze with one of frustrating neutrality.

"Now see here," Jamie objected. "I've no quarrel with Hitch."

"Oh, that's quite all right." Even the old man's eyes were dancing. "He holds none with you."

Jamie turned to Julia. "Any ideas for pulling me from this fiasco would be most welcome right about now."

But she could think of nothing to do but shrug in reply.

Stiffly, Hitch inquired, "Would you care to take your position, Mr. Lowell?"

"Truthfully?"

Julia knew that she had the power to stop this catastrophe from taking place. It was only proper. Surely, she had not the right to risk the lives of both Jamie and Hitch, all in the name of a purpose only she understood and cared about.

And yet, she recalled the anguished words in Miriam's letter, begging for a salvation that could only come through the rather tangled path of Jamie becoming a temporary marquis so that they could marry and so that her Uncle Collin might release Julia's inheritance. When she thought of the way Miriam had pleaded for Julia to save her, the choice no longer became as clear.

Jamie and Hitch stood back to back, pistols raised to their chests, ready to march ahead forty paces. Jamie glared at Julia, noting stiffly, "This was hardly part and parcel of our agreement, Miss Highsmith. I daresay such a breech of conditions qualifies me to turn tail and flee."

"Don't you dare."

If Hitch was bothered by their shouting in the middle of his duel, he didn't show it. He just continued counting paces, voice growing progressively louder in an attempt to be heard over Jamie and Julia's quarrel. "Seventeen, eighteen, nineteen."

Jamie said, "If I had wished a speedy death, I could have happily remained on the gallows."

"There you had no options. Here, at least, there is a half chance of survival."

"Twenty-four, twenty-five, twenty-six."

"If I decide to drop this pistol and head for the woods, that half chance grows proportionally greater."

"If you head for the woods, I will see to it that every Bow Street runner in England is on the lookout for you come nightfall. By morning you will be back at Newgate. And your chance of survival will once again shrink down to none."

"Thirty-three, thirty-four, thirty-five."

Julia couldn't believe the harshness with which she was pushing Jamie to his potential death. Yet, what choice did she really have in the matter? It was imperative that he acquire a title, and this was the only way she could conceive of doing it.

Watching him march the requisite number of steps, Julia felt her heart starting to beat all the faster. Momentarily forgetting Miriam and Alexia, and the lie Lady Emma had forced Julia to offer Gavin, Julia thought, *But it doesn't matter. None of it matters. I just don't want Jamie to die.*

She opened her mouth to scream for them to stop, resigned at that moment to sacrificing anything and anyone she had to if only to prevent Jamie's being harmed in any way.

But it was too late.

"Forty." Hitch's final shout was nearly obscured by the explosion of gun powder from his pistol, and the sickly sound of Jamie crumpling and crashing to the ground.

6

He hit the dirt, face down, feeling the familiar, suffocating sting of earth clogging up his eyes, mouth, and nose. But Jamie's ears remained clear enough to hear Julia's undisguised gasp of horror, and the scream she managed to stifle by covering her mouth with both hands. His pistol lay beneath him, digging into his stomach at a most uncomfortable angle. Yet, he didn't dare reposition it. He didn't dare move, or so much as breathe.

With cheek pressed to the ground, he caught the echo of Hitch's boots moving closer. His heart hammered so madly against his throat that Jamie feared it would escape out his mouth. Yet he forced every muscle in his body to remain limp and lifeless.

With one mammoth hand, Hitch grabbed Jamie by the shoulder, yanking him a good foot and a half off the ground, and turning the body over, before carelessly dropping Jamie on his back.

He then saw his presumed shooting victim unexpectedly open his eyes, grab at his pistol, and, smiling so sweetly he might have been offering the footman another scone with his tea, remark, "I do believe that it's my shot."

To his credit, Hitch's sole show of surprise consisted of a brief, bewildered blink of his eyes, and a swift, guilty glance over his shoulder at the marquis of Martyn who was no longer quite so delighted. The old man's pupils had grown as round as his ears. He stared, perplexed, from Hitch, to Jamie, and back again. He tried to speak, but found a few specks of dry spittle easier to produce than saliva, and finally settled for a cock of his head, and a helpless shrug of both shoulders in lieu of a verbal apology. Hitch took a deep breath, swallowing so hard that his Adam's apple ballooned to the size of a melon, and, straightening his uniform, prepared to accept his fate.

Except his assassin-to-be was no longer looking in Hitch's direction. Because Jamie couldn't tear his gaze away from Julia.

She had gone absolutely pale, her skin blanching so white that it had turned a deathly shade of greenish gray. She had chewed the nail on her thumb down to the quick, drawing a drop of blood.

It was the most vulnerable Jamie had ever seen Miss Julia Highsmith. He felt certain that, if he wanted, Jamie could finally seize the upper hand over her with an ease equal to none other.

At the very least, he now possessed the perfect opportunity to hurl a series of barbs in Julia's direction, in justifiable compensation for all the insults and patronizing remarks she'd sent his way in the past week.

Except that, for a reason Jamie could barely identify, much less admit to, he found himself unable to do it.

Watching Julia so obviously frightened—and over his welfare, no less—Jamie felt his initial urge to exploit the situation completely overshadowed by another very different emotion. He wanted to protect her. To take her in his arms and stroke her hair until her terrified shaking finally stopped for good. He wanted to kiss her injured finger, wrap his palm around the wound until the warmth from his hands magically healed every ache, every hurt that plagued Julia not only today, but throughout her entire life.

This, Jamie decided, was not a positive development.

Bad enough he was in debt to the woman for his clothes, his meals, his life. If he allowed her dominance over anything else, Jamie might as well roll over right then and there, and offer Hitch another shot at the target. He couldn't risk handing Julia such an advantage. And yet, deep down, there remained a part of Jamie that wondered whether capitulation might not have its pleasant side.

"I say, sir," Hitch said while he uncomfortably cleared his throat, and waved one hand in front of Jamie's face, hoping to recapture his attention. "If you do not mind, I would prefer you, well, getting on with things, as it were. This anticipation, it truly is the most uncomfortable of all. Do shoot, now. I am waiting."

Forcibly ripping his eyes from Julia's gradually calming figure, Jamie stared down at the pistol in his hands. He turned it this way and that, studying the barrel and the trigger with near childlike curiosity. Finally, he confessed, "The truth is, I've never fired a pistol before."

Hitch closed both eyes, pained. "Marvelous." Sighing, he told Jamie, "You line up the target—in this case, that would be me—along the sight."

"That's this little bump on the end?"

"Precisely." He raised Jamie's arms to chest level. "Line up the target, aim, and pull the trigger. It would be a great help if you were facing me at the time."

Jamie did as Hitch instructed, holding the pistol at arm's length, but already half turning away and squirming, face wrinkled in reluctance, as his finger rubbed the trigger.

"Please, sir." Despite his radically changing fortunes during the course of the last quarter hour, Hitch had yet to alter his tone. "I would prefer to die from a single bullet to the heart, rather than from a prolonged, agonizing, infected, not to mention messy, hemorrhage to another area. Do aim carefully, Mr. Lowell. You are at point-blank range. I would hate for you to miss."

Jamie nodded thoughtfully, reassuring Hitch that he understood his point completely. Then, as if the thought just came to him, he turned to the marquis and inquired, "Have I won yet?"

The old man's quickly fading brows both burrowed together to form a single eyebrow of average length and width. He sputtered, "What? What did you say, boy? Won? Won what?"

"Our wager. May I go about London proclaiming myself the future marquis of Martyn, with no fear of your denying the fact?"

The present marquis waved his question away with an indifferent toss of one hand. "If you wish. I, personally, have grown rather tired of the moniker."

Jamie snuck a peek at Julia over his shoulder. He expected her to be ecstatic at the news. Finally, she would get exactly what she wanted. And it hadn't cost her a farthing.

He thought she would be leaping for joy, throwing her bonnet in the air, or whatever it was the upper classes did to express happiness. But she hardly appeared to have heard the marquis' approval. Instead, Julia remained where she was, blinking furiously to keep back what, if Jamie didn't know better, he could have sworn were tears. But hardly ones of joy.

Her eyes met Jamie's, and for that instant, he was once again awash with the same sensations that, only a moment earlier, Jamie had personally decreed thoroughly inappropriate.

"I am sorry." The quiet tone was so unfamiliar, he could hardly believe it to be coming from Julia. "I am so sorry. I did not want anyone hurt because of me."

He didn't know how to respond. Neither did Hitch nor the marquis, so they merely swiveled their heads to stare at Jamie, looking for some clue on how to proceed.

In response, he stood up straighter, squaring his shoulders, until his posture was that of the silly dragoon Jamie had acted out for Julia on a previous occasion. He turned his back, tossing the pistol over his shoulder and into the hands of a most unprepared Hitch, who had to fumble to catch it. "Lovely meeting all of you, I'm sure. But the fictitious Marquis would like to go home now."

For part of the carriage ride homeward, Julia sat still and silent, neither agreeing nor disagreeing with her aunt, who, for the first time since Jamie intruded upon her life actually deigned to speak *to* him, rather than at him. He supposed the fact that Jamie were now sitting between the two ladies, as opposed to at their feet, may have had something to do with it.

At the first words out of Salome's mouth, Jamie instantly recognized where Julia had learned that imperious tone she so liked to toss in his direction. Salome lectured, "If we meet someone along the way, you are to introduce yourself as the marquis of Martyn's nephew. His heir, and my godson. Your mother left England many years ago to marry a wealthy foreigner."

"Now would that need be a citizen of a particular country, or will any foreigner do?" Jamie, who did not appreciate being treated like a fool either by young ladies or their dowager aunts, snapped irritably. The bulk of his attention, anyhow, lay focused on Julia and her uncharacteristic silence. Jamie wished that he might lean over and ask Julia what was wrong. But he doubted her aunt would approve of such forward behavior.

"New Zealand," Salome announced. "We shall tell people that you were raised in New Zealand."

"Australia is better," Jamie said, because he simply felt like annoying her. "Larger continent. Easier to have remained anonymous."

She allowed his suggestion a moment's thought, then finally conceded. "You are visiting your uncle. But, since the Marquis lives so far out in the country, he feared you might grow bored, and so he asked me, a family friend, if you might spend some weeks with us, closer to the London social scene."

"I am sorry, Mrs. Weiss," Jamie said with mock formality, over-enunciating each word, "but you are certainly no friend of mine. I would have thought, your being on such good terms with the marquis, you might at least have voiced the tiniest of objections whilst he were making plans to mount my head in his trophy case."

"It were you who agreed to it. You are a grown man, surely, you are fit to make your own decisions."

Unexpectedly, Julia turned to face Jamie, her eyes wide. As if only now waking from a deep sleep, she whispered, "That was a dreadful chance you took. He might have killed you."

Jamie reminded, "Despite what your aunt asserts, I wasn't given a lot of choice in the matter, m'lady. From somewhere in the deep recesses of my mind—or maybe it were from a few feet behind me—I heard a voice, female, as a matter of fact it was, telling me that if I did not accept the challenge, I would be quite dead by morning, either way."

"Did you really believe I would do that to you?" Julia rested her hand on Jamie's arm, reaching across Salome's lap to do so.

Through the layers of fabric, he could feel the warmth of her fingers against his skin. And so much softer than he ever could have imagined. He wanted to rest his cheek against her palm, and hear her say his name in anything but a command. But, instead, Jamie merely answered, "I've known a great many desperate people in my day, Miss Highsmith. Desperate people often do desperate things. And only regret them later."

She accepted his scolding, admitting, "All my life, if I wanted something, God help anyone who stood in my way. I rarely stopped to think how my actions affected other people."

"So why now, Julia?" If she heard his impertinent use of her Christian name, she didn't react to it. "What was so different about today, that it made you respond in such a manner?"

She looked away, using one finger to slowly trace the outline of her carriage window, pretending to be engrossed in the moving countryside. Finally, Julia confessed, "You. It was you."

"Me, Miss Highsmith?"

"I've never put a person in mortal danger before. At least I hope I never have. It made me realize how selfish I have been."

By the time they reached Picadilly, Julia had apparently either made peace with her guilt, or decided to simply ignore it. Jamie sensed the improvement in her mood the moment Julia's power of speech returned with a vengeance.

It were her idea that they stop at Monsieur Andre's, a

tailor her late father had been particularly fond of, to order Jamie's fashionable new clothes.

Sweeping into the shop with Jamie and Salome running to catch up, Julia barely waited for the proprietor, Monsieur Andre himself, to kiss her hand and exclaim over what a beautiful young lady Julia had grown into, before she launched into the tale of her houseguest, Mr. Jamie Lowell, who had arrived in England for a visit. Unfortunately, the paperskull coachman, minding his stage, foolishly piled all of Mr. Lowell's baggage in the rear boots, forgetting to cover the lot when it began to rain, and allowing every stitch of clothing Mr. Lowell owned to be soaked and ruined.

Did Monsieur Andre think he might be able to help them? They needed an entire wardrobe of men's clothes as soon as possible. And did Julia mention that money were no object?

She was about to launch into a list of items they would need, when Jamie, voice level but unmistakably authoritarian, gently rested his hand upon Julia's arm. "Do forgive me, Miss Highsmith, but I have been dressing myself for quite a few years now."

Julia blushed, realizing the impertinence of her actions, and the manner in which such impertinence could be interpreted. Gritting her teeth, she attempted to apologize, furious both at herself for making such an error, and at Jamie for the terribly polite way he'd chastised her. Now she would not even have the satisfaction of thinking him arrogant or condescending.

Seeing Julia's thinly veiled fury, Jamie allowed himself only the briefest of smiles, before telling Monsieur Andre, "Although, of course, on the other hand, whom do I dress for, if not the lovely ladies of London? Perhaps it would be wise, after all, for me to consult Miss Highsmith."

Julia stared at Jamie in surprise, unsure of whether or not he were teasing her.

Jamie continued, "Australian fashion, I am afraid, is quite behind the styles of England. I would not wish to offend anyone by making an incorrect choice of garment."

They spent the rest of the afternoon picking out material, arguing the merits of silk and wool berege versus Circassian cloth, and the aesthetic advantages of grenadine versus lutestring. While Jamie and Monsieur Andre retired to the back room for measuring, Julia and Salome made a list of garments to order. He would need a variety of coats, of course, in varying lengths and colors to suit the occasion. Pantaloons, hats, gloves, shirts, boots. And all had to be in the first state of elegance.

As the four of them labored over making Jamie Lowell a Corinthian in prime twig, either Julia or Salome would occasionally be interrupted by friends and acquaintances who spotted them through the shop window and popped in to say hello.

To each of them, the women introduced Jamie as the marquis of Martyn's nephew, exclaiming with delight that he had "finally arrived." They spoke as if Jamie's visit had been common knowledge among the *ton* for weeks, trapping their audience in the unenviable position of either claiming ignorance and thus admitting to a seat outside the know, or of going along with the fabrication. Predictably, everyone whom Julia and Salome introduced Jamie to chose the latter.

As they left Monsieur Andre's, both footmen loaded down with packages and instructions to return next week for the rest, Jamie complimented Julia and Salome on their deviousness.

Niece and aunt exchanged looks. "You are not the only one practiced in the art of living a deception, Mr. Lowell."

That evening at tea, Jamie waited until Salome had excused herself to check up on supper preparations, before asking Julia, "Is there a particular reason that your aunt seems to so despise me, or is she just practicing in anticipation of a future evil?"

Julia thoughtfully stirred her tea, tapping her spoon against the cup's rim and shaking off the final drops of brown liquid before resting it upon the blue and white patterned saucer. "I do not think that Aunt Salome hates you, Jamie. It is the idea of you that she does not like. You remind her of things that she would, all the same, rather forget."

"What things?" He crossed his legs, balancing the saucer and cup on one knee, and leaning back in his chair.

Realizing that she had already confessed more than she ever intended to, Julia attempted to pull back, waving the question away with one hand, and proceeded to lead the conversation towards a less probing topic. Julia said, "Did you see the faces of those ladies we met this afternoon at Monsieur Andre's? They were quite taken with you, Jamie. Quite taken. Why, this entire masquerade might prove to be easier than we thought."

She looked to Jamie, hoping for a word of confirmation on her prediction. But no agreement proved forthcoming. Instead, he remained as he was, sitting across from her, arms crossed against his chest, watching Julia with an intensity that seemed to bore right through her. He wasn't smiling, and in response she felt her own smile fade. His eyes fastened on hers, making it impossible to look away or hide. For a moment, Julia actually believed Jamie capable of seeing through the facade she'd worked so hard to erect around her true thoughts and feelings, and into her very soul.

She knew that she should be offended by his brazen invasion, but, strangely, the only sensation Julia seemed capable of summoning was a most unfamiliar consciousness of relief. How long had Julia been waiting for someone, anyone, to cut through all her lies and defenses and finally discover the true Julia Highsmith? How long had she been praying for the day when, at long last, Julia could stop pretending and just be?

The romantic in her wanted to believe that such a moment had at long last arrived. But the pragmatist knew better.

Drawing on all her strength, Julia ripped her gaze away from Jamie's, reminding herself that she was probably reading much too much into the entire exchange. No one, not even Jamie Lowell, could ever know a person simply by looking at them.

But, for the rest of the evening, just to be safe, Julia conscientiously avoided meeting Jamie's eyes.

With a few days to pass while they waited for the finer items in Jamie's new wardrobe to be completed, Salome told Julia, "My dear, you had best begin thinking of how exactly you intend to spring Mr. Lowell upon your uncle. Remember, the gentleman-to-be is allowed only one chance to make a first impression, and, for all our sakes, it should be no less than spectacular."

"Why, Aunt Salome," Julia teased. "And to think that you once judged my entire scheme a thoroughly horrid idea."

Salome refused to crack a smile or admit to a change in opinion. Stiffly, she said, "I still insist that it is most horrid. Unfortunately, as long as you appear so set on going through with it, my task is to insure that, at least, it is the best-executed horrid idea in London."

Julia beamed, impulsively kissing her aunt on the cheek. She felt as if a load the weight of a small pony were being lifted off her shoulders. At least she no longer had to face the upcoming trials alone. At least there would be someone to support her and warn Julia that she were getting too far out of line. Not that Miss Highsmith had any intention of listening to the latter.

She answered Salome's earlier question with a shrug and, "I suppose I shall merely arrive at my Uncle Collin's door, Jamie in tow, and hope for the best."

"No," Salome said.

"I beg your pardon?"

"No. Julia, you simply cannot thrust a potential husband upon a man with standards as stringent as your uncle's, without first laying a bit of groundwork towards his acceptance."

"But I intend to introduce him as the marquis of Martyn's nephew and heir. Won't my telling him of Jamie's potential wealth, and of the lands his father owns in Australia, won't that do enough to impress Uncle Collin?"

Salome smiled. She patted Julia upon the hand as if her

niece were still a child, and solemnly educated, "My darling, Julia, if I have told you once, I have told you a dozen times, never complete any task yourself when you can get the *ton* to do it for you."

Reasoning that any biographical information the duke of Alamain heard about Jamie Lowell would carry much more weight coming from seemingly impartial sources, Julia and Salome set about the task of innocently disseminating information.

While visiting the Princess Esterhazy for tea, Salome waited until their hostess concluded a most delicious story regarding Beau Brummell referring to their prince regent as the second baron of Alvanley's "fat friend," before she happened to mention her houseguest, the marquis of Martyn's nephew, and proceeded to launch into a detailed description of his fictitious Australian holdings.

At the opera, in between a heated discussion that carried to their adjoining boxes, regarding whether the Philharmonic Society had acted generous or foolish in offering Ludwig van Beethoven three hundred guineas to come to London and bring with him two new compositions, Julia and Salome made certain to also discuss, equally loudly, that recently arrived nonpareil, Jamie Lowell, and his instant fascination with Julia.

As Salome said, if, by the end of the evening, the entire hall did not have its curiosity whetted, it were not for niece and aunt's lack of trying.

By next afternoon, a half-dozen women came calling. Julia held her breath, watching every moment of Jamie's initial introduction to society with the intensity most reserved for rabid animals and particularly intense cricket matches. Every time Jamie opened his mouth, she expected him to blurt out something inappropriate. At one point, when talk turned to the Spa Fields riots, Julia felt certain that, any moment, Jamie might utter some phrase that would brand him on the side of the poor who'd rioted instead of with those who condemned the entire uprising.

But he never so much as wavered.

Instead, Jamie chatted with the ladies about his uncle,

the marquis, that delightful character Hitch, and Australia, painting verbal pictures of a land that, if it did not in actuality exist, certainly should have, from the beauty of Jamie's description.

He discussed Byron's leaving England, and the illicit rumors surrounding his departure, as if such were the most common of topics for him, nodding politely when the Viscountess Lark expounded her opinions on both Anabella Milbanke and Augusta Leigh.

He agreed wholeheartedly when the duchess of Westlake praised the House of Lords recent abolition of income tax on land owners, and Jamie responded with, "Do not you also find that a twenty-one-pound tax on those owning four-wheeled carriages, coupled with the nine-pound tax on possessing three horses to be terribly steep? After all, how ever are those attempting to subsist on a mere fifty thousand pounds or so supposed to bear it?"

The ladies left still singing Jamie's praises, and issuing more invitations to social events than there were hours in the day. He thanked each one graciously, promised to try and attend, and kissed their hands in a manner that made even the oldest among them, fifty-two-year-old Lady Langly, blush and titter.

Following their departure, and still flying from the success, Julia eagerly asked Salome, "What shall we do next? What now?"

"Now, my lovely Julia, we sit back and we wait for word of your delightful Mr. Lowell to reach the duke of Alamain. And then we wait for him to issue the both of you an invitation to visit."

The last instance Jamie remembered his appearance being so fussed over, his mum was spitting on her handkerchief and wiping his face clean for church.

Before they set out for the visit with her uncle, Julia must have ordered Jamie to change garments six times, until she finally settled on the picture she wanted him to present, circling Jamie no less than a dozen times, smoothing down the fit of his coat in the shoulders, wiping away imaginary dust specks, and tugging on the folds of his shirt to make them lay down right. Her hand brushed his waist, fleetingly at first, then returning to actually dig her fingers into the fabric.

Accusingly, she asked Jamie, "Why aren't you wearing the Cumberland corset Monsieur Andre sent over?"

Jamie stepped back, so that Julia might receive a better view of his figure. "I'm afraid that I have no use for one, m'lady. Everything, I am happy to report, stands straight by itself."

It took a beat for the full meaning behind his words to sink in. Julia ordered herself not to blush or comment.

Her resolve on the former managed to last a good few seconds, after which she ducked her head, hiding both scarlet cheeks from Jamie's gaze, and proceeded to spend one half hour arranging his cravat, folding and unfolding and discarding, until Jamie's neck felt raw from all the ministering.

"If I did not know any better, I might begin to suspect all this attention to be of a more personal nature," Jamie said.

"You flatter yourself, Mr. Lowell."

"No." He turned Julia about so that both faced the full-length mirror. He slipped one hand around her waist, and placed the other on Julia's shoulder. Their reflection glimmered back to present a most handsome young couple. "On the contrary, Miss Highsmith. It is *you* whom I flatter."

She could feel the heat of his hand through the thin cotton sleeves covering her shoulder, and the sensations seemed to travel down the length of her body. Even through the mirror, the magnetic pull of Jamie's eyes that had so captivated Julia a few days earlier tugged as hard as ever, filling her with a warmth the pleasure of which far outweighed the unfamiliarity. It was as hypnotizing as staring at a fire, and, somehow, equally as dangerous to approach.

"Well?" Jamie whispered. "What do you think, Miss Highsmith?"

Think? He wanted her to *think?*

Julia licked her lips, forcing moisture into her mouth in the hope that, once she were once again capable of speaking, her muddled brain might actually conceive of something for her to say.

"What?" Julia asked. "Think about what?"

Hardly a particularly brilliant utterance, but certainly an improvement over staring blankly into the mirror.

"Us." Jamie stretched himself to full height, as if both of them were posing for a formal portrait.

"Us." Julia repeated, simultaneously thinking that, judging from the caliber of this conversation, the celebrated wits of London could certainly sleep soundly at night, secure in the knowledge that Miss Julia Highsmith would never be a threat to their positions. "What do you mean, us, Jamie?"

"I mean," he smoothed down an imaginary wrinkle in his coat. "What do you think of how the pair of us look, Miss Highsmith? Why, what in the world might you have thought I meant?"

If it weren't for the incident at the marquis's home, the most nervous Jamie ever spied Julia would have been in the moments before the door to her uncle's drawing room opened, and the duke of Alamain stepped out to greet his niece. She had to link her fingers to keep from biting her nails, and Julia's feet refused to stay in one place, forcing her to dance a very small mazurka, constantly shifting her weight from leg to leg. She wore a pale yellow dress, with matching bonnet and parasol. The pastel color brought out the rich blackness of both her eyes and her hair.

"My precious Julia!" The duke raised both arms to embrace his brother's daughter, a task made difficult by the fact Collin Highsmith was a man so rotund that, by the time his arms outstretched his midsection, there was little room left for Julia. "And who might this be?" The duke turned his attention to Jamie, the smile beneath his mustache twisting into a potential frown.

"This is Jeremy Lowell, Uncle. The marquis of Martyn's nephew. From Australia. I wrote you of him. In reply to your invitation to visit."

Jamie tried to stand taller and look simultaneously wealthy, titled, and Australian. He said, "I have come, Your Grace, to ask for your niece's hand in marriage."

"Hrmph."

Jamie wondered whether to interpret it as a grunt of approval or disdain.

"Australia, did you say?"

"Yes, sir."

"Sydney?"

"No."

"Melbourne?"

"No."

"Surely you did not reside among the kangaroos, Mr. Lowell."

"No, sir. I did not."

Geographically, Jamie's plan was simple. He had no intention of revealing his alleged birthplace until his inquisitor had finished calling off every township and city he was familiar with. That way, once he eliminated the treacherous, Jamie could proclaim himself a native of some obscure area no one had ever heard of.

"Well, then?" the duke demanded. "Whereabouts in Australia?"

"Queen's Rock, sir." Jamie had no idea whether such a place even existed. But it certainly sounded like a good name for a town in a British commonwealth country that, as far as he knew, was covered in desert and stone.

"Queen's Rock?" Now the potential frown was, without a doubt, sliding towards the real thing. "Never heard of it."

"It is quite small, sir. My father ran a sheep and cattle station. Up north. Very, very, up north."

The duke rested his hands on his belly, the fingers barely touching, and sighed. Finally, he turned to Julia, "I wish to have a talk with your young man. In private."

"But, Uncle." Julia all but blocked the door to the drawing room with her body. "I have already told you everything you need to know about Mr. Lowell."

"Cannot the gentleman speak for himself?"

"Certainly," Jamie donned his most confident face, and stepped forward toward where the duke was beckoning.

As he moved into the drawing room, he heard, behind him, Collin Highsmith whisper to his niece, "I do not like this, Julia. I do not like this one bit."

7

For a man who did not like him one bit, the duke of Alamain certainly took great pains to ask Jamie what sort of sherry he preferred, to offer him a cigar, and to favor his niece's intended with a brief history of the Highsmith family.

Pretending to be deeply engrossed in the tale, Jamie arranged his features in a show of attentiveness, all the while proceeding to study his surroundings. Because, without a doubt, this manor was by far the grandest home he'd ever been in.

Starting off in a single-room hovel, and then proceeding to charm his way gradually upward by means of the daughters of the middle class—merchants, clergymen, civil officials, and the like—still never prepared Jamie for the life enjoyed by England's aristocracy. If he had believed Julia's home something to behold, then her uncle's residence quite simply made him dizzy.

Instead of a single crystal chandelier, this room hung three, every piece of glass a work of art within itself. The furniture stood covered with a rich, velvet-textured black damask. The intricately carved wood gleamed from a decade of conscientious polishing. Two mirrors, each in a flowering golden frame, hung on opposing walls, making the room appear filled with an infinite amount of treasures.

And the quiet. Despite all he had already seen, it was

the peace and serenity of these isolated manor houses that still appealed to Jamie the most. No couples breaking rolling pins over each other's heads, no drunks staggering home and passing out in the alleys, no peddlers hawking their wares at the tops of their lungs. Until he'd come to the country, Jamie had possessed no idea that birds actually made an audible sound when they opened their mouths. And such a pleasant sound at that.

Which, sadly, was more than Jamie could say for the duke of Alamain. For next to ten minutes, Julia's uncle droned on and on about no topic in particular, requiring nothing more of Jamie than an occasional nod of the head.

Swishing the sherry about in his decanter, the duke took a final swallow, throwing his head back and sucking the final drop out of his glass, before finally turning towards the matter at hand. "You seem like a fine lad," he said. "Good future, fine family, a pleasant income and title to look forward to. Yes, yes, don't look so surprised. I've heard quite a bit about you these past weeks. All of it favorable, let me assure you. Why, all of London is talking about the marquis of Martyn's charming nephew."

Jamie made a note to compliment Salome on her handiwork.

"So, tell me then, why in the world would you want to marry my niece?"

"Because I love her, sir," Jamie answered with the sincerity of someone who'd been practicing for such a question all week.

"So? What matters that?" The duke moved to stand beside the fireplace, underneath a nearly life-size portrait of himself in leaner days. "Why should a promising young gentleman like yourself wish to tie himself down with the likes of Julia?"

"I do not understand, sir." A moment ago, Jamie had come in expecting to be asked to defend himself. Now, he was facing the task of speaking up on Julia's behalf.

"The girl has no positive attributes. She is stubborn, rude, argumentative, domineering, surly, ill-mannered, and, Lord help us all, how that girl can talk in circles until even the strongest go begging for mercy."

"You say that as if it were a bad trait." Jamie offered the duke his most innocent, beguiling smile.

The Duke peered at him queerly. "You find her complete lack of decorum charming, do you, Mr. Lowell?"

"In all honesty," Jamie was surprised to realize how true the words sounded to his ears, "those are exactly the traits I find most appealing about your niece."

"Hrmph." Twice, in ten minutes. Jamie really must be displeasing His Grace now. Apparently exasperated with his young guest's refusal to follow the prepared text for this dialogue, the duke drew his chair closer to Jamie's, leaning over until they were practically sitting face to face, and whispered, "The girl comes from bad blood, you know."

"Bad blood?" The only bad blood Jamie knew of, was the kind that refused to stop dripping from your nose, mouth, or eye after a tavern brawl. "What sort of bad blood?"

"Suffice it be for me to explain that my brother, God rest his soul, made a most unwise choice in his marriage. He wed for love, you understand. The girl was thoroughly unsuitable. I am afraid that Lyle was a bit like Julia in some respects. Absolutely impossible to stop once a particular bee landed in his bonnet. They were able to hide the truth, of course. He forbade her to so much as speak of it to another living soul. But, well, I feel that it is my duty as a gentleman to warn you. There's bad blood on the mother's side, Mr. Lowell."

"Is that why Julia refused Lord Neff's proposal?"

All three of the duke's chins wagged in synchronized surprise. "Told you about that, did she?"

"Julia and I are very honest with one another." *We only lie to everyone else.*

The duke nodded thoughtfully. "Indeed. I counseled her to do so. You cannot begin to imagine the scandal and heartache it would have caused Gavin if the truth ever came out. Why, he would have been ruined. Absolutely ruined. And his children. Goodness gracious, it might have meant the end of the entire Neff line."

* * *

Considering how long and how hard she had been staring at the drawing room door, Julia felt the least she ought to be able to do was see through it by now. Or at least hear through it.

What could Jamie and Uncle Collin possibly be talking about this entire time? All the duke needed to do was utter either yea or a nay to the marriage. How long could such a simple task take?

Surely, after the fiction Jamie had performed for Hitch and the marquis's benefit, how hard could it be to pass for a living, breathing peer?

Julia shivered, remembering just how real Jamie's death act had seemed. A second after Hitch fired, Jamie actually flew backwards, landing on the ground in a crumpled, seemingly lifeless heap. His performance was so good, Julia actually imagined that she had seen the bullet enter his body. She imagined she saw the blood that came spurting out of his chest on point of impact.

She'd wanted to scream then. But, like in the worst of nightmares, no sound was forthcoming. She wanted to run to him, pick him up off the ground, tend to his wounds, and beg Jamie not to die. But, in the end, Julia did none of those things.

She tried to tell herself that it was due to fear. Her legs felt rooted to the spot, cold, and as heavy as two columns of Roman marble. She couldn't move, much less run anywhere. Her breath stayed trapped in her throat, also frozen into a block of ice that refused to move either up or down. Her head spun, necessitating Julia's grabbing onto a tree branch for support. That was why she could not follow her heart and run to Jamie. At least, that was what Julia spent the last week trying to convince herself was the reason. But even she no longer believed her own rationalizations. Because Julia knew that the reason she had stayed where she was, even as she stood convinced that Jamie were bleeding to death in front of her eyes, was because Julia felt terrified of running to Jamie, only to have him reject her. She couldn't bear the humiliation of reaching out to Jamie and having him push her away.

And yet, the impulse to do so was undeniable.

So, naturally, Julia fought it by treating Jamie shabbily. So that he would grow angry with her.

Because it was a great deal easier for Julia to keep her distance from him when Jamie was shouting at her, than when he was acting as sweet and compassionate as he had during the ride back from the marquis's house. In fact, if Julia had her way, Jamie might remain perpetually cross in her presence, so that he might not seem any more appealing to Julia than he already was.

After what felt like a decade of nervous waiting, but, in actuality was barely three quarters of an hour, the drawing room doors finally opened, and her uncle returned to the foyer, followed by an uncharacteristically somber Jamie.

Immediately, Julia feared the worst. They had been denied, found out, exposed. And yet, her uncle didn't appear angry. In point of fact, he was positively beaming with self-satisfaction.

"Well?" Julia demanded, looking from the duke to Jamie. "Have you come to an agreement?"

"Not yet," Jamie said. "Your uncle tells me that he still needs to give some more thought to this matter."

"Thought? Thought? What is there to think about?" Julia shouted her queries so loud, Isaac warned her to stop, lest she spook the horses. Slamming the carriage door shut behind them, Julia demanded of Jamie, "What did he say, exactly? Did he sound well disposed to your proposal? Did he sound skeptical?"

"He sounded," Jamie told her truthfully, "like someone who wishes to make sure that you never marry."

"Don't be daft. Why in the world would my uncle not . . ." Julia's voice trailed off as even she recognized the obvious. Slowly, she said, "He does not want to pass on my inheritance. He wants all of my father's lands and wealth for himself."

"That would be my guess, yes."

Julia fought the instinct to order Isaac to turn around and head back to her uncle's home, so that she might throttle him. Instead, she settled for asking, "What did he tell you? To keep you from wanting to marry me?"

Jamie fidgeted, hesitantly running his tongue against his upper lip before answering, "He told me that there was bad blood on your mother's side of the family. That it had been passed on to you. And that you would, in turn, pass it on to your children."

Bad blood.

He'd told her as much six months past, when Julia came running to her uncle, dizzy from the thrill of Gavin's proposal, and so certain that the duke would give his consent to her marriage that she'd never even contemplated what Julia might do if he refused.

But he didn't refuse. That was Collin Highsmith's brilliance. Instead of forbidding his niece to marry Gavin Neff, he merely warned her against it. Cryptic, at first, forcing her to all but beg for details, then, finally, with an oh-so-sincere sigh of regret, the Duke confessed all.

About Julia's mother. About Salome. And about Julia herself.

She hadn't believed him.

He told her to ask Aunt Salome.

And it were Salome who, after cursing her brother-in-law with words Julia never even suspected the older woman of knowing, much less uttering, confirmed Uncle Collin's tale. Bad blood.

The phrase echoed and multiplied in Julia's brain until she feared it overflowing. Of course, to Uncle Collin, that is exactly what it was. He had despised her mother. And he had cursed Lyle for dooming them all to living in constant fear of discovery.

Cautiously, Jamie inquired, "What did he mean, then, your uncle? About the bad blood? What was he talking about?"

"That," the answer came automatically to Julia, "is none of your concern, Mr. Lowell."

"Fine." Jamie crossed his arms and turned away.

Was he pouting again, or merely complying? With Jamie, it were so hard to tell just what was going on behind those infuriating eyes. His pupils were a shade of blue so light, they reminded Julia of brightly gleaming mirrors. No matter how deeply she peered into them, all she saw back was a noncommittal reflection. Every sincere emotion, she suspected, was firmly locked up behind that impenetrable mask.

He said, "Your uncle's words may be none of my business, but his actions most certainly are. He is determined to prevent your ever marrying. When he realized that I was not about to be frightened away, he appeared ready to simply veto our union."

Julia grabbed Jamie's arm. "He wouldn't dare."

"Aye, he would."

"What did you say to him?"

"I told him that I needed more time to consider his warning, and convinced him to postpone his official decision."

"Thank God." Julia felt free to breathe again. Awkwardly, she tried to compliment Jamie. "That truly was quick and clever thinking on your part."

He shrugged, indifferent. "It is what you hired me to do."

His use of the word *"hired"* surprised Julia. Or, rather, she was surprised by how much it affected her. Somehow, she found the fact that he considered their circumstance a job rather insulting. Although, she couldn't for the life of her decipher why.

Jamie continued, "Unfortunately, we cannot stall him forever. Eventually, when he realizes that I still intend to marry you, all your uncle needs to do is formally forbid it, and you will be back at the same spot you were weeks ago. He holds the ultimate power over you." Jamie couldn't help himself from adding, "Rather, in the same manner as you do over me."

Julia chose to ignore his closing barb. Although, sadly, she was forced to admit the validity of all that came before it. Jamie was absolutely right. Her uncle did have the power to make sure that she never received her father's inheritance. And, since that was obviously the duke's plan, there was no reason why he couldn't go on rejecting every suitor she presented him with as unsuitable.

Her only option was to intersect him. To trick the duke into publicly voicing his approval for her marriage. Or at least to maneuver him into a situation where he had no choice but to do so.

Over dinner, Julia barely had a chance to taste the delicious broiled chicken and kidney pie Cook had served them. She was too busy watching Jamie eat.

At first, Julia thought her fascination stemmed from simply wishing to monitor his table manners. She still suffered nightmares of their going into society, and of Jamie reaching for the wrong piece of silverware, or committing some other unforgivable *faux pas*. However, after becoming convinced that he had done an exemplary job of absorbing every lesson she had drummed into him, Julia realized that the reason she so enjoyed watching him eat was because Jamie was the first person in her life whom she'd ever truly seen enjoying his food.

Everyone else she knew merely cut, chewed, and swallowed. The scrumptious breakfasts and luncheons and dinners and suppers in front of them had so long ago become predictably routine that no one even tasted them anymore.

But Jamie relished each bite.

Every morsel was a new experience, every slice a dream come true. He noticed everything, from the tender flakiness of the pie's crust, to the rich juices spilling out of its meat, to the sweetness of the baby potatoes. He cut his dinner into small pieces, chewing each one long enough to drain every last bit of taste pleasure. He didn't hurry through the food, but rather reveled in all the sensations available.

Julia watched, nearly mesmerized, the sleekness with which he handled the cutlery. It amazed her that someone as big as Jamie could so sensitively manipulate the delicate silverware, managing to make a simple, simultaneous raising of his fork and knife look almost balletic in its beauty.

The backs of his hands were deeply tanned from the sun, the palms covered with work-induced callouses that only now were starting to soften. She could see the veins underneath his skin flex with every flick of the knife. To Julia, they seemed almost flirtatious in their constant appearance and reappearance.

The pie in her throat froze on its way down, as the full impact of her thoughts finally sunk into Julia's brain.

Truly, she must be going mad.

What other answer could there be?

After all, sane people certainly did not first grow hypnotized by forks and knives, and then interpret perfectly natural body rhythms as flirtations. What in the world was wrong with her?

Noting Julia's preoccupation with his eating habits, Jamie awkwardly lay down the cutlery. "Did I do something wrong?" he asked.

It took a supreme yank of will for her to look into his eyes and force her features into a charade of indifference. "What? Wrong? No. I—I was just . . . thinking. About my uncle. And what I can do. To stop him."

Wonderful. Now she was even incapable of speaking in complete sentences. A few more days like this and Julia could forget marriage and France, and concentrate instead on keeping her uncle from committing her to the insane asylum.

But Jamie did not appear to notice. He nodded his head thoughtfully and agreed, "The duke of Alamain will not be an easy bloke to budge once he's got his mind made up."

"It runs in the family," Julia said.

"That it does." Jamie saw the expression on Julia's face unexpectedly change from a frown of frustration, to the beginnings of a foxlike smile. He asked eagerly, "You have thought of something to cross him?"

She rocked her head mischievously from side to side, the grin growing wider with each bob. "Possibly. Very possibly."

"Well, go on then. Out with it."

Julia rubbed her hands one against the other, tapping both middle fingers against her lips. She turned to Jamie, eyes shining, and said, "You are a charming fellow, are you not?"

Raising his eyebrow, he slowly replied, "Some individuals have been heard to agree with that, yes."

"Individuals, yes, I know. But how skilled are you at charming large crowds?"

He shrugged. "A large crowd is just a mass of individuals. I don't foresee a particularly great difference."

"Excellent." Drowning in excitement, Julia couldn't continue sitting still. She leapt out of her chair and proceeded to pace up and down the room, amazed that Jamie didn't suffer a stiff neck from watching her. "We'll throw a ball. A huge ball to introduce you to society. We'll invite everyone we know. Well, perhaps everyone I know, not everyone you know."

"A wise decision, I am sure."

"And we will invite my uncle."

"Somehow that does not sound nearly as wise."

"You don't understand. At this ball, you are going to be so charming and so appealing and so, well, irresistible, that the whole of the *ton* will fall in love with you on the spot."

"Or at least by the stroke of midnight."

"Don't you see? If you make the *ton* accept you, then my uncle will possess absolutely no feasible reason for refusing you my hand in marriage, without risking painting an absolute fool of his own self in public." Julia paused in front of Jamie's chair. She could feel her cheeks blazing red with enthusiasm, and suspected that her hair—barely manageable under the calmest of circumstances—was, no doubt, currently flapping about her face in a plethora of ebony curls. She probably looked a mess, and would never have dared to appear in public in such a manner. Yet, strangely, in front of Jamie, Julia felt no embarrassment. She asked him eagerly, "What do you think of my plan?"

He cocked his head to one side. "It might work."

She grinned ear to ear, as if he had paid her the grandest of compliments. "I'll go start the guest list."

Julia turned away, already hurrying towards the parlor,

trying to remember where she had last seen her best stationery, when she heard Jamie's voice calling out to her, "Make certain that you do not forget to include Lord Gavin and his lovely bride on that guest list of yours, Miss Highsmith."

8

As a Chinese opium trader once told Jamie, "Be careful what you wish for. You just may get it."

He seriously considered that bit of wisdom as, exactly one week after she first conjured the idea, Jamie stood before a mirror, dressing in preparation for Julia's ball.

What in the world had possessed him to insist that she invite Lord Gavin and Lady Emma? Like many of Jamie's remarks, that one had shot out of his mouth without stopping to consult with Jamie's brain on the prudence of the utterance. And then it just hung there in the open air, like a sleeping bat.

What did Jamie care if the Neffs came or not?

His only acquaintance with both consisted solely of the moments spent peeking under the door at their footwear. Hardly the most intimate of friendships. And yet, even though he tried denying it to himself, Jamie knew why he had so insisted. Because Jamie wanted another opportunity to watch Julia with Gavin.

He considered himself an excellent judge of people. He boasted that, based on the things they said, the things they didn't say, the way they moved, and the way they stood, that Jamie could see through societal convention and instantly discern the true nature of a couple's relationship. And now Jamie wanted a chance to apply that skill to Julia and Gavin.

The only thing he didn't understand was why Jamie found either one of the pair worth his efforts.

Two weeks, and Julia thankfully was no longer supervising every article of clothing that Jamie put on. In fact, her only comment upon seeing him descend the stairs, dressed for the ball in a rich, purple buff coat, black pantaloons, and a pair of top boots, was, "Finally. Our guests are due in at any moment."

Her own gown was a demure white, with rose-petal embroidery on the puffed sleeves and bodice. She wore her hair swept up, mimicking the latest fashions, and emphasizing the graceful curve of her neck. Although in Jamie's opinion no dresser's artificial creation could match the beauty of her curls when she allowed them merely to fall loose about her shoulders.

However, any compliment Jamie may have wished to offer Julia on her appearance died from the angry expression in her eyes. Ever since Jamie brought up Gavin's name in Julia's presence, she had acted distinctively cold towards him, going so far as reverting to the imperious "Mr. Lowell."

Yet, to her credit, Julia proved nearly as convincing at play-acting as Jamie. The moment their first guest crossed her threshold, the anger in Julia's eyes was instantaneously replaced with seemingly sincere warmth. She greeted everyone by name, asked about their families, and presented Jamie with such devotion, introducing him simply, yet coyly, as the marquis of Martyn's nephew, that even he was almost fooled into believing she truly adored him. The only time Julia's expression of perpetual joy ever wavered was in the instant Gavin and his wife strolled up to pay their regards.

Appraising the fellow for the first time at eye level, instead of from the boots up, Jamie found very little to be impressed by in Gavin Neff. He was of average height, solidly built, and with blond hair that looked as if it had been wet down with a damp comb. His clothes, of course, were of the finest sort, but Gavin's abnormally wide shoulders made even the most specifically tailored shirts nevertheless appear slightly ill-fitting. He wore a cravat starched so stiffly that Jamie doubted the gentleman could see over it in either direction, or down at his sparkling Hessian boots.

Lady Neff, however, invited no such derogatory observations. In Jamie's opinion, Gavin's wife was quite possibly one of the handsomest women he had ever seen. Although small in stature, her presence filled up the room. She sparkled, not only from the diamond and emerald necklace at her throat, or from the sheer brilliance of her silver-threaded green gown, but from the manner in which she appraised her surroundings, indicating instantaneously that she considered herself superior to every other soul on the premises. Hers was the quality Jamie perpetually associated with the truly confident. It was an attitude he had put great efforts into developing. And, like any pupil, he was enchanted and honored to see a master at work.

Julia introduced Jamie to both Emma and Gavin simultaneously, although her standard expression of adoration was not nearly as enthusiastic on this go-around. Gavin and Jamie shook hands, and then he bent from the waist to kiss the glove of Lady Emma. She smiled charmingly at him, perhaps resting her arm in Jamie's grip a split second longer than required.

"It is," she purred, "truly a pleasure to meet you, Mr. Lowell."

Jamie waited until Lord Gavin and his wife seamlessly blended into the ballroom full of guests behind them before confronting Julia. "Isn't there something written in the Bible about not coveting your neighbor's husband?"

"I believe the tenth commandment is thou shalt not covet thy neighbor's wife, Mr. Lowell."

"Ah. Well, then, that makes all the difference." Jamie glanced over his shoulder, making sure that they were safely out of earshot, and asked, "You are in love with Gavin Neff, aren't you?"

"That's Lord Gavin, to you." Julia refused to look in Jamie's direction. She stood with her back to him, eyes fastened on the dance floor, where a flurry of dresses and black evening coats were performing yet another quadrille.

"What I don't understand, though," Jamie persisted, "is why, if you love him so, you turned down his proposal of marriage?"

"Do try to keep your memory at least relatively current, Mr. Lowell. My uncle warned me against marrying Gavin, for the same reason that he attempted to discourage you."

"Yes, of course. Bad blood and all. But Lord Neff's proposal took place before you needed your inheritance so badly."

"Yes. So what of it?"

"Why did you not simply say to hell with your uncle, forfeit the inheritance, and wed Gavin on the sly?"

Julia spun around, her skirts swishing so sharply that they slapped Jamie across the shins. "First of all, Mr. Lowell, you will watch your language in this house. Second of all, I could not just disregard the words of my uncle and elope with Gavin. That isn't how things are done among civilized people. And, if you were a civilized person, you would know that." The color in her cheeks was swiftly racing to catch up with the rosy shade of embroidery decorating Julia's dress. "And thirdly, Mr. Lowell, it was my decision, not my uncle's, to refuse Gavin's proposal. I could not do such a thing to him. He is a very important man. His family has a history and tradition going back a hundred years. Each of the sons is not only a peer, and an exemplary member of the House of Lords, but also a graduate of Oxford and a student of the law."

"So?" Jamie mimicked Julia's previous statement. "What of it?"

"If I were to have married Gavin, no son of his could ever do any of those things."

"Why in the world not?"

"Because, he would also be a son of mine."

Be careful what you wish for. You just might get it.

Well, there he had it. Jamie asked Julia for the truth, and she had given it to him. Julia loved Gavin. It was that simple. Seeing her talking to him only confirmed it.

Jamie leaned against the ballroom's far wall, a glass of champagne in one hand, and watched his fiancée and the man she loved, exchanging conversation in the opposite corner. They weren't alone, of course. Julia's sense of social decorum would never allow her to, in good conscience, ignore the bulk of her guests in favor of a single individual. From the first moment, she'd made certain to surround herself and Gavin with a neutral crowd of friends and acquaintances.

They weren't alone. But they might as well have been.

For it didn't matter whom Julia was talking to, her gaze never left Gavin. She laughed at his wit, agreed with his opinions, and complimented his tastes. She did everything but crown him king.

Her eyes danced as she spoke to him, and, every few moments, Julia would reach over to affectionately straighten his coat, or touch his wrist while she spoke. Her entire face, despite the harsh lighting of the ballroom, appeared softer somehow, no longer as crowded with worry and anger, as when she spoke to Jamie. She looked years younger. And so undeniably beautiful, that it were as if Jamie were seeing a completely different person.

"May I?" A woman's voice interrupted Jamie's reverie, and nonchalantly slipped the champagne glass out of his grasp. He watched silently as Lady Emma took a sip of Jamie's sparkling wine, taking care to place her lips exactly in the spot Jamie had recently touched, and smiling sweetly at him over the rim.

"Good evening, Lady Emma."

"Mr. Lowell." With a nod of her head, she indicated Gavin and Julia across the room. "I daresay that our respective escorts have come to the conclusion that two is but the perfect number to make this evening a smashing success."

"I understand his lordship and Julia are childhood friends."

"Yes," Lady Emma sighed, obviously very tired of hearing about it. "But neither one is a child anymore."

Jamie shrugged. Under no circumstance did he intend to

find himself trapped in the middle of whatever strained relations passed between Gavin and his wife.

Lady Emma continued, "Of course, in your case, it isn't
you who should worry about Julia, but rather, I suspect,
Julia who needs to worry over you."

"I beg your pardon?"

Emma returned Jamie's champagne glass to him, taking
the opportunity to run one hand appreciatively down the
length of his arm. "You are a very handsome man, Mr.
Lowell. This room must be filled with hundreds of women
who would love to snatch you away from right underneath
her nose."

Jamie smiled to himself. It certainly was pleasant to find
a kindred spirit in the room. The only difference was,
while Jamie manipulated for a living, Lady Emma did it
for the sheer spite.

He carefully disentangled his arm, placing one hand
over his heart and announcing in all seeming seriousness,
"I'm afraid that's impossible, Lady Emma. I am quite de-
voted to Julia."

Her ladyship looked across the room at Gavin. "You
aren't the only one, Mr. Lowell."

The lady had a point.

As far as Julia and Gavin were concerned, there didn't
seem to be another soul in the room. They probably didn't
even know which tune it was that the orchestra was playing.

But Jamie was hardly about to give Lady Emma the satisfaction of seeing that the fact bothered him. Instead, he
merely continued smiling, and, keeping his tone level, reminded, "It is me that Julia has agreed to marry."

"Yes. I suppose she didn't think Gavin good enough for
her. Why settle for a viscount, when you might win a marquis?"

Win, Jamie laughed to himself, being the operative
word.

"Unfortunately," Lady Emma continued, "Gavin has
never quite gotten over it."

"He married you, my lady."

"His father was dying. Gavin needed to marry someone,

to assure the old man of there being an heir. Sometimes I suspect that I was simply the woman standing closest to him, when he decided a proposal must be made."

Jamie laughed out loud, turning to face Lady Emma, both hands on his hips. "Come, come, now, Your Ladyship. Our acquaintance may currently be limited to a scant few minutes, but please, please, do not think me such a fool as to be convinced by this show of self-conscious modesty."

Lady Emma gasped in what Jamie supposed was intended as proper indignation. But, to him, the puff sounded exactly like what it was—a lifelong charlatan shocked at finally being realized.

"Please, Lady Emma, do not take my words in any but the sincerely complimentary manner with which they were intended," he reassured. "It is merely that I see you as a beautiful woman. What is more, I know that you see you as beautiful woman. Under such circumstances, it is very difficult for me to believe that you truly think you might be any man's second choice."

Unsure of whether he was insulting, mocking, or praising her, Lady Emma allowed Jamie's explanation to pass without comment, and, instead, insisted, "But I *was* second choice. For Gavin. He wanted Julia. It was only when she turned him down that he focused his attentions to me."

"And you are never going to forgive him for it."

"No," Lady Emma corrected, "I am never going to forgive Julia Highsmith for it. I would like to see her suffer. Well, actually, I would like to see her dead. But I will settle for suffering."

"I see."

"Do you?"

"Yes," Jamie told Gavin's wife. "I understand perfectly."

And, to be honest, he didn't find the proposition unappealing. Lady Emma was certainly a lovely woman, and, undoubtedly, discreet. And as for that pompous little bastard, Neff, it was no less than what he deserved for all but abandoning his wife at Julia's ball, while he went off chasing after another woman.

"So, Mr. Lowell?" With one finger Lady Emma turned Jamie's chin even more to her direction. "What say you?"

What say he, indeed.

Jamie smiled and took Lady Emma's hand from his face, cupping it between both his palms. He opened his mouth, meaning to say a great many things, among which would be cleverly, but not indecipherably, hidden the word, yes.

But then, a most fantastic event took place.

Instead of uttering a single syllable of what he had planned, Jamie, as if in a trance, heard his own tongue and lips most distinctly form the solitary reply. "No."

Julia's uncle, the duke himself, made his appearance at the ball a good three hours beyond the time invited. By then, the dining room table previously loaded with tureens of mulligatawny and turtle soups, plates of roast beef, salmon, beef tongue, sausages, saddle of mutton, and a host of vegetables in accompanying sauces, stood all but empty. In Jamie's book, that sort of behavior long passed the fashionably late stage, and sledded downward into simple rudeness.

But, of course, he didn't dare say so to the duke of Alamain. Although, considering how his tongue had behaved earlier, Jamie no longer felt certain that he possessed any control over what came out of his mouth.

As the duke handed his top hat and coat to Moses, he told Jamie, "Rather irregular, isn't it, hosting a ball before receiving permission to marry?"

"It was Julia's wish, sir."

"Uncle Collin." The lady in question swept past the other dancers to greet him, embracing him as warmly as if her fury at the duke were merely a figment of Jamie's imagination.

Before her uncle even had a chance to say hello, Julia was escorting him to the dining room, insisting that he sample what was left of Cook's buffet, and urging him to join in the dancing. Then, she promptly excused herself and disappeared, thus saving herself the discomfort of having to answer any awkward questions.

She swept past Jamie on her way to rejoining Neff, but Jamie grabbed Julia by one arm, pulling her back.

Under the cover of music and contented guests chattering away, Jamie told Julia, "So kind of you to tear yourself away from His Lordship for a few moments."

"I am merely acting the proper hostess." Julia jerked out of his grasp, smoothing down her hair with one hand, and her dress with the other.

"Really? How interesting, when I could swear that there must be entire families of guests at this affair who have yet to see you. It isn't very polite to spend all your time exclusively entertaining a single gentleman. Especially when he is someone else's husband."

"The only thing you know of politeness, Mr. Lowell, is what I've taught you. So I would hesitate before deciding to instruct me in proper etiquette."

"Touché, Miss Highsmith. And may I compliment you, as one actor to another, on that splendid performance of perceived affection for your uncle."

Despite her anger at him, she beamed. "I was good, wasn't I?"

"You are learning. A little more practice, and you might actually prove as adept at hiding your obvious affection for one certain gentleman, as you are at counterfeiting it for another."

Now that neither Julia nor Lady Emma were speaking to him, Jamie was finding the entire party rather dull. And exhausting. Never having been faced with charming such a huge mass of people at one time, Jamie had failed to take into account how tiring it would prove. Traditionally, it wasn't unusual for Jamie to spend weeks, sometimes months, charming a single young lady. With such a schedule, Jamie not only had the time to learn enough information about his mark to render the complete seduction easier, but he also had at least a few hours a day to himself.

It was one thing to play his role for the space of a summer afternoon, quite another to live the lie around the clock. For nearly six hours now, he'd been Jeremy Lowell.

Not Jamie, but Jeremy. Six hours without a single reprieve.

And, even more peculiar, it had been Jeremy Lowell whom Lady Emma Neff had propositioned so coquettishly. But it had been Jamie Lowell who inexplicably turned her down.

Growing tired of the monotonous music and conversation, Jamie escaped for a few moments into the garden, his mind still obsessed with figuring out just what it was that had come over him with Lady Emma. Why had he turned a woman as beautiful as Mrs. Neff away?

The obvious answer, of course, was simply that Jamie didn't dare risk damaging his bargain with Julia. After all, she had warned him that a single impropriety would be grounds enough to send him back to Newgate. Swinging.

But somehow, Jamie didn't believe that to be the exclusive reason. Because he hadn't been thinking about Julia's money as he refused Lady Emma. He had been thinking simply about Julia.

Julia and the way she looked when she thought he'd been shot.

If Jamie hadn't known better, he might have thought the look in her eyes to be one of true concern. And not merely the sort of concern that accompanied guilt, but the kind of feeling that only bloomed when there was sincere—dare he think it?—affection involved.

Jamie shook his head violently, hoping to toss the idea out of his consciousness. He was a fool for even considering such things. And he was a bigger fool for feeling so strangely touched by the mere possibility. Especially when, in the next moment, Jamie turned around to see Julia, accompanied by Gavin, of course, stroll out into the garden. And Lord Neff was holding her hand.

9

Julia didn't slip her hand out of Gavin's grasp in the moment he took it—as she very well knew that she should have—because there was something so pleasantly sinful about it all.

As they walked along the garden, Julia watched the shadows on Gavin's face. Freshly blooming flowers wrapped the night in a cocoon of sweetness.

And, for a reason obviously known only to God himself, Julia found herself thinking of Jamie Lowell.

It was ridiculous. Here she was, out on a full moon summer night with Gavin, and Julia's mind was inexplicably on a man she barely knew. Even worse, unlike previous occasions on which she'd been unable to drive Jamie from her thoughts, Julia wasn't even dwelling on some insult that he'd sent in her direction, but rather on the compliment he'd paid her.

He had told Julia that she did a good job manipulating her uncle. Certainly, a professional rascal like Jamie would know when such a task were completed properly. And he had applauded her for it. So she must have done it well.

How strange that Julia should take such pleasure from this most peculiar of venerations, coming as it had from that most peculiar of men. But, for some reason, she truly did.

"And what is my beautiful Julia thinking about on this

most lovely night?" Gavin stopped their walk to perch upon the edge of a ceramic bird fountain carved in the shape of a soaring swallow.

"Oh. Nothing very important." Julia was certain that Gavin would neither be amused, nor would he approve, if she did tell him exactly what had been occupying her thoughts.

"It is a splendid ball, Julia. You look ravishing."

"Thank you."

"I must admit, I did feel a bit put out. Here you are, barely six months after turning down my proposal, and you are announcing your engagement to another man. Whatever happened to that beautiful child who swore to me that she would never marry anyone."

A pin pricked at Julia's confidence upon hearing Gavin refer to her as a child. Considering everything she'd been through in the last month, a child was the last thing Julia felt like.

"Views change," she said. "Once, you swore that if you couldn't have me, you wouldn't want any other woman. Yet barely a month later you were engaged to Emma."

"But surely you see how different that is, my dear. I am a man."

Julia wasn't certain how exactly he expected her to reply to that remark, so she let it pass.

"I changed my mind about marriage when I met Jamie."

"Ah, yes. Mr. Lowell, your Aunt Salome's godson. The future marquis of Martyn did you say he is?"

"Yes. The marquis of Martyn."

"That's quite a grand piece of property the old man owns. Between the money you'll inherit from you father, and the marquis's estate, why, you'll be one of the wealthiest families in England."

While he spoke on about the many things Julia would soon be able to purchase with her newfound wealth, a single thought ran through her head. *The only thing I really need to buy is Miriam and Alexia's safety.*

Gavin was saying, "And my wife tells me your intended is a most handsome chap."

She stared at him queerly. "Can you not see him your-self?"

He laughed. "Oh, Julia, men are no experts at judging the appearance of other men. However, Emma could speak of nothing else save how attractive your Mr. Lowell was."

After five months, Julia was already used to the mental jab to the stomach that she felt every time Gavin mentioned his wife. Yet she was completely unprepared for the intensity of the blow that came when he mentioned Emma and Jamie in the same sentence.

She had seen the pair of them talking earlier in the evening, and the fact bothered Julia even then.

"Yes," she said, slowly. "I suppose Jamie is attractive. He doesn't look very much like the other men of the *ton,* does he?"

"And what an odd name that is. Jamie. His Christian name's Jeremy is it not? Most peculiar. I've never heard of Jamie as a diminutive for Jeremy, before."

"Actually, that started when he was a small boy. He couldn't pronounce his name. Jeremy is quite the mouthful for a toddler. All he could say was Jamie. So that's what they called him."

Funny, but when Jamie first told her that story, Julia barely paid any heed to it. Yet now, relaying it to Gavin, she felt strangely touched by the image of a tiny Jamie, probably already sporting a head full of that bright red hair, stammering and stuttering over those dreadfully complicated sounds in his name.

"Gor," Gavin said, looking at Julia's face "You really are head over heels for the fellow, aren't you?"

She stared at him as if he had suddenly gone mad. What in the world was he talking about? Surely, she wasn't that gifted of an actress. How could Gavin think that Julia loved Jamie, when, all evening, it had been a Herculean effort to hide from the world just how much she adored Lady Emma's husband.

"I am pleased for you, my dear. Myself, no matter how hard I try, I just can't seem to make myself feel the same towards Emma."

No, Julia decided, this was not happening. She was not

standing below this exquisitely full moon, listening to Gavin proclaim his inability to love Emma. This was a dream. Any minute now she would awaken and it would all blow away like a fog.

"She doesn't love me either, of course. We both knew ours was to be a marriage of convenience. Why, I even told her about us." Gavin scratched his ear thoughtfully. "In retrospect, that might have been a mistake."

Julia was still trying to collect her wits and come up with an adequate response to his confession when Gavin unexpectedly trailed off in his speech, gesturing instead towards an open window and inquiring, "What in the world is that?"

Julia turned and listened. As far as she could discern, the orchestra had changed tempos, switching from a one-two-three-four beat to a one-two-three-four-five-six. And the shift was causing a great deal of commotion on the dance floor.

Gavin's face hardened, and, with the expression of a man at long last identifying the origin of a particularly foul stench, he rolled his eyes and pronounced, "The waltz. Really, Julia, I hardly expected a woman of your breeding to grant respectability to such a common, public fancy."

Feeling as sincerely surprised by her musicians' unexpected change of program as he was, Julia hurried inside. Gavin followed.

What they both found was Jamie, standing before the orchestra, conductor's baton in one hand, patiently humming the new melody out loud, while her musicians attempted to follow.

Sidling up to him, Julia demanded, "What exactly is it that you think you are doing?"

"The waltz!" Jamie announced, sweeping both arms grandly over his head to emphasize his point.

Simultaneously speaking for the benefit of both Jamie and the curious crowd beginning to gather all around them, Julia slowly emphasized each word, explaining, "I am afraid that I must claim ignorance with the mores and customs of titled life in Australia, Mr. Lowell. However, you see, in England, this dance of yours, the waltz, it simply is not—is not—we do not do it."

"But I saw the Russian ambassador's wife and Czar Alexander dance it Almack's not two years past," he insisted.

"Oh, you did, did you?" Try as she might, Julia suspected that a bit of her incredulousness had managed to squeeze through what she otherwise hoped might pass for a neutral tone.

"Indeed, I did." He was smiling broadly, clearly enjoying himself for the first time all evening. Jamie ducked his head and whispered, "I would suggest though, that you refrain from inquiring what exactly it was I was doing at the aforementioned function, and we shall both lead longer and happier lives."

Helpless in the face of his relentless cheerfulness, Julia turned towards her guests, hoping that someone among them might speak up to help her out of the awkwardness. A pond of faces stared back, their intrigued eyes sliding from Julia to Jamie.

"And just what does this waltz look like, Mr. Lowell?" Lady Emma's voice carried easily from where she was standing, cutting through the crowd like the tip of a boat through the Thames. "I am afraid that I was not fortunate enough to have been in Almack's on the night you mentioned. And while, I have certainly heard of the waltz—after all, who among us, has not?—I cannot seem to recall its every intricacy."

"It is very simple. I'll show you." Jamie moved to the center of the dance floor. "The waltz is a whirling dance. At the function where I spotted the Russians dancing, I also noted Lady Jersey enjoying this identical waltz with Mr. Cupid Palmerston."

His mentioning one of the most respected women of the *ton* in conjunction with this faddish dance caused an audible ripple of murmurs among the guests.

"That is true," Julia said. "I heard people speak of it."

"Well, Miss Highsmith?"

Unable to make up her mind, Julia glanced over one shoulder at Gavin. He stood, stiff-lipped, arms crossed, back pressed against the pair of doors leading out to the garden. She'd known him too long not to recognize Gavin's face of extreme disapproval.

Coolly, he stated, "I cannot imagine that anyone, save the lowest sort of woman, would allow herself to partake in such a sinful, wicked, devilish dance."

Refusing to budge from his stand, Jamie requested of Gavin, "Please, Lord Neff, do not beat about the bush so. Tell us what you really think."

Julia was still trying to make up her mind how best to respond to Jamie's offer, when a woman's voice, clear as a set of crystal wind chimes, called out from across the floor, "I would be honored to dance the waltz with you, Mr. Lowell."

Every head in the room turned in time to enjoy the sight of Lady Emma parting the crowd with one elegantly gloved hand, and making her way towards Jamie. She smiled pleasantly at Gavin, then took an even longer moment to linger over Julia's shocked features, before presenting herself to Jamie. "Do refresh my memory, Mr. Lowell. Was that step, step, glide, or turn, turn, step?"

"Turn, glide, step." He corrected, gallantly.

"Oh, yes. I'm afraid that you shall have to bear with me. I am going to require quite a lot of personal assistance before I master this—did you call it devilish, Gavin?—dance of yours."

"It will be my pleasure to assist you, Lady Neff."

"No." The violent denial shot out her mouth without Julia possessing the slightest say in the matter. She spoke before she thought, and then felt at a loss over why she'd done it, or what she intended to do next.

"I beg your pardon, Miss Highsmith?" Jamie was already resting one hand on Lady Emma's waist, in preparation for the waltz.

"I said . . . no." Now everyone was watching her. Especially Gavin. But she had already gone too far to back away. Besides, the sight of Jamie and Lady Emma was quickly making Julia feel sick. And thus angry. And thus foolish.

"I am sorry, Lady Neff, but I should like to reserve the right to this dance with Mr. Lowell."

Reluctantly, Gavin's wife stepped outside of Jamie's embrace, making an exaggerated show of handing him over to Julia. "You are our hostess for the evening, Miss Highsmith."

Julia courteously accepted this ceremonial passing of the prize, but then, unable to help herself, she winningly suggested, "Perhaps your husband would agree to partner you for at least some of the dances, Lady Emma."

Behind her, Jamie loudly commanded, "Maestro, the waltz!"

Without an instant to prepare herself, Jamie swept Julia into his arms, the strength of his upper body nearly lifting her off the ground. He pressed Julia against him, a huge smile lighting up his features, as Jamie counted out loud, "And one, two, three, one, two, three, turn, glide, step, turn, glide, step," and guided Julia effortlessly across the dance floor.

She might never have guessed that a man of his size could not only be such a graceful dancer, but also an equally skillful partner. Unlike most males, whose idea of leading a dance was to forcefully drag their ladies from one corner to the next, Jamie made Julia feel as if she were floating. Or flying.

And yet, whenever it started to seem as if all the swift whirling about were growing dangerously out of control, there was Jamie's arm, securely wrapped around Julia's waist, to make her feel safe and protected and wonderfully cared for.

Gradually, other couples at the ball grew convinced that a single waltz would not brand them degenerate, and joined in with Jamie and Julia's dancing, until the entire room became a marvelous blur of kaleidoscopic colors. Men and women laughed and twirled to the soul-lifting strains of an Austrian waltz, while the few guardians of public morality shocked by the sight of couples embracing so in public retired in a huff to another room. So engaged was she in the wondrous freedom and joy of the buoyant movements that Julia did not even care to note whether or not Gavin went with them.

Instead, when the music stopped, she was among the

first to urge her musicians to play, "A waltz, another waltz, please. And faster this time."

Jamie threw back his head and laughed, spinning Julia into a new, more difficult series of steps, and acclaiming, "You, Miss Highsmith, are by far the most able pupil I've ever taught."

"The same could be said for you, Mr. Lowell."

"What? Oh." He tilted his head to indicate the presence of the *ton*. "That. I am doing my best to be charming. And to remember which fork to use for which course."

"You're doing marvelously. Every woman in this room has already fallen in love with you."

"Every woman?" Jamie slowed down his dancing, so that his face was no longer a blur, but rather an inescapable presence. "Are you certain of that, Miss Highsmith?"

His mirror-blue eyes bore into her with such force that Julia felt certain Jamie could not only read everything that she was thinking, but also see through to all those things that she felt too scared even to think. His right thumb softly massaged the inside of her left palm, while the rest of his fingers gently stroked the back of her hand, sending a current of delicious sensations through Julia's body. Dancing so closely, Julia found herself wondering what it might feel like to lean completely against him, to rest her head on Jamie's chest and listen to his heartbeat. To wonder whether, at this moment, it were beating as frantically and as loudly as her own.

She barely noticed it when Jamie stopped dancing, taking Julia by the hand and leading her away from the dance floor, towards an unoccupied balcony. Outside, the darkness swallowed his features, blending one into the other until only the intensity of Jamie's blue eyes seemed to shine like a beacon.

Julia could not tear her gaze away from his. It was almost as if he had bewitched her in some way, leaving Julia so completely under Jamie's power that she no longer felt certain of her ability to resist. Or of her desire to do so.

He lowered his head ever so slightly, this time whispering the words, "Surely, not every woman?"

So eager was Julia to feel his lips upon hers, that she

imagined already feeling them there a moment before it happened. Yet, in the instant he did touch her, there was no doubt in Julia's mind that even the most passionate hopes of her fantasies were a mere raindrop in a storm compared to the actual thing.

Jamie pulled her to him, parting Julia's lips with his tongue and proceeding to stroke her from the inside out, until she felt herself growing limp in his embrace. Julia wrapped her arms about Jamie's neck, wanting to draw him in even closer, wanting to make certain that nothing, no one, could ever pull him away again.

"Julia, really!"

The voice reached to her as if traveling in slow motion and through a heavy London fog. Still, it was enough for her to recognize the disapproving tone of her Uncle Collin.

Julia opened her eyes with a start, breaking Jamie's embrace, and spinning around to find the balcony doors leading into the ballroom opened, and not only Uncle Collin, but Gavin, and Emma, and even Moses, along with a good dozen party guests, staring straight at them.

There was a lot of whispering going on behind cupped hands.

And no one was smiling.

10

Guessing that, of the two of them, he was the more experienced in talking his way out of uncomfortable situations, Jamie turned towards their visibly curious audience, and, resting one hand to his cheek in imitation of thoughtfulness, innocently asked, "Did I forget to announce that Julia and I are to be married?"

A beat, and then the entire room broke into spontaneous laughter and applause. As if acknowledging a curtain call, Jamie took Julia by the hand and bowed deeply, indicating for her to curtsey as well. He accepted congratulatory handshakes from the men, and embraces from the women, all the while keeping one eye on dear Uncle Collin. Because Uncle Collin did not look happy.

Gradually making his way through the crowd and towards where the duke stood keeping watch over the buffet, Jamie stretched his hand forward and inquired, "Don't you want to congratulate me, sir? Or should I say, Uncle Collin?"

"You're a bloody fool, Lowell."

"It is within your prerogative to think so."

"Were you not listening to a word I said? Your life will be ruined if you marry Julia. Ruined, do you hear me?"

"If you shout any louder, sir, His Royal Highness in London will be able to hear you." Turning his back on their guests, Jamie forced the duke into a corner out of sight. Darkly, he warned, "Don't you ever speak in such a manner about my wife-to-be again, or I will personally introduce you to the sport of wrestling, Australian style. That, in case you are unfamiliar with it, is the game where only one winner lives to walk away from a match."

Sincerely terrified, the duke swallowed hard, and, in a much meeker voice, whined, "I am only trying to help you, son."

"Your Lordship's sort of assistance I can live very well without, thank you kindly."

"She's got the devil in her. Heretics, witches, all of them. You'll see. Just wait until your first child is born. You'll remember me then. But by that time, it will be too late."

The further Jamie moved up in society—and, to date, his rise could be truly called meteoric—the less he believed the myths, folklore, and ghost stories that had played such a large part in his upbringing. But the duke's rambled warning about witches and the devil forced Jamie to remember all sorts of tales that he had long ago thought a part of his past. And, despite his successful show of indifference, Jamie had to admit to the slightest stirring of fear.

From the first day, he'd known that Julia was hiding things from him. Such was her right, and Jamie had let it be. But now . . . what if her secrets were genuinely something sinister? Truly, she had all but brought Jamie back from the dead once. What sort of a trap was he getting himself snared in?

Jamie didn't even know why they were going to France, save Julia's insistence that she had matters to settle there. What sort of matters? And why the infernal secrecy?

Making the decision to untie this knot once and for all, Jamie marched himself back into the ballroom.

Julia stood surrounded by a crowd of female well-wishers. With a smile guaranteed to melt even the most resistant, Jamie charmingly asked the young ladies to excuse them. He and Julia had a few personal matters to discuss.

Pulling her away, Jamie sequestered them in the kitchen,

where even Cook could hardly overhear their words above the clatter of pots and plates.

"Jamie, what is it?" Julia rubbed the arm where he had previously grabbed her. "You're scaring me."

"Well, it's no less than what your uncle did to me." Taking a deep breath, Jamie demanded, "Why did you refuse to marry Gavin? I know you love him. I saw you walking in the garden hand in hand."

Julia gasped, "You were spying on us?"

"Don't flatter yourself. The entire scene so sickened me that I escaped as soon as possible. But you still have not answered my question. Why did you refuse to marry Gavin?"

"I—I told you, Jamie."

"Yes, yes, I know. Bad blood. But what does it mean? No one will tell me what it means. Your uncle only speaks in riddles."

"He is afraid of besmirching his own reputation."

"Why? I thought it was your mother's family that festered under this dark cloud, not his."

"My uncle does not wish to be tainted with the tar-brush of his older brother's folly."

"What about me?"

"What about you?"

He grabbed her by the shoulders, shaking Julia not hard enough to hurt, but with enough feeling to get his point across, and charged, "What does your uncle mean when he swears that you have the devil inside you?"

"The devil?" Julia pushed Jamie away. "Is that what he said? And is that why you are acting like such a madman?"

"Where I am from, we take the devil very seriously, Miss Highsmith, seeing how we live next door to the fellow day to day."

"Well, where I am from, Mr. Lowell, we save such superstitious nonsense for children's bedtime stories and church sermons."

"Your uncle didn't think it was nonsense."

"My uncle was trying to scare you. He succeeded beautifully."

Jamie challenged, "You obviously believed his superstitious nonsense enough to sacrifice your own happiness, and save Gavin."

"You don't know what you are talking about."

"Enlighten me."

"No."

The simplicity of her response took Jamie by surprise. "No?"

"No." Julia coolly puffed up her sleeves where Jamie had crushed them. "Nowhere in our arrangement did I promise to tell you anything that is no concern of yours. In fact, I distinctly remember warning you against asking too many questions."

"Our arrangement," he repeated.

"Yes. You do recall it, do you not? The initial conversation that put us on this merry path?"

"So everything that has happened up to this point, was all a part of some *arrangement?*" Jamie made sure to put enough emphasis on each word, so that Julia understood exactly what he was asking.

When she didn't snap back with an easy answer, he even allowed himself to suspect that perhaps he had finally gotten through to her. That Julia, as well as he, was willing to admit that they had already gone beyond and above some insignificant arrangement, and were moving into an area and a situation that couldn't be charted, predicted, or planned. One that required complete honesty on behalf of both participants.

Yet, in spite of Jamie's hopes, ultimately, Julia looked him straight in the eye and boldly replied, "Yes."

"Yes, what?"

"Yes to your question. Yes, this has all been a part of our arrangement. And you were marvelous, just as I suspected you would be when I chose you."

Jamie snapped his arm back to eye level, feeling the blood shooting through his finger, ready to strike and strike hard.

But it wasn't until Julia, frightened, ducked her head out of his reach, that Jamie realized what he had almost done.

He froze, looking at his hand as if it belonged to a complete stranger, and slowly lowered it to his side.

He'd never previously wanted to hit a woman. Not because Jamie was any more gallant or self-possessed than the average man, but because in order to hit, you have to feel angry. And, in order to feel angry, you have to care. And Jamie had never before cared enough to raise his hand to any woman.

Sensing that the moment of danger had passed, Julia slowly released the breath she was holding, as anger swept in to replace the previous strokes of terror in her expression.

"What were you trying to do, Mr. Lowell?" Julia pointedly demanded. "Beat the devil right out of me?"

Stiffly, they walked out of the kitchen side by side, and returned to the ballroom. The duke of Alamain lay in wait for them, hissing to Jamie and Julia, "How dare the both of you make such an announcement without my blessing?"

"I thought that we had already been granted it, Uncle. After all, you did not refuse Mr. Lowell's request when he came to ask for my hand at your home this past week."

"But neither did I approve it."

"Do you wish to withhold your blessing now, sir?" Jamie asked.

"Well, I, you must understand—"

"On what grounds would you refuse us, Uncle?"

"Attention, please, everyone, attention," Jamie left the duke sputtering for an appropriate answer, and raised his voice to be heard in every corner of the room. "Miss Highsmith's uncle has an announcement that he wishes to make, regarding our marriage."

The guests turned to listen, causing Collin Highsmith to flush a deep red, and briefly glance behind him, apparently in the hope that every eye might possibly be centered on another. Alas, no one magically appeared, and the duke realized himself to be stuck.

He yanked a handkerchief embroidered with his initials out of one pocket, and dabbed at the droplets of sweat gathering along his eyebrows. He coughed, he pounded his chest a few times, he took a sip of wine. Still, the guests watched and politely waited.

Sighing resignedly, the duke cleared his throat for a second time, and, albeit without much enthusiasm, raised his glass.

"A toast," he said finally. "A toast to my lovely niece, and to her future husband."

It was nearly dawn by the time the final guests bade them good-bye, wished Julia and Jamie all the best, and climbed into their carriages for the return trip home. As soon as the last titled waistcoat crossed the threshold, Jamie figured his part in the affair to be at an end. Exhausted, he gratefully pulled the slightly wilted cravat from around his neck, using it to dab at the moisture on his face, and began walking up the stairs towards his bedroom. It was only when he realized that Julia were no longer behind him that Jamie paused, turned, and, puzzled, sat down on the steps, watching through the banister as Julia continued standing where she was, peering out into the darkness.

She'd run one hand through her hair, tugging at the knots and swirls her maid had so toiled over all afternoon, and letting the jet-black curls spin carelessly past her neck and shoulders.

From the back, she suddenly looked much smaller than Jamie ever could have guessed at head on, especially after Julia kicked off both shoes behind her, tapping the pair into a corner without so much as turning her head to look where they went. She sighed, the gesture causing her shoulder blades to snap up, then slowly lower back into place. The hem of Julia's dress swished against the floor, rustling slightly from the wind.

Jamie wondered how she didn't catch cold, standing without a wrap, and wearing a gown with gossamer, puffed sleeves that only reached to the tips of her elbows.

He stood, meaning to close the door, or at least suggest that she take a few steps back from the wind when Julia, hearing Jamie's footsteps behind her, unexpectedly said, "When I was a little girl, I used to love sneaking downstairs and watching my parents after all their guests had gone home. They would wait until the last carriage pulled out of sight, and then my mother would close the door, and turn around, and my father would be standing there. Looking so handsome. And he would reach for my mother's hand, kiss it, smile, and then he would say, 'I hope the most beautiful girl at the ball saved her last dance for me.' And my mother—oh, Jamie, my mother was so beautiful. Like those models that the painters hang in museums. My mother would squeeze my father's hand, and she would say, 'Always.' Always. And then he would lead her to the dance floor, and they would dance. Just the two of them. As if there wasn't another soul left in the world." She turned around to face him, and Jamie realized that there were tears in her eyes. "I still expect to see them. Isn't that terribly silly of me? I am hardly a little girl anymore. But every time the last guest disappears over the horizon, I still expect to turn around and see my parents. Dancing."

He didn't know what to say. Whatever anger Jamie had felt towards Julia earlier than evening inexplicably dissipated into a foreign emotion of equal strength, but more ambiguous identity. He could not empathize with Julia's feelings of loss, because, to be truthful, Jamie could not recall a single person or incident in his past that might have prompted a similar sense of bereavement. And yet, she had described it all so beautifully, that, strangely, Jamie could almost see the way it had once been, and an unfamiliar twinge of regret tugged at his heart, as if he too had lost something infinitely precious.

Swallowing hard, Jamie took a step towards Julia, gently closing the door behind her.

He stretched out both arms, reaching for Julia's hand and bringing it to his lips. Softly, Jamie said, "I hope the most beautiful girl at the ball saved her last dance for *me.*"

She looked up at him with moist-bright eyes. Hesitantly, Julia brought her right arm, palm up, towards Jamie, resting it ever so carefully on the side of his shoulder. She bit down on her lower lip, needing to exhale deeply before replying in a voice barely audible, "Always."

He took her hand and led her to the silent dance floor, their footsteps echoing against the scuffed parquet.

And then, for a while at least, the two of them danced in the Highsmith family ballroom as if there wasn't another soul left in the world.

Unfortunately though, such was not the case.

Not more than five minutes after they began, Aunt Salome blew into the room, directing what looked like an entire fleet of servants to collect and polish the silverware, store the tureens and plates, scrape the meats and vegetables into combined dishes to conserve space, and see to it that the bottles of sherry, hock, port, and claret were all returned to their proper places. She stopped with a start upon spotting Jamie and Julia.

In spite of the fact that they'd done nothing wrong, the pair instantly dropped hands and guiltily moved away from each other, allowing Salome to step in between them.

She turned to face Jamie, cocking her head to one side and observing, "You are full of surprises this evening, Mr. Lowell. First dancing to music most would be afraid to hum in private, then dancing to no music at all."

"I find that it saves the expense of hiring an orchestra."

Salome sniffed imperiously at the remark. "I suppose, young man, that you presume yourself to be amusing."

"I am amusing. You just never noticed before." Jamie refused to let the condemnation upon her face shame him into thinking he'd committed an act worth apologizing for. "Your niece, on the other hand, has grown in appreciation for my talent by leaps and bounds."

"Well, fortunately for us all, I possess a few years ahead of Julia, and a bit more life experience. I've known men like you, Mr. Lowell. I know your tricks and your games. And I am not about to let my niece become another bit of muslin in your collection."

Incensed by this accusation of chicanery amidst one of his rare moments off, Jamie fought to control his temper. Squeezing both fists at his sides in an attempt to remain in control he carefully said, "I believe, Mrs. Weiss, that you owe me an apology. I committed no crime this past half hour, save asking your niece to stand up with me."

"And how long, Mr. Lowell, would it have been before you asked her to lie down with you, as well?"

The insinuation was more than Jamie could bear, although the query did cross his mind as to why he should find this particular charge of plying his trade so disturbing. Jamie turned to Julia, hoping, no, expecting her to defend him, to insist that Jamie had meant no harm. But she would not even meet his eyes. On the one occasion when he ached to hear her speak, Julia Highsmith had chosen to remain uncharacteristically silent.

But he would be damned before Jamie allowed either woman to see how much they had wounded him.

Face neutral, Jamie took a step backwards, bowing deeply from the waist. "Good evening, Miss Highsmith, Mrs. Weiss." And, controlling his urge to storm out of the room, calmly walked past the dance floor, through the main hall, out the front door, and out of sight.

Jamie waited until he felt certain that both Julia and Salome were in bed before returning to his opulent prison. Yet, considering how tired he felt after an evening spent trying to act like a future marquis, Jamie found it exceedingly difficult to fall asleep. He tossed and turned, even going so far as to hurl his pillows on the floor in the hope that a return to the unadorned surroundings he was used to dozing in might make things easier.

By morning, Jamie had been up a dozen times, fiddling with the window curtains in an attempt to immerse the room in blackness. In all honesty, the bed chamber was already dark enough, and a few random streaks of sunlight were hardly the reason for his insomnia. When he felt like it, Jamie could fall asleep at noon, on the noisy sidewalk in front of the House of Lords.

The only reason that he was experiencing so much trouble slumbering now was because every time Jamie closed his eyes, he saw Julia staring back at him.

Jamie couldn't understand it. She was hardly the first woman with whom he'd played romantic games. And he could state so with certainty, because, in fact, Jamie still remembered the very first woman.

He had been fourteen years old, and completely on his own. One week earlier, Jamie's father had, in a drunken binge, picked up his only son and threw the lad into the street, cursing a warning never to return. It wasn't the first time Pa had done such a thing, but it did prove to be the last. Not even his mother's hysterical pleading could convince the old sot to reconsider.

He slept for the first few nights huddling next to the back wall of a bakery, where a stove operating on the inside could provide at least some sort of warmth. Hungry, Jamie spent half the morning eyeing a peddler's fruit and vegetable barrow. He knew that, if he actually got close enough to snatch an apple or two, then he could scurry away through the alley and avoid being caught. Unfortunately, the barrow's proprietor watched everyone who came near like a hawk. He rarely looked away for more than a second. And that didn't leave Jamie enough time to make his move.

But it did give him enough time to learn that his target possessed not only a fine assortment of fruit and vegetables, but also a young daughter.

Her name was Philipa, and, like her father, the bulk of the girl's face was dominated by a pair of murky gray eyes that, when suspicious, turned into disbelieving slits.

And it were just those slits that Jamie encountered the first time he managed to get Philipa alone. Knowing that, in her father's line of work, she must have heard every beggar's story invented by man, Jamie chose to take a completely different approach. Rather than groveling or playing on her sense of charity, he instead introduced himself as a public school boy playing hooky and slumming in the East End, reinforcing the charade by jumping just such a boy and robbing him of his clothes prior to approaching Miss Philipa.

When she appeared unconvinced, Jamie launched into a series of riotous tales describing life at his thoroughly fictional boarding school, culminating with a reluctant admission that Hensley Hall was holding its first formal ball

Saturday next, and Jamie truly didn't know any girls who would be willing to go with him—seeing as how small he was for an eighteen-year-old—and, well, would Philipa, would she, could she ever consider, well, going with him?

By the time they finished setting up the details, including where to meet and who would be chaperon, Jamie was clutching in one arm a complimentary bag full of apples, plums, and berries to share with his mates back at school.

And, after that, it was all so easy.

Practicing his trade on a series of East End girls, Jamie eventually moved up to the more respectable classes. In his experience, daughters of ministers, country doctors, storekeepers, and other such honest chaps were rarely prepared for a confrontation with a born liar, and they were the ones easiest to get around on.

As a supplement to his natural abilities, Jamie made a point of improving himself through education.

An ape-leader librarian introduced him to all the great poets and philosophers to be found between two book covers. She bought Jamie newspapers, and they would spend the evenings going over every story page by page, with her filling him on history, vocabulary, and other relevant details.

A seventeen-year-old seamstress taught Jamie about color and material and fine clothes.

He took a job driving a dandy's rig, so that he might receive an understanding of what sort of dressing women found attractive, and lost the bulk of his Cockney accent by convincing a pretty upstairs maid to sneak him into her master's study, where Jamie spent days hidden behind the porticos, listening to how the well-bred spoke, then wandering the streets until all hours, repeating and rehearsing what he had heard.

He soon discovered that nothing disarmed a proper, middle-class young woman more than a man claiming to be aristocracy. Not very major aristocracy, of course. Surely nothing as grand as a marquis or even a duke. The highest title Jamie ever bestowed upon himself—and he did it back then without benefit of a duel, thank you—was that of a baron.

Nevertheless, despite Jamie's success at fooling the middle classes into believing him a peer, never in his wildest dreams would he have presumed to pass himself off as one in front of actual members of the *ton*.

No, Jamie was perfectly content to move from countryside to countryside. A vicar's daughter here, a schoolmistress there. Small dowries, but they added up. And, as long as he never actually legally married any one of them, Jamie could still feel more or less like a simple rogue, rather than a true scoundrel.

His only mistake came in wooing a young woman who, he found out a hare's breath too late, turned out to be the sister of a London Bow Street runner, who made it his life's goal to see Jamie dragged before a magistrate's bench, and charged with a docket full of crimes half of which Jamie had never even heard of, much less committed. He could no longer remember which—or maybe it was cumulative—of them he had been sentenced to hang for.

Which all went to prove Jamie's stand, that he hadn't treated Julia Highsmith half as badly as he had some others.

So, why then, did her silent refusal to deny Salome's charges continue to haunt Jamie through the night, leaving him to pace the floor, and to wonder.

11

When Julia was younger and angry, she threw things. Now that she were older and angry, she . . . still threw things.

The only difference was, as a child, Julia had smashed breakable objects against the floor for the sheer audible pleasure of hearing them break into a million pieces. At twenty, she understood that such behavior would be considered inappropriate. And so Julia, when infuriated, now consoled herself with the wholly unsatisfactory act of flinging, one by one, an entire shelf of books at her pillow. But they only made a muffled thump upon impact and then just lay there, pages flapping, leaving Julia to seethe in infuriating silence.

The only problem was, she hadn't the faintest idea whom she was angry at.

Jamie for enticing her into that scandalous, silent waltz, or Salome for stopping it?

Salome for accusing him of only toying with her affections, or Jamie for refusing to vehemently deny it?

Befuddled, Julia sank down on the bed, sliding a pillow onto her lap, and mindlessly tugging at both corners until the white cloth started to tear at the seams.

Or was she angry at herself, for the excited trembling that shot through her in response to Salome's question about Jamie's true intentions, and for the pictures that leapt into her mind, making it impossible for Julia to so much as meet Jamie's gaze.

Strange how Julia and Gavin had done little more than hold hands and exchange secret glances across the room, and she had believed herself in love with him. But years of knowing the young lord hadn't managed to ignite in Julia an ounce of the passionate sensations that had so overwhelmed her after a brief moment in Jamie's arms.

It was all so puzzling. Julia noted the hole she had started in her pillowcase, and hooked one finger over the edge, tearing it further and enjoying the sound that it made.

Julia didn't love Jamie. She felt certain of that. And yet, obviously, a great many women before her had.

Admittedly, he was handsome. Especially when scrubbed and combed and dressed in some of the best men's clothes money could buy. And he was smart. Maybe not terribly learned, and certainly grossly undereducated, but undeniably in possession of a keen mind. In only a few short weeks he'd committed to memory everything Julia had taught him, sometimes surprising even her with his uncanny ability to recite, word for word, an order she'd given him as far back as half a month ago. And he was terribly witty. He made Julia laugh. And fume. Sometimes at the same time. He was charming. He could be sweet. He could even, she knew, be gentle.

The sooner they got married the better.

Once Julia collected her money, traveled to France, appraised Miriam and Alexia's situation and performed whatever task necessary to set it all right again, then Jamie would be free to go on his way and she would never have to set eyes on the rake again.

Yes, Julia decided, tomorrow morning they would set a wedding date, and move towards bringing this farce of a betrothal to an end once and for all.

"Sunday."

Jamie looked up from his breakfast of fried eggs and sausage to agree, "It is the day following Saturday, and preceding Monday. What of it?"

"You and I." She settled across the table from him and poured a cup of tea. "We are to be married. Three Sundays from now."

"Very well." He hardly bothered to look up from his plate.

The complete nonchalance startled her. Julia was not accustomed to Jamie's accepting her words without argument. "Did you hear what I said, Mr. Lowell?"

"Sunday. Wedding. You and I. Yes, I heard every word."

"And?"

"And, what of it? What do you wish me to say? It's no less than what I have been waiting for. After all, marriage was the primary objective of our little charade, was it not? I knew it was coming eventually. Now it is here. Don't chastise me for refusing to act like the traditional nervous groom."

He possessed a definite point. What was it that Julia wanted for him to say?

Nothing, really.

Then why was she finding the few phrases that he did deem worth uttering so completely unsatisfactory?

"Don't you—wouldn't you like to know anything of the arrangements?" The moment she said it, Julia knew that the last had been a most unfortunate choice of words.

Jamie slowly lifted his head, one eyebrow raised in obvious disparagement. "Why, no, Miss Highsmith, I thought that I would leave all the *arrangements* up to you."

She resolved not to allow him to make her as angry this morning as he had managed to last night. That was the last thing she needed. If Jamie knew he had the power to manipulate her emotions, he would become thoroughly unbearable. So, avoiding his sardonic expression, Julia prattled on, "We shall have to order you a wedding suit, I suppose."

"Very well."

"I'll send for a tailor from town."

Julia tapped her fingernails atop the dining room table. Jamie returned to his breakfast, making a great show out of cutting his eggs in an exaggeration of perfectly proper behavior.

Knowing that she were treading into a potentially deadly trap of quicksand, Julia hesitated before asking him, "And what religion is it that you practice, Mr. Lowell?"

This at least managed to capture his attention away from the apparently fascinating slices of sausage.

Jamie shrugged, "Why, the Church of England, of course. At least, that's what I remember from the few Sunday mornings my mum proved able to catch me running out the door before services. Why do you ask? What else could I possibly be?"

She forced herself to sound neutral. "It is only that we will be having an Anglican service. I just thought that I would inquire, in case that you were a practicing Catholic or, or a Mason, or some such thing."

"Rest assured, m'lady, an Anglican service is well and good. I am neither Catholic nor Mason nor Hindu nor Muslim nor Jew."

Once again, his extensive knowledge of matters Julia hardly suspected to be common fodder on the streets of St. Giles, took her by surprise. She said, "You were merely pretending, weren't you?"

He did not know what she was referring to, but, nevertheless, answered, "Most likely. I would have to go back quite a few years to find a time when I wasn't pretending something or other."

"While I was teaching you manners and such, you were only pretending not to know them. Confess, Mr. Lowell, no man could be as ignorant as you claim in the doings of proper society, and yet be able to rattle of a list of world religions as if fresh from a schoolroom lesson in geography."

Jamie raised both arms in the air, capitulating. "Very well, Miss Highsmith. I surrender. You have found me out."

"What?" She leaned forward across the table, sincerely intrigued. "What have I found out?"

"You are right. I was playing the fool to gibe you just

a bit. You are most attractive when patronizing. The truth of the matter is, I already received all the education in manners that I needed, from women intimately acquainted with *ton* etiquette."

She exclaimed, "Surely, Jamie, you haven't been plying your trade on ladies of the aristocracy? The magistrate assured me that it was only ladies of the service-class that you beguiled. Don't you realize what sort of a quagmire that places me in? What if someone were to recognize you?"

He shook his head and waved one hand from side to side in denial. "Calm yourself, Miss Highsmith. I said that I were taught by ladies merely acquainted with *ton* etiquette. Maids, cooks, seamstresses, dressers. All of them close enough to high society to understand their rules and habits, yet far enough away to insure my continuing to live unrecognized."

"But what if a lady's maid were to spot you, and what if she tells her mistress?"

"In such matters, just who do you think will be believed by the *ton,* lady's maid, or the future marquis of Martyn?"

"I suppose you are right . . ."

"Actually, Miss Highsmith"—now it was Jamie's turn to lean forward with a question— "it would seem to me that a much greater threat to my charade being uncovered rests not with the company I've kept in the past, but rather with a few of your own more recent acquaintances."

"My acquaintances?"

"If anyone can recognize me for the fraud, it would be the magistrate who sentenced me, and the hangman whose work you compelled to go unfinished. Now, granted, executioners rarely travel in society's finest circles, but I have heard of the presence of a magistrate or two."

"Your magistrate received adequate financial remuneration for remaining silent, as did the hangman. Furthermore, I can sometimes barely recognize the future marquis of Martyn as the same man whom I dragged out of Newgate covered in filth. I doubt that those who remember you from your months in prison would do much better."

"So everything is in order, then?"

"I do believe that I have taken care of everything. All that remains now is for us to marry. My uncle will be signing my inheritance over to me immediately after the wedding ceremony."

"Congratulations," Jamie said.

"We leave for France the evening of the marriage. Isaac will drive us down to Brighton, and then a ship across the Channel to Le Havre. I hired a carriage there to take us to Nogent-le-Rotrou."

"And where may that be?"

"Two provinces outside of Paris."

"Rather odd spot for a honeymoon, don't you think?"

"No, Mr. Lowell, I do not."

"And what shall we do there, upon our arrival in . . . where?"

"Nogent-le-Rotrou."

"Yes, correct. What shall we do when we get there?"

"That is singularly my concern."

Jamie finished eating and pushed his plate away in disgust. "Do you ever get the feeling, Miss Highsmith, that every conversation we start inevitably twists itself into a perpetual circle, until we are literally parroting the same sequence of sparring questions and answers, day after day into infinity?"

"If you stop asking, I will gladly refrain from answering."

"But that is just my meaning. You do not answer. You stall. You hedge. I daresay, on many an occasion, you simply out and out lie. Why is that? What could be so damning that you have to expound the bulk of your energy just keeping it from coming into the light?" His voice softened. "I know what all that is like. I am hardly a stranger to subterfuge. It is very difficult. It sucks the life out of you, until you find it impossible to decipher where the lie ends, and where the actual person begins again. It can be soul-destroying, Julia."

Julia barely saw Jamie in the weeks leading up to their wedding. There were simply too many details to take care of. She still needed to send out invitations, order a wedding gown, arrange for a church and minister for the ceremony, and meet twice with Uncle Collin to insure a smooth transfer of money into her name.

Or rather, as Julia discovered much to her shock, into the Marquis Jeremy Lowell's name.

Her uncle had explained, "It is the provision of your father's estate. He did not trust a woman's ability to manage a fortune of such magnitude alone, and thus insisted that it only be bestowed upon you once you were married. And that your husband shall then take charge of your affairs."

"Does that mean I will be forced to go to Jamie whenever I need to purchase the smallest item? Why, that is almost as bad as needing to seek your permission," she had retorted bitterly.

At least handling her guest list proved a much simpler affair. Julia was stunned by how many people who'd met Jamie at the ball were terribly eager to come to their wedding.

She had to hand the rascal credit. He had done exactly what Julia demanded of him, and then some. Practically all of London was talking about what a charming, handsome, and delightful match Julia Highsmith had made for herself. A few mothers with daughters at home of debut age had even whispered behind cupped hands to Julia, "Where in the world did you find such a man?"

Wisely, she refrained from telling them everything.

The night before the wedding, Julia sat at her writing desk, penning a letter to Miriam. She wrote quickly, head so filled with everything she wanted to say that her hand moved hardly fast enough across the paper.

My darling Miriam;

Do not despair. I am coming soon, and bringing with me money enough to insure saving both you and Alexia from your dreadful situation. I have written to you before of the steps I felt obligated to take to acquire these funds. I beg, do not think too poorly of me for having taken them. I, myself, try to view them not as a sacrilege or a betrayal, but as a necessity.

The man I am to marry knows nothing of my plan, only that it includes travel to France.

Julia hesitated, then slowly she added:

He is a good man. With, I suspect, a finer heart than he allows seen, and possessing a depth of understanding of the human soul that I have never before encountered in such abundance.

For the remainder of the night, Julia wrote to Miriam about Jamie, unaware of the hours sweeping by her.

It wasn't until Moses respectfully knocked on Julia's door, that she sat up with a start, and realized, with a combination of horror and a most peculiar anticipation, that her wedding day to Jamie Lowell had finally arrived.

12

Considering how many times he had talked of marriage, promised to marry, and come frighteningly close to actually being married, Jamie hadn't expected that finally participating in the ceremony would so greatly affect him. In that, he were mistaken.

It was one thing to discuss the institution in abstract. It were quite another to don the appropriate clothes, stand at attention while being fussed over by a quartet of valets, and then be driven to the church, where, if nothing else, the splendor and solemnity of the surroundings was enough to overwhelm any man.

Jamie's first view of the cathedral came the morning of his wedding. He stepped out from his decorated carriage, only to come face-to-steps with possibly the tallest steeple in England. Why, even the bell in the belfry had to weigh in at ten stone. But even the sheer size of the building quickly paled in comparison to the two-hundred-year-old stained glass window that was the pride and joy of this particular church.

Titled "Jonah Window," it featured a man dressed in a blue robe and red cape, resting beneath a tree made heavy by dozens of ripe golden apples, while at his feet, a brook bubbles joyously over time-worn rocks, and a thriving town of brown and white buildings peeks over the hills in the distance.

As far as Jamie could see, the art's only flaw came in that the leading holding together the hundred or so square sheets of glass produced an effect of looking at the picture as if it were set behind a rectangular grid.

Still under the impression of the window, Jamie could only gape once he was led inside the church itself. Everywhere he turned his head, gold trim sparkled like the sunlight. A pipe organ dominated one entire wall, each glistening tube the size of a fully grown man. Yet, for Jamie, the church's grandest feature had to be the fact that each of the pews facing the altar came with a sturdy back against which to lean, in case the minister felt particularly long winded. After a childhood spent trying to glorify God while sitting on hard, splintery, wooden benches; benches where one leg, inevitably, proved shorter than its twin, Jamie and his aching back sincerely thanked the Almighty for at last providing them with this splendid reprieve.

He could not even begin to guess at how much money had been spent to erect such a fine structure. Obviously more than he would ever encounter in a lifetime.

Which was a shame really, since money, truly, was such a convenient thing to possess. After all, look at all it had done for Julia. Not only had her wealth bought her a convict from the gallows, but it also enabled her to afford the twenty-eight guinea special marriage license from the archbishop of Canterbury, enabling them to get married any place they wished, any time they wished, without the pesky paperwork—such as, say, a birth certificate—demanded of less financially fortunate couples.

Publicly, they claimed the reason for the extra expense, instead of Jamie and Julia's simply acquiring a regular license from the Doctors' Commons, was due to the difficulties of sending for Jamie's birth certificate from Australia.

Inside the church, Jamie asked Moses, "Where might Miss Highsmith be?"

"Upstairs, I believe," the butler replied and reluctantly added, "sir."

Jamie slapped him heartily on the shoulder. "Don't strain yourself with all that civility now, Moses."

"I shall try not to, sir. Thank you."

Smiling less at the man's discomfort, and more at himself for provoking such a reaction from a person who, only a month earlier, might have arguably been considered his social superior, Jamie repeated, "Miss Highsmith is upstairs, you say?" And turned towards the door leading to the second level.

Moses grabbed Jamie by the arm, and sternly shook his head.

"You may not see the bride before the wedding."

"May I see her after?"

"If I possessed the slightest say in this matter . . . no."

"You do not approve of Julia's reasons for marrying me?"

"I approve of her reasons. Not her methods."

"So you must know what those reasons are, then." Jamie clapped his hand against Moses' arm, hoping against hope that, finally, he'd stumbled upon the person capable of offering him some answers.

"Allow me to explain a small matter to you, Mr. Lowell." Moses distastefully removed Jamie's arm from his shoulder. "There is very little that goes on within Miss Highsmith's household that I do not know about. In advance."

Jamie lowered his voice. "Then tell me. Tell me what she is plotting. Damn it, Moses, if I am to be involved, I at least possess the right to know. Is it illegal, what she intends?"

Moses eyed Jamie up and down as if he were a stray cat dragged out of the river, and dryly remarked, "I am certain that you, sir, would be acquainted with the extensive list of just what is and what is not illegal in this country, much more than either Miss Highsmith or I. Furthermore, if you will forgive my saying, I hardly believe that you of all people any longer possess the right to claim moral outrage when confronted with the possibility of legal impropriety."

"So she *is* up to something bootlegged, then?"

"I am not at liberty to say. And, if I recall the details of your arrangement correctly, you are not at liberty to ask."

The door leading to the second flight of stairs opened

with a barely perceptible squeak. Julia, wrapped only in a
dressing gown, looked both ways to assure that they were
the only ones about, before poking her head through the
doorway, and waving, annoyed, at Jamie to stop his ha-
rassing of Moses.

Jamie said, "I thought there reigned a penalty of death
if I so much as caught a glimpse of you prior to our nuptials."

He turned to address Julia, noting, in spite of himself,
how pleasantly the sheer, heaven-blue, silk gown clung to
every curve along her body. She hadn't yet found the time
to fix up her hair, and it hung just the way Jamie liked it,
tumbling in loose curls all down her back, and framing
Julia's face into a perfect oval. Those stray wisps that she
was constantly brushing out of her eyes, the ones that Julia
found such a nuisance, Jamie thought her most appealing
feature. Something about the fact that even she, the imperious Miss Julia Highsmith, could not control a few free-
floating strands of hair, made her appear ever so much
more human to Jamie, and thus, a great deal more engag-
ing than when she presented herself all spit and polished,
and indistinguishable from every other young lady of the
ton.

Julia said, "We have no time for such nonsense, now. I
am afraid there was something I overlooked in planning
this affair."

"I can think of one most important thing," Jamie said
softly, wishing desperately that she might comprehend his
meaning.

But Julia proved in too much of a tizzy to bother with
anything but the common-faced meanings of every statement. "Oh, do stop whining over being kept in the dark,
would you, Jamie? What I meant was, I completely forgot
that you would need a groomsman for the ceremony."

"A groomsman?"

"An attendant."

"I know what a groomsman is, Miss Highsmith. I was
merely repeating your words in confirmation that I were
listening."

"Well, stop repeating, and commence thinking." She

sighed, "It will look rather odd, don't you think, when you stand at the altar without a single attendant. Already, I worry what people may think when they realize that the only guests invited are those from my circle of acquaintances."

"I had assumed we would explain that all of my friends and family remained behind in Australia."

"Along with your groomsman?"

"He," Jamie beckoned her forward with one finger and whispered conspiratorially, "was eaten by a kangaroo."

In spite of herself, Julia smiled.

Moses sniffed distastefully, and, when Jamie asked him what was wrong, he replied, "I suppose that you presume yourself to be frighteningly clever, Mr. Lowell."

"He's always been frighteningly clever," Julia piped up before Jamie even had a chance to defend himself. "You've just never noticed it before, Moses."

He wanted to sweep her off the ground and hug her. He wanted to laugh, he wanted to thank Julia, even though Jamie himself wasn't sure exactly for what. But, mindful of just what sort of reaction such an act on Jamie's part might provoke from Moses, Jamie settled for merely winking at Julia, grateful when she returned the gesture with a mischievous smile of her own, and said, "Actually, Julia, you are wrong. A member of my immediate family will be in attendance. Have you forgotten? The marquis of Martyn has accepted our invitation."

"Actually, he accepted Aunt Salome's invitation. I fear those two are up to something. Although, I am certain that, if she asks, he will agree to stand up for you this morning."

"The last time your aunt asked the marquis of Martyn for a favor on my behalf, I ended up face down in the dirt, listening to the sound of bullets shooting over my head."

Julia saw Jamie's point. "Perhaps then I should ask him."

Promptly at noon, the pews began to fill with wedding guests. Jamie thought that he had never seen so many buff coats, and evening coats, and riding coats, and tall-crowned hats, not to mention the rainbow-colored gowns with their two dozen underskirts, beneath a single church roof before. With the abundance of ladies' stylish, high-set hats and bonnets, Jamie doubted anyone but the front row would ever get to see more than the very tip of the minister, or of the ceremony.

He stood on the second-floor church balcony, obscured well enough by the heavy drapes to prevent anyone seeing him, yet in possession of a glorious, bird's-eye view of his guests. He heard a rustle behind him, and turned around, surprised to spot Julia, still clad only in the dressing gown she'd modeled earlier. She stood on her tip-toes, attempting to peek over Jamie's shoulder and into the church below.

He asked, "Shouldn't you be dressed by now? Fashionably late for a rout is one thing, fashionably late for one's own wedding . . ."

"Salome and her seamstress are arguing over the best way for me to climb into my wedding dress. Salome thinks that I should step in through the neck and then pull it up, and Mrs. Tally insists that, if we're careful, I should be able to slide it on over my head." Julia shook her head and shrugged, indicating her indifferent preference towards either method. "So I thought I had best leave them be to discuss it."

Jamie nodded understandingly and stepped aside, giving Julia broader view of their turnout. When she appeared to be having trouble seeing—a good foot or so shorter than Jamie, she couldn't quite reach the peephole break in the curtains—Jamie easily lifted Julia off the floor, sitting her on his shoulder.

Her hip was only inches from his cheek, one hand clutching the top of his head for balance, and yet, Julia fit so comfortably atop his shoulder, it were as if the two had been chiseled exclusively for each other. He wrapped one arm about her legs, steadying Julia against his chest, enjoying the temporary intimacy that sprung from such an act. Yet, even though Jamie took great pains to keep his hands confined to the most neutral of areas, he nevertheless expected her to object, or at least to issue a perfunc-tory protest against his stealing such a liberty.

But Julia only giggled in delight at her view of the church, and, after a few moments, said, "Thank you, Jamie, but you may put me down now. I've seen enough."

He acquiesced, albeit reluctantly. Sneaking a final peek at their audience, Jamie observed, "Not much to look at, is there?"

She glanced up from smoothing down her hair. Jamie's impulsive bit of gallantry had shaken loose a few strands, leaving them to billow about her neck like a slipped halo.

She dismissed his concerns. "They're only the same people we saw at the ball. The same people I've seen at every ball since I were old enough to stay awake past ten."

Jamie nodded thoughtfully, then, rather self-consciously, he asked Julia, "Those people down there, do you think that they are better than me?" Before she had a chance to respond, he hurried to add, "Certainly, they are wealthier than me, and better dressed than me, and with finer man-ners than me. I do not argue any of that. It is only to be expected."

"Then what exactly are you asking?"

He wished he knew the answer to that one himself. "I guess, I suppose what I am asking is, all those people, all the people in the peerage, do you truly think that they are better than anyone else? That there is something inside them, a birthright, or a kiss from God, that actually makes them superior?"

She wasn't certain how to answer his query, although even Julia could see how important the correct reply were to him. "Well. Do you think so, Jamie?"

"I don't know. Maybe."

Briefly, Julia catalogued in her head the assortment of guests she'd assembled for her wedding. The arrogant vis-counts who pawned their wives' family heirlooms to pay off their gambling debts. The hypocritical earls and dukes who forced every tenant on their estate to attend church every Sunday, while simultaneously supporting both a wife in the country and a mistress in London. The great ladies and baronesses with a half-dozen children resembling neither each other, nor their mother's legal husbands.

When stacked up against the hypocrisy gathered below them, Julia felt no qualms about assuring Jamie, "I refuse to acknowledge any sort of moral or personal superiority within the peerage." When he still appeared less than convinced, Julia took a deep breath, and, looking both ways lest they be overheard, beckoned Jamie forward and whispered, "My mother was not born into the peerage, either. And I never knew a grander lady."

Jamie's head bobbed in surprise at her admission. "Truly?"

"I swear it. She was the daughter of a merchant. A wealthy merchant—he was the first to import porcelain pots and pans from Germany to England—but a commoner just the same. The best my father could do was eventually arrange a knighthood for him. For services rendered to England's kitchens."

Seeing that Julia found the tale equally as amusing, Jamie allowed himself a smile. "Well, isn't that slap up to the echo."

Buoyed by Jamie's enthusiasm, and still as enchanted by the story now as she had been upon first hearing it, Julia elaborated, "My father met my mother at my grandfather's store. She kept the books there. She was very smart. He fell in love with her at first sight, and asked for her hand barely a fortnight later." Julia's face momentarily darkened. "She refused him at first. Wouldn't tell him why. But Papa persevered. Collin was furious."

Jamie nodded. "Is that what your uncle meant, then? About the bad blood? He meant that your mother wasn't of the peerage?"

"Yes." Julia seized on the answer with such force, Jamie took a step back in surprise. "Yes, that's it. That's all of it. That's what he meant." She glanced nervously over her shoulder. "I think I hear Salome calling me. I'd best be going. There is still the minor matter of a wedding for the pair of us to attend."

* * *

No matter how much he tried to ignore it, Jamie could feel a familiar stirring in his stomach. The same beginnings of fear that he usually experienced immediately before embarking on some new con. He told himself that it were to be expected. After all, was not this wedding the biggest fraud of Jamie's professional career?

And yet, it was hard to continue thinking of it as nothing but a subterfuge, while standing inside a holy church, surrounded by Jesus looking down in judgement from all sides, and about to recite vows that included the words "swear" and "forever."

It was one thing to lie to fellow people. But Jamie thought it were quite another to out and out try to outwit the Almighty—which, after all, was what this wedding boiled down to. He and Julia were attempting to con God.

And that did not sit too comfortably with this bridegroom.

In his line of business, Jamie's major attributes were his looks and his words. Which was why he were always very careful, and took great pains to select just the right verbs, nouns, and adjectives to precisely relay his exact meaning. Despite what he'd been accused of in the past, Jamie never swore to God or made any promises that he did not intend to keep. Granted, he may have, at one time or another, carefully arranged his words so that, later, the young ladies may have sincerely believed they heard him make a proposition. But he could not help what someone else did or did not hear, now could he?

Contrary to what people believed, Jamie had standards. They were very low, but he had them. And he had never, ever, in his life, made a literal promise while already knowing that he would not be following through on his words.

Lying to God did seem like a most unfortunate place to start.

Everyone rose for the wedding march, and turned their heads to watch Julia walk down the aisle on the arm of her Uncle Collin. She moved slowly, one foot evenly spaced in front of the other, but her face, at least to Jamie's experienced eye, was that of a woman who wished she could just dash up the aisle and get this blasted thing over with.

She took her place beside him on the altar, and, when the duke passed Julia's hand to Jamie, he felt surprised to find it shaking. Jamie grasped her gently by the fingers, soothingly rubbing them between his thumb and palm. He tried smiling reassuringly at Julia. She did not return the expression.

From their guests, Jamie could hear the murmur of ladies commenting on what a handsome couple the two of them made.

Certainly, Jamie had never seen Julia look lovelier than she did at that moment in her wedding gown. White was the perfect color for her. It brought out the ebony of her hair and eyes, and the rose in her complexion. And it surrounded her with an air of vulnerability that Jamie might otherwise never have suspected.

His heart sped up, beating in tune with the last few notes of the wedding march. Jamie stood straighter, wanting to look his very best in order to feel worthy of the loveliness around him. And before him.

The minister spoke, and Jamie forced himself to look away from Julia, and to listen. With their vows looming closer, Jamie again felt assaulted by nerves. He swallowed hard and let his eyes wander, as if in the hope that an answer to his dilemma might magically write itself upon the walls.

One option, of course, would be for Jamie to reword the vows in his own, noncommittal style. But he did not think that either the clergy or Julia would appreciate it.

He could cross his fingers out of sight. But, surely, such juvenile tricks would not carry very much weight with the Savior.

Even as the minister read aloud their vows in preparation for Jamie and Julia repeating them, the bridegroom still desperately searched for a way to insure that his words would not be noted in heaven as deliberate, deserving-to-go-to-hell-for, lies.

But it was only as he actually began to make his vows to Julia, promising to love, honor, and obey until death did them part, that Jamie finally understood why it were that he was no longer in any danger of burning for eternity.

Because, as he held Julia's hands in his own, looked into her eyes, and pledged his lifelong devotion to her, Jamie realized—much to his horror, delight, and every other emotion that fell in between—that he honestly, truly, meant every word he was saying.

For Jamie, the reception following passed in a blur.

There were hands to shake, toasts to make, and congratulations to graciously accept, when all he really wished to do was to go off somewhere quietly by himself, and take a moment to sort out the conflicting emotions that had so assaulted him during the ceremony.

There was no doubt about it, the wedding vows had come from Jamie's heart. The big question, of course, was why?

Hoping that maybe Julia understood better than he why being in a church in front of so many witnesses should make an event they'd bantered about for weeks all of a sudden feel so serious, Jamie waited until they rode in the carriage heading towards home from the church, before asking, "Julia? Did you—rather, well, when you were taking your vows, did you feel, even slightly, did you feel like we might be doing something sinful?"

"Sinful?" she asked. "In what way?"

"We were, both of us, we were, in effect, lying to God, were we not? We promised things falsely. That's a sin."

"Nonsense," Julia said. "It would only be a sin if we actually meant what we swore, and then went against it. That would be a lie. But, since neither of us meant what we said, when we break the vows, it won't be a sin. Do you understand?"

"Yes. And no."

"I beg your pardon?"

"I understand what you are saying. I am not daft, you know. But I am not asking what you thought. I am asking what you felt." Jamie felt like a puppy with its teeth sunk into a piece of meat. No matter what Julia said, no matter what his own common sense said, he simply could not let this topic go. "Surely, you felt something. Regardless of the peculiar circumstances, we were in a church, taking our vows before God. We are married, Julia."

"Are we?" She hesitated, asking a question that, under other circumstances, Jamie might have interpreted as sarcastic. But the curiosity in Julia's voice, the way she swiveled about in the carriage, arms crossed, facing him, head cocked pensively to one side, convinced him of her sincere ambiguity. "It were only words that we said, after all, Jamie. Are words really all that powerful? For instance, let us say that you went about your entire life thinking that you were, oh, say, a duke. And then, one day, someone comes up to you, and they say, 'Do pardon me, terribly sorry, but we seem to have made a mistake. You're not a duke after all. You're not even a peer, but rather the son of an itinerant gardener.' Should that change the person that you believe yourself to be? Would that change who you were, deep down inside?"

"It would certainly narrow your social circle."

"Exactly. But you would still be yourself. A few words couldn't change that. And it is the same with our wedding. You say that we were married in the eyes of God. But God knew that we were lying. After all, if He is supposed to see everything, it is a bit much to hope that our little sham escaped His notice." Julia sighed, "In fact, what we were actually doing was getting married in the eyes of the *ton*. For my purposes, their approval was certainly more vital than God's."

"I am sure that the lords and ladies of the beau monde would be ecstatic to hear it."

Julia's eyes clouded over. "I cannot imagine, Jamie, that something as important as marriage could be a matter of words. Surely, it must carry far more weight to feel married, than merely to verbalize it. How can a third party, any third party, pronounce someone man and wife, if their hearts do not shout it so first?"

13

Jamie, Julia decided, was most definitely not acting like himself. From the moment they'd set foot on the steamer heading for France, it had felt as if she were traveling with a complete stranger. Jamie did not mock Julia. He did not chastise her. He did not lecture or argue with her.

And, truly, she wished that he would stop. Such a sudden turnaround in attitude was most discombobulating.

On the one occasion Julia felt certain Jamie could not let pass without a quip to make her face redden, he infuriatingly insisted on behaving as the perfect gentleman. All it took was a subtle raising of her eyebrows for Julia to indicate that, on this voyage, Jamie would be sleeping in the dressing room adjoining their cabin, for him to understand and silently comply.

So stunned was she by Jamie's acquiescence, that Julia could only stand and stare at the firmly shut door behind him. Her gaze narrowed on the stacked rows of hand-fastened, lacquer-dyed twigs that, tied one on top the other, made up the hatchway between them. She wondered whether one might be able to see through such a door.

Ten minutes of pressing her eye to the wood and squinting answered Julia's question in the negative. You most definitely could not see a thing. But you might hear quite a bit.

Switching senses, Julia placed her ear against the twigs, and listened. On the other side, she could make out Jamie moving around. The lock on his trunk snapped twice as Jamie opened it, followed by the rustle of clothes being rummaged by a pair of impatient hands. She heard the thump of Jamie taking off his boots and dropping them on the floor one by one. Then, a creak of tired bedsprings, and finally, a most peculiar, muffled, clapping sound, followed by a click-click-click the likes of which Julia had never previously encountered.

Burning with curiosity over what activity might inspire such strange noise, Julia impulsively knocked on the door, and, when no reply proved forthcoming, walked on in.

Jamie lay atop the bedcovers, head and shoulders propped up by a trio of stacked pillows, right leg bent at the knee, left leg stretched out in front of him. He'd discarded the evening dress of black Jamie had worn for the ride from church, and now lounged in merely a pair of white trousers with a blue stripe down each side. And no shirt whatsoever.

Julia stopped short, looking. Well, no, if one wanted to use the correct terminology, Julia suspected that a more apt word for her actions just might be gaping. She stood, gaping.

His chest rose up and down with every breath Jamie took, the triangle of silken, golden-red hair pulsating, and all but drawing an arrow from the width of his shoulders down to Jamie's muscular stomach and ... Julia forced herself to look away. Surely, this wasn't what she'd come in for. Was it?

No. Julia shook her head, grateful for the blurring vision that produced, and sternly reminded herself that she only had an innocent curiosity about the source of that most peculiar clicking sound. And it, unfortunately, seemed to be coming from the vicinity of Jamie's chest.

Lying on his back, elbows by his sides, Jamie held, by each end, a two-foot piece of rope. When he moved his hands just a little, a golden ring hanging from the rope began to spin, making the same click-click-click Julia had heard through the door.

She recognized the ring. It belonged to her late father. Julia had given it to Jamie to wear for their wedding ceremony.

Unsure of how to react to such a blatant display, Julia remained silent. Jamie continued with his game, seemingly oblivious to her presence.

Palm up, Jamie moved the threaded ring atop his palm, and closed four fingers over it. Flipping his arm, he crisscrossed the dangling rope ends over the back of his palm, and, with his free hand, tugged hard on the rope, pulling it free and simultaneously unclenching his fist. The gold ring was gone.

Julia gasped in surprise. He repeated the trick. This time, her father's ring appeared threaded back on the rope without Jamie seeming to so much as touch it. Enchanted, Julia inched closer, watching in awe as Jamie continued his magic, passing a solid gold wedding ring through what appeared to be solid rope, tossing it from hand to hand and making it disappear mid-journey, tying it in a knot at the bottom of the rope without once needing to handle the ring, until, finally, Julia was sitting on the bed beside Jamie.

She didn't dare take her eyes off his hands for even a second. The nimble fingers seemed like a seperate life form as they danced about the rope and ring. Every time Jamie moved, Julia felt her body responding, as if it were her that his hands were so gently caressing and effortlessly bending to his will.

The air around them grew hotter, and Jamie sped up the pace of his efforts, working faster and faster to that insure Julia remained unable to make out the trick that created the magic, until her face lay inches from his, Jamie's breath warm against Julia's cheek.

He was moving with the speed of lightning now, every action a blur to the naked eye. Julia's heart beat in rhythm with the flashing of his fingers, her hands trembling in anticipation. And then, unexpectedly, Jamie stopped. The rope fell limp in his grasp. He turned sharply, lips all but brushing against Julia's.

Her head spun. Her vision blurred, bright yellow bursting in front of her eyes, as if she'd stood up too quickly. She couldn't see, couldn't breathe, couldn't speak. She couldn't do anything but feel Jamie's presence beside her.

And then, just as suddenly as he'd approached, Jamie pulled away. He stood up from the bed, moving to the porthole across the room, and remained there, staring out at the sea, until Julia managed to compose herself.

Awkwardly, she pressed her hands to her cheeks, noting that, while Julia's face was warm, her palms felt ice cold. She looked at Jamie, hoping for a word of explanation or clarification. But now it were he who refused to even meet her gaze.

Not trusting her voice to produce so much as a steady good-night, Julia only nodded in Jamie's direction, feeling foolish for the action since he obviously did not wish to see her, but certain that there ought to be some sort of acknowledgement between them. Wordlessly, she retired to her room, taking great pains to soundly shut the door behind her.

For the rest of the night, Julia lay awake, half-expecting Jamie to burst in. But, despite what Julia felt certain had almost happened earlier that evening, no bursting in, not even a knock on the door, proved forthcoming.

The next time Julia saw Jamie, it were on deck before breakfast, whereupon his actions and manner proved to be those of a perfect gentlemen, with no indication of anything out of the ordinary having taken place.

He kept Julia, as well as the rest of their dining companions, laughing with bulls-eye imitations of their wedding guests, from the duke of Lancshire, whose eyepiece was forever slipping down the front of his cravat, to the widow Banbury, who, having buried four husbands, nevertheless, at the age of nine and fifty, continued eyeing every unattached gentleman at the reception.

On the one hand, Julia felt thrilled, of course, that he had decided to behave. It certainly made things easier, especially now that she had so many other more important details on her mind. But, on the opposite side of the coin, she couldn't help feeling ... disappointed? No, that was not it.

Rejected? Good God, certainly not that.

Unaccustomed?

There. That was the word Julia sought. She was feeling unaccustomed. After all, who might have guessed that Jamie Lowell would prove himself to be such a pleasant traveling companion?

Not only was he never at a lack for conversation, but Jamie also knew a great deal about such things as what amount to slip the steward—not too little, lest they miss their mark, and not too much, or he would expect the same for every service.

And fortunately, for the remainder of their journey, there was no repeat performance of their wedding night.

But then again, there *was* the minor matter of the kiss.

For the whole of the week leading up to their wedding, Julia had dreaded the moment Jamie would be prompted to kiss the bride. Mainly because she still shivered whenever she remembered the way Jamie's lips had felt pressed against hers at the ball. The sensation proved so pleasurable, that, often at night, before she fell asleep, Julia would relive the moment over and over again, until she felt positively light-headed.

Although in the harsh light of day, the last thing she wanted to feel was light-headed. It was bad enough that, lately, some of her exchanges with Jamie had possessed the power to turn a woman her father always called "much too quick of mind for a girl," into a simpering, blathering idiot incapable of putting together thoughts any more complex than "And what shall we eat for dinner?" Now, with Miriam and Alexia's fate so close to being resolved by her timely assistance, the last thing Julia needed was to risk another attack of Jamie-induced dizziness.

And yet, at the wedding that was exactly what happened. Despite Julia's steeling herself in advance, despite her constant repetition that this was all part of their act—or, as Jamie might sneer, their "arrangement" —the moment that Jamie reached for her, the moment his fingers no more than brushed her cheek in preparation, Julia had felt willing to forget everything and everyone, if only he might promise to never stop.

* * *

Julia and Jamie had barely settled at their inn in the French countryside at the outskirts of Nogent-le-Rotrou, before she informed him that she would be going out, and that Jamie, under no circumstances, was to accompany her.

"Very well." Jamie barely glanced up from the book he was reading to wave in her direction as Julia headed out the door.

She knew she should feel pleased by how easily he accepted the situation. Yet, Julia was still *unaccustomed* to this more serious Jamie.

Offering him one final chance at a protest, Julia took her time collecting her hat, gloves, and reticule, then spent a moment hovering at the door, glancing over one shoulder at Jamie, hoping that he might start to wonder why she was still there.

He did not. Wonder, that is.

Resolving to put the entire infuriating paradox out of her mind, Julia slammed the hotel room door loudly behind her, marched down the stairs, and climbed into her hired carriage, offering the driver Miriam's address in Chateaudun.

For the length of the journey, she concentrated on her cousin's dilemma, and on the best way to handle it. Yet, with every inch of distance stretching between then, Julia could not help but feel her mind wandering in speculation about what her husband was doing at the same moment.

Her husband.

In the first instant that Julia instinctively thought of Jamie in those terms, the effect of her words made the dizziness experienced from his touch, feel like but a minor splash in a bucket the size of the Channel.

Jamie Lowell was her husband.

So what if she had told him back in England that the words they'd dutifully recited were meaningless to her? Julia knew that it weren't due to the vows they'd taken or the documents they'd signed that she now felt married to Jamie.

Now the only question remained, whether, after everything that had happened and everything that was about to happen, could Jamie ever begin to feel the same way about her?

The maid who opened Miriam's front door at once raised a finger to both lips and warned Julia to keep her voice down. "Madame de Mornay is . . . ill."

Something about the way she pronounced the final word sent a shiver up Julia's spine. Remembering the French drilled into her in the schoolroom, Julia demanded, "Ill, or hurt?"

"Ill," the woman stubbornly insisted. Then, lowering her voice, confided, "No one in the house can understand it. We all thought he loved her so. And then, three months ago . . . With no reason, madame. I have never seen anything like it."

Pushing past the housekeeper, Julia rushed up the stairs to Miriam's bedroom, knocking on the door, and then cautiously peering inside, after hearing a feeble *"Entrez."*

At the far end of the curtain-drawn room, Miriam lay in bed, propped up on a half-dozen pillows. Her hands, atop the blankets, seemed to have shrunk to the width of flower stems, with only the tips remaining swollen and frighteningly bluish in color. She barely had the strength to fully open both eyes, but, when Miriam saw Julia, she attempted a smile. The tightly drawn skin across her dry lips cracked, and she winced, coughing.

Julia pulled up a chair, sitting by Miriam's bed, taking her hand, and leaning in closer so that she might hear her words.

"You came," Miriam whispered. Her cheeks had sunk so deeply in the folds of her face, they formed a pair of hollow crevasses on either side. "I feared you would not be able to come."

"After the sort of letter you sent?" Julia could hear herself speaking, and she wondered what in the world was possessing her to sound so jovial while in a sickroom.

And then Julia understood.

It was like whistling while passing a cemetery. As long as Julia continued speaking as if her cousin were perfectly well, then she did not have to contemplate the alternative.

"One look at your mother's devastated face, and I knew I had to come. You sounded so desperate in your letter, I almost swam the distance. Fortunately, I remembered in time that I never learned to swim."

A corner of Miriam's mouth twitched. Eyes closing, she breathed, "You always were skilled at making me laugh."

Julia stroked Miriam's forehead, brushing away hair that looked as if it hadn't been combed in days. "If you think that I am amusing, then you should hear my husband. He can even make the duke smile. And you recall how perpetually stern my uncle can be."

"I should have liked to meet your husband." Miriam rallied briefly, raising her head and surveying the room. "Is he here?"

"No." Julia urged Miriam to lie down and rest. "Jamie is waiting for me at the inn. I . . . I did not tell him where I was going. Or why."

"Would he disapprove, then? Of me?"

"If he so much as tries to disapprove of you, darling, I will personally see him hanged for it." Julia wondered how Miriam would react if she learned that her threat was not merely a colorful exaggeration for effect, but a legitimate possibility. She said, "Tell me instead what has happened. Your letter did not even begin to suggest matters growing this bad."

Simply, Miriam said, "I thought I could trust him. We have been married for ten years, I believed that he loved me. And I was so very tired of lying. I confessed everything to him. I knew that he would be cross, but I never suspected, I never suspected he would grow so . . . violent." Miriam closed her eyes, pained, and looked away, blinking back tears.

Thinking to comfort her, Julia reached to pat her cousin's arm, only to feel Miriam stiffen and pull away. Gingerly, Julia rolled up the sleeve to Miriam's dressing gown. The flesh of her arm lay red and inflamed, crimson streaks dotted with swollen, purplish welts. Julia gasped, bringing one hand to her mouth.

"Henri did this?"

"He was angry. He said I betrayed him."

"But surely you must have summoned a doctor to treat it."

"Not at first," Miriam said. "At first I was too ashamed. And so I waited. They say I waited too long. There is no way to stop the infection once it has spread this far."

"So you did finally see a doctor, then," Julia clasped on the first bit of good news she'd heard since arriving. "When does he predict you well enough to travel?"

"Julia," Miriam painfully squeezed her cousin's hand. "I beg of you, stop. I wrote you what my doctor predicted, and when."

"Oh. That. Well, naturally, I assumed you had gotten rid of that particular prophet of doom, and switched to someone a bit more helpful. And optimistic."

"How many doctors will it take to convince you that I am dying, Julia? And that not even you can do a single thing to prevent it happening."

Julia looked away, blinking furiously to keep the tears from spilling down her cheeks. She pretended that her effort to remain stoic was being conducted for Miriam's benefit, when, in fact, both knew that it was Julia who needed help acting brave.

Miriam continued, "My concern now is with Alexia. Henri is incensed by the idea of my tainted blood poisoning his child. He wants her sent to a convent. But that is not the worst of it. He talks of—of beating the devil out of her. As if she were possessed by an evil spirit, or a demon. And I am afraid that, after I am gone, there will be no one to stop him from trying."

"Your mother would try to stop him. Salome would never let anyone hurt her only grandchild."

"My mother has no influence in France. She has no title, no powerful friends, no money. And Henri is adamant. He believes that he is doing God's work." Miriam's breathing continued to grow more labored, until Julia could see the effort it cost her to suck in every gulp of air, and how painful it was to release it again. "I cannot protect her from him anymore. I had thought of snatching my daughter and fleeing. But I haven't the strength. Henri would send the law in pursuit of us. And what sort of protection could I depend on from the law? He is my husband. He possesses complete control over my person. And as for Alexia. Oh, Julia, I live in a Roman Catholic country. What sort of sympathy do you expect them to extend for a Jewish mother who refuses to let her child be forced into a nunnery?"

A nurse wearing a starched white pinafore swept into Miriam's room, ordering Julia to leave and let Madame de Mornay rest. Julia departed reluctantly, promising Miriam that she would still be there when her cousin awakened, and for however long afterward that Miriam desired.

Needing to fill the time while Miriam slept, Julia decided to pay a visit to the nursery, where she watched, unobserved, Mademoiselle Alexia De Mornay, being drilled in her daily English lesson by a most pompous-sounding tutor.

At nine, her cousin's child was almost a perfect miniature replica of Miriam. She wore a gray dress trimmed with lace at the collar, and a neck-to-knees row of shiny silver buttons down the front. Her ruler-straight blond hair, the sort that turned golden in the summer and brown when wet, was held off of Alexia's face with a silver band. Listening, Julia marveled at the girl's charmingly French-accented English.

As Alexia patiently repeated her tutor's teachings, Julia found herself being reminded of Jamie. Had she sounded as patronizing while quizzing him on etiquette? Had she really treated an intelligent, full-grown man like a child?

Julia would have liked to offer an indignant, "Of course not," to such a question. But she knew that it would be a lie.

Her behavior towards Jamie had truly, from the first day, been abominable. And the worst part was, Julia could no longer even recall why that was. It were as if the woman who had fetched Jamie from his jail cell, and the woman that she had somehow, over the past months, transformed into, were not even distantly related, much less had ever been the same person. Thinking back on past conversations, Julia grew more and more uncomfortable as she realized just how much she'd sounded like Alexia's tutor.

She had belittled Jamie, berated and insulted him. And, when he expressed the audacity to protest, she had threatened him with a hanging. Why, not even Julia's frantic worry over Miriam and Alexia's fates could justify such behavior.

Now that she had the hindsight to step away and look at herself as if from the side, Julia felt amazed that the one time Jamie raised his hand to her, he had hesitated to follow through and give her the slap that she so soundly deserved.

Promising the nurse that she would see to it Miriam ate every last morsel of dinner on her tray, Julia rushed the imperious woman out of the room and turned back to her cousin. She helped Miriam sit, arranging the pillows so that she might be propped up from all sides, and then balanced the tray across Miriam's lap, cutting her food into smaller pieces for her to chew.

She said, "I can spirit Alexia to England. If Henri tries to take her by force, he will have to go through the English courts, and, with anti-French sentiment so high after the war, I doubt that he could count on a successful litigation. Besides, in London, Salome does have the powerful friends, and I have the money to ensure a judgement being handed down our way."

Miriam nodded weakly. "Yes, that is the best idea of all."

"Tomorrow then. I will return tomorrow morning, pack up Alexia's things, and we will be on the ship heading for England by dinner time. Even if Henri does hear of our absence from your servants or the like, it will be too late for him to stop us."

"And your husband?" Miriam spent the last of her strength to inquire "How will you explain all of this to him?"

Her cousin's question continued to plague Julia, even as she bade her farewell, and left the house, walking towards her hired carriage. How would Julia explain all this to Jamie? Or maybe a better question was, how much of this would she explain?

Signaling for the driver to bring his rig around, Julia hiked up the right side of her skirt with one hand, and opened the carriage door, stepping inside.

A male hand reached out from the depths, firmly clasping Julia's fingers, and offering the extra tug necessary for her to easily slide inside the carriage. Surprised, she fell against the cushioned seat, needing to catch her breath before turning to identify the mysterious figure.

"What a surprise to run into you here." Jamie crossed his legs and leaned casually against the opposite wall. Politely, he asked, "Now, would you care to explain the reasons as to why?"

14

The moment Julia stepped inside the carriage, Jamie knew that, finally, he would be getting the answers he wanted. She looked exhausted. She moved slowly, letting her head fall back, and sharply rolling her shoulders in an attempt to ease the painful stiffness in her spine. Julia's mouth was set in a straight, grim line, and all ten of her nails had been bitten down to the flesh.

Seeing her in such a state, Jamie felt tempted to soften the aggressive questioning he had planned for while following Julia from the inn to this chateau. But he did not dare pull back, for fear that it would be too far, and then Jamie might never learn just what sort of plot it were that Julia had dragged him into.

He gestured for the driver to start his team, then grabbed Julia by the arm, and demanded, "Now, that we have all the time in the world, perhaps you would care to begin at the beginning."

She no longer possessed the strength to fight him. Lying on her side against the carriage seat, and rubbing her eyes with the back of one hand, Julia looked less like the co-conspirator of an intricate inheritance plot, and more like a little girl desperate for a good night's sleep. Julia yawned, covering her mouth with one hand, and sighed, looking at Jamie with eyes so beaten, they lacked any other expression whatsoever. Tonelessly, she told him,

"This chateau belongs to my cousin, Madame Miriam de Mornay. She is dying, and she needs my help to save her child."

In as few words as possible, Julia told him about Miriam's situation vis-a-vis Henri, and his threats to put Alexia in a convent, as well as her promise to protect the girl.

Jamie listened silently, only to, at the end of her tale, point out, "I asked that you start at the beginning. This, my dear Mrs. Lowell, sounds suspiciously like the very end."

"What else is it that you wish to know?"

"How does all this fit in with your reluctance to marry Gavin, and with your uncle's most dire predictions of doom, and with his cryptic warnings of 'bad blood' in the family?"

Julia took a deep breath, forcing herself to sit up at least a wee bit straighter. She opened her mouth to answer, but no sound proved forthcoming. She tried again, confessing, "This is most difficult for me. After so much time spent training myself not to answer, it is almost as if my mind were blocking upon my tongue."

"Try harder."

Julia looked down at her hands, squeezing them into fists so tight her knuckles turned white, and, refusing to meet Jamie's eyes, said, "The bad blood that Uncle Collin spoke of, it is in Miriam, as well. My mother, and Salome, and Miriam, and—and I—we are all of the Jewish race."

Jamie blinked in surprise, peering closer at Julia. He'd been given so much time to imagine the worst that his brain stood prepared for a multitude of explanations, ranging from the medical to the legal to the occult. Yet, never in a million years, would he ever have guessed at this. A part of him, childish and superstitious to be sure, but a genuine part nonetheless, instinctively searched Julia for the horns his old man claimed all Jews had growing from the tops of their heads.

Noting Jamie's surreptitious interest, Julia snapped, "Do stop it, Jamie, I haven't any horns, nor a tail either."

He swallowed guiltily, and claimed, with false bravado, "Of course not. I did not really think that you would."

"Have you never met any other Jews before?"

"Only the ones I saw living in the London ghetto. And they all wear those heavy dark coats and hats, and the women kerchiefs. So who knew what they might be hiding."

Julia said, "They tell me Uncle Collin put up such a wail when my father dared marry my mother, that those pair of mirrors in his parlor fell down from their walls. He called her a heretic, and a witch, and every other epithet that he could think of. Even when my mother swore that she would never tell another living soul what she was, Collin still did carry on so."

"I don't understand." Jamie, over the initial shock, now felt merely intrigued. "If your mother swore never to confess, why did she and your father bring you up in the Jewish faith, all the while knowing England to be filled with nincompoops like your uncle and I, who believed you to have horns, or worse."

"They didn't. I was baptized and raised Anglican, just like anyone else. I did not even know about my mother's faith, until Collin told me. To prevent my marrying Gavin." Julia shook her head, marveling at her own naivete. "I grew up in the same house with my mother, and Salome, and Miriam, and I never knew. No one ever told me. They all wanted to protect me, they said. They did not want to force me into a life of lies, like theirs. My mother had to deny who she was until the day she died. Salome is still denying. My grandfather—"

"The commoner who sold pots and pans?"

"Yes. He lived two lives. A Christian one for his customers, and a Jewish one at home. He went to church every Sunday, and prayed in private Friday night, begging for forgiveness. I can't blame him though. A few untruths does seem like a small price to pay for a path out of the ghetto." Julia turned to face him. "Have you ever been inside the Jewish ghetto, Jamie? After Collin told me, I went to take a look. It was horrible, such conditions those people live under. But, at the same time ..." She hesitated, warning, "You'll laugh at me."

"I've been laughing at you for weeks. What's another chuckle, more or less, between friends?"

"But, at the same time, it was wonderful. All my life, I felt like I never belonged with my peers. Physically, I am much darker than, for instance, Gavin or Lady Emma. Or you. I barely look English. But the ghetto is filled with people who look like me. Not in how they dress, or how they act, but in their eyes. Even when our eyes were of a different color, they were the same. Can you understand?" She shook her head. "Oh, of course, you can't."

He took offense at her assumption. "Certainly. How in the world could I possibly understand what it feels like to circulate among people you are only pretending to belong with, all the while fearing they might find you out?" Noting her chastised expression, Jamie added, "What I do not understand, however, is why this should have altered your desire to marry Gavin. After all, if your mother kept her origins secret, why could not you do the same?"

"There is a tradition in Gavin's family of the eldest son going to university, studying the law, then taking his rightful seat in the House. Our child would never be able to do so. Jews are not allowed at Oxford, nor may they study the law anywhere else. And as for the seat in the House, the oath every new member must take requires a swearing of abidance to the Christian faith and the Christian Savior."

"And you would not wish a child of yours taking such an oath?"

"No." Julia cleared her throat, and, feeling that she had nothing more to lose, attempted to explain to him exactly why she continued clinging to such uncomfortable principles, rather than taking an easier route. "After I returned from the ghetto, Salome warned me never to speak of it to anyone. She said that I had no concept of the sort of violent reaction I might provoke from people if ever they found out I had deceived them."

"I presume she was referring to a violent reaction along the lines of the one your cousin Miriam received from her husband."

"I suppose. Only, you see, I could not obey Salome's order."

"A rule that you could not obey," Jamie said, not unkindly, "What a stunning shock."

Julia smiled. "I sought out my mother's family. I badgered Moses and Isaac for every bit of information they knew."

"Moses and Isaac? Our Moses and Isaac?"

"They are my mother's cousins. That is why they take such fine care of me."

"And, no doubt, why they watch me like such hawks."

"Moses went against Salome's orders to teach me, not only about Jewish customs and traditions, but also about Jewish history in England. They never teach such things in school. Did you know that, in 1144, in Norwich, an entire town of Jews were hanged after a Christian boy was found murdered? One hundred years later, an Oxford University student who converted to Judaism and married a Jewish woman was burned alive for his crime."

Lightly, Jamie said, "That certainly makes me feel secure."

"I had such nightmares afterwards."

The fear on her face was genuine. It made Jamie want to reach out and comfort her. It made him want to take on every fool, like himself and dear old Uncle Collin, who once thought her, and those like her, to be some sort of devils in disguise.

Julia said, "But the odd thing was, instead of my being frightened away by Moses's stories, I became even more determined. I became determined that if the world and England hated all Jews so much, then that's exactly what I would become. If only so as not to allow those who try to purge us a posthumous victory. No matter how much Salome tried dissuading me, I had my mind made up. I would live a Jewish life, in the name of all those who had been killed trying to defend it."

"A very noble sentiment, Mrs. Lowell," Jamie still found it difficult to, one hundred percent, accept her words at face value. "However, you are hardly living this Jewish life out in public, where you can be seen. Could it be that, noble sentiments aside, you are not yet ready to sacrifice all the posh and privilege that comes with being the wealthy *Anglican* daughter of a peer?"

She glared at him so ferociously that Jamie felt certain he had hit his intended target.

"True," Julia spat out, but Jamie was no longer sure whether her anger were directed at him, or at herself. "I am a hypocrite. There, I have admitted it. Are you happy? I love the life of the *ton*. I love its balls and its fox hunts and its nights at the ballet and the opera. I love the beautiful clothes that my money buys me, and I love the way I am bowed to when I travel into town. Sometimes, I wish that I were two people. That I could lead two lives. Or that, at the very least, that I might decide which one it was that I really want." A tear trickled down Julia's face, and she wiped it quickly, telling Jamie, "You must think me horrid."

"Why? Because you were born Jewish? Very few of us are allowed to choose whom we would like to be born. I, for one, was given the option of springing to life either as prince regent, or as the son of a sot in the East End. How do you like my decision?"

She smiled. "You do not think me a silly skitterwit, for being unable to decide what sort of life I wish to lead?"

"On the contrary, I commend your honesty."

"My honesty? You are commending my honesty? Now, there is something I never expected to hear you say."

"You could have continued lying to me. It is a very brave soul who will admit to their shortcomings and doubts."

"I feel so confused, Jamie. Who is Julia Highsmith? Am I the daughter of a peer? Am I a Jewess? Do I deserve a manor home? Do I deserve banishment to the ghetto?"

"No one deserves banishment to a ghetto. Furthermore, there is no reason why you cannot be a Jewess and the daughter of a peer, simultaneously. It is what you are already."

"But I do not act it. I act either one, or the other. Never both at the same time."

"I have acted enough different roles simultaneously to field a cricket team and a half."

Inexplicably, Julia burst into giggles. Jamie recognized the sound as the beginnings of nervous hysteria, and attempted to calm her, but Julia insisted on sputtering out the words, "Between all the people you have been, and all the roles I have acted, I am amazed the lot of us fit so comfortably into this one carriage."

She barely noticed it when her unnatural laughter somehow turned into an agonized flood of tears, but, when Jamie reached for her hand, Julia allowed him to take it, gratefully collapsing into his comforting embrace, and clinging to Jamie as if he were the only dependable thing still left in her world.

She felt so exhausted when they arrived at the inn that Julia nearly stumbled while stepping out of the carriage. Catching her by the waist, Jamie easily swept Julia into his arms, carrying her inside as he might have done for a sleepy child.

Too tired to fight him, Julia merely rested her head against Jamie's chest, wrapping both hands about his neck for better balance. Her hair tickled his chin, smelling so sweetly of Julia herself that Jamie wanted to stop and deeply inhale its fragrance.

However, such an act would look rather silly on the stairs to their room, so Jamie waited until they had gotten inside. Gently, he laid Julia on the bed, and reached to remove her shoes.

She jumped as if he had bitten her, demanding, "What is it you think that you are doing?"

A million responses swam through Jamie's mind, ranging from the sarcastic to the patronizing to the heartbreakingly sincere.

But Julia wasn't the only one feeling tired. After months of playing games, and wrestling for the upper hand, Jamie's limbs carried a weariness no amount of rest would ever be able to cure.

Unable to summon up the energy to spar with Julia—or force himself to keep coming back every time she so roughly slammed him away—Jamie, instead, hurled her shoe against the far wall with such impact, that the windows shook.

Julia jumped, terrified, and opened her mouth to apologize.

But Jamie had already stormed out the door.

A part of her believed that he might never come back.

Instead of spending her night ironing out the final details for fooling Henri de Mornay and whisking Alexia out of the country, Julia spent it worrying about Jamie.

What was wrong with her, anyhow? Why did she constantly continue saying and doing the wrong things in front of Jamie?

He must probably hate her by now. And Julia could not blame him. Just once, why couldn't she treat him with some kindness, instead of constantly looking for hidden motives in his actions?

She had felt so safe in his arms. So comfortable and secure, and . . . loved. Yes, that was the word. She had felt loved. Loved and protected, the way it used to be on all those mornings when she rode in the saddle in front of her father, and felt his strong, masculine arms wrapped around her shoulders. Only, with Jamie, the feelings that swept through her were all those and more. She not only felt safe, she felt . . . alive.

All her perceptions heightened, until every breath she took felt clearer than ever before, with the surrounding sounds of night coming through crisper, and tactile sensations, such as the way the skin of his neck rubbed against her cheek, and the warmth of his palm supporting her waist, increased in their power, until Julia could feel Jamie in every pore of her being.

And it was the overwhelming quality of the pleasure that so frightened her. Although by nature emotional, this evening with Jamie was the first time Julia had ever felt as if a given sentiment had actually grown larger than she was. That it were big enough to control her, instead of the other way around. And she felt terrified at the prospect.

Julia could not afford such a calamity. Leading a double life required her remaining in possession of all of her faculties at all times. She did not dare risk a distraction. Which was exactly what Mr. Jamie Lowell turned out to be. She'd known it from the first day at the prison, when his relaxed, mocking attitude had so befuddled Julia that she barely knew what to say.

He'd done it again at the ball, and at their wedding. Both times, Julia had felt willing to succumb to him, rather than stubbornly continue on with the path she had chosen, the one that she knew it were imperative to follow.

In her head, Julia suspected that Jamie's choosing never to return would be the best thing that could happen to her.

But, in her heart, she suspected that it might also, quite possibly, kill her.

She awoke the next morning, after a night spent tossing and turning, feeling as if a tree trunk were lying across her chest. She could still remember the way Jamie had looked at her, in the instant before throwing her shoe against the wall. He had been angry, yes. Disgusted, tired. But also disappointed.

Julia dunked her head in the basin of cold water, hoping that it might shake off some of the lethargy that so plagued her. It succeeded only in making her teeth chatter, and standing the hair in back of her neck on end. She wiped her face vigorously with a towel, then quickly dressed, stuffing the rest of her belongings in a trunk in preparation for returning to England as soon as she fetched Alexia. No item in the room stood disturbed. Obviously, Jamie had not come back while she slept.

Resolving not to think of her missing husband, Julia took a final glance at her face in the mirror, deciding that, under the circumstances, this was the best she was going to look, and opened the door of her room.

On the other side, arm raised as if to knock, stood Jamie.

15

Julia blurted out, unthinking, "You came back."

"I would welcome any thoughts you might harbor on the possible reasons as to why." Jamie blocked the doorway with one hand.

"I—I don't rightly know."

"The closest I can figure, is that I am terribly afraid of your botching this entire job, and leaving me to pick up the pieces. In case you've forgotten, I do have a criminal record."

"What has that to do with anything? I am the one committing the crime."

"And I will be the one they call an accomplice. Should the law catch up with us, I offer you one guess as to which party will end up with a slap on the wrist and a trip back to jolly old England, and which party will be living out the rest of his life in prison. A French prison. Where they do not need nooses, because the richness of their sauces will probably kill you." He sighed, rubbing one hand against the other. "But, unfortunately, I am a professional. And it would be a breach of trade ethics to allow an amateur to perform a task I alone possess the specialized training to complete."

If anything, Miriam looked worse on the morning of Julia's second visit than she had during her first.

This time, she barely found the energy to raise her head when speaking to Julia. When being introduced to Jamie, she requested that he stand at the foot of the bed, where Miriam did not have to turn her head to look at him.

Unsure of what Jamie's reaction might be to a woman so ill, Julia kept a close eye on him. But she need not have worried. Within a moment, Jamie had turned on enough charm to have even Miriam smiling weakly, as Jamie acted out for her the nuptials she had missed last week. He appeared not to notice the infectious, open sores dotting Miriam's arms and lips, or the grotesque manner in which her sunken face now resembled a living skull.

And, after only a few minutes of Jamie speaking to her as if she were still the beautiful woman of weeks past, Miriam even appeared to rally a little. While Jamie spoke, Miriam's gaze briefly shifted to Julia, and she winked, offering a final stamp of approval on her cousin's choice of a husband.

Reluctant to interrupt what was probably the most pleasant time Miriam had experienced in months, Julia nevertheless indicated the clock on the mantelpiece, and reminded, "We had best fetch Alexia. It is almost time for us to go."

Miriam nodded and asked Jamie, "Would you kindly call my daughter? She should be in the schoolroom right now."

"Certainly." A gentleman to the end, Jamie bowed and kissed Miriam's hand before departing.

"Such a handsome man," Miriam said. "And so dear. You are very lucky, Julia. A man like that would never betray you."

Julia wondered if Jamie believed the same to be true about her. She certainly hoped so.

"*Maman?*" Little Alexia appeared in the doorway, clutching on to Jamie's fingers as if they'd been friends forever.

Miriam beckoned her child closer, gesturing for Alexia to sit on the edge of the bed, and proceeding to whisper in French.

After only a few words, Alexia grew agitated. She

looked over her shoulder at Julia and Jamie, then violently shook her head no, grabbing Miriam's arm and hugging it tightly.

Tears in her eyes, Miriam nodded yes, and tried to untangle herself from Alexia's grip.

"*Non,*" Alexia's voice rose to a desperate shriek, and she clutched Miriam even tighter, kicking her legs against the bed. Switching to English, Alexia screamed at Jamie and Julia, "No, no, I do not want to go. I want to stay. I do not want to go."

Julia tried soothing the girl by embracing her, but Alexia threw off Julia's hands, and buried her face in Miriam's chest, sobbing hysterically, and holding on with all of her might.

"Alexia, darling, please," Julia pleaded. The child's torment was upsetting Miriam to where she was having trouble breathing.

"No, let me be, let me be. I want to stay home with *Maman.*"

"Alexia!" Jamie grabbed the little girl around the waist with one arm, pulled her off of Miriam, and set her down on the ground, a hand on each shoulder. She tried wriggling to get out of his grip, and, when that failed, commenced kicking and biting. Jamie merely continued holding Alexia at a harmless distance, waiting until she was spent and exhausted from struggling.

"Listen to me, Alexia," he finally said.

If Julia thought she had heard every tone available in Jamie's arsenal, then she was mistaken. The voice he used for Alexia was firm, no-nonsense, a little bit intimidating, but also kind and caring. He said, "I want you to hear what I have to say, young lady, because, as your Aunt Julia will tell you, I hate to repeat myself. Now. Do you love your mother, Alexia?"

The little girl sniffled, looking from Miriam to Jamie, and whispered, "Yes."

"Yes, what?"

"Yes, I love my mother."

"Do you believe that your mother loves you?"

"Yes."

"Do you want your mother to be happy?"

"Of course, I do."

"Well, then, can you try and understand how your mother loves you so much, that the only way she can be happy is to know that you are safe." Jamie brushed a strand of damp hair from the girl's face, and loosened his grip. "And you cannot be safe in France."

The last of her sobs escaped Alexia's chest as a dry gasp. "I know. *Maman* told me what Papa wishes to do."

"Then you know why it is so important that you come to England with your Aunt Julia and myself. We will take care of you, and we will love you. Although, you and I both know, that no one in your life could ever love you as much as your mother does."

"He is right, Alexia," Miriam said softly. "He is right."

Jamie peered into the girl's eyes with a hypnotic intensity Julia recognized from previous occasions. "This is the most difficult thing you will ever have to do, Alexia. But you must do it. Not only for your sake, but for your mother's as well."

"I do not want to leave my home." Alexia wiped her lashes with a damp sleeve.

"Leaving home is never simple. But, believe me when I tell you that it does grow easier. You learn to carry everything that is important in here," Jamie tapped Alexia's chest over her heart. "And you learn not to give away pieces of yourself to other people, so that you do not have to leave pieces of yourself behind."

Now it wasn't only Alexia wiping away tears. Julia had to bite her lip to keep from making a noise and shattering the tentative rapport Jamie was building with Miriam's daughter.

"I know what you are feeling, Alexia, and I know that, for a long time, you are going to continue feeling angry, and lost, and determined never to trust another soul, until the pain inside becomes like a heavy fog that you believe is never, ever going to blow away." He was squatting now, nearly at the child's eye level. "But do you know what, Alexia? It does blow away. One day, just when you are certain that the heavy feeling in your chest is something that will be there, be a part of you, for the rest of your life, you will meet someone unexpected. Someone with a smile so beautiful, that it will cut right through all the pain inside, and lift it away without so much as a scar. And that, Alexia, is when you'll know that you have finally come home again."

When it came time to leave, Julia could do no more than brush Miriam's cheek with her lips, then hurriedly turn away, lest Julia completely collapse. It had proven difficult enough to watch the tearful, murmured good-byes between Alexia and her mother, and Julia feared, should she start crying again, that this time she would find it impossible to stop.

So it fell to Jamie to take Miriam's hand and reassure, "I swear to you, Madame de Mornay, your daughter will want for nothing. Julia and I will do everything we can to ensure her comfort and happiness."

"I know, Mr. Lowell," Miriam pressed Jamie's hand to her face. "You have already assured mine."

In the past, whenever Jamie surprised her and did something so sweet, so considerate, that it made her heart ache, Julia managed to halt the avalanche of sentiment that his tenderness involuntarily stirred within her by growing quarrelsome and goading Jamie into doing the same. But his consideration for Miriam, his gentleness with Alexia, and Jamie's general willingness to help Julia with a task he might have simply maligned, stripped her of any and all traditional defenses.

Instead of rejecting the sentiment, or feeling threatened by it, Julia cherished the memory of Jamie's kindness, hoarding it in her breast like a last bit of coal on a cold day, and returning to it again and again to revel in the pleasurable warmth of its glow.

On the carriage ride back to the inn, Julia watched Jamie with Alexia. He held the little girl on his lap, letting her cry against Jamie's chest until there were no more tears left, and then gently rocking her back and forth, whispering things in Alexia's ear that Julia could not hear, but guessed, from the gradually peaceful expression on Alexia's face, to be of great comfort.

Looking at Jamie now, so pleasing with the child in his arms, Julia could not, for the life of her recall what had ever made him appear so threatening to her in the first place. Why had she feared Jamie so, to the point of deliberately making him angry, lest he somehow break through her defenses? Why had she gone out of her way to make him act in a provoking manner to her, when, in reality, there was no sensation sweeter than the understanding and acceptance of his true nature.

Miriam and Alexia recognized the good in Jamie immediately. It were only Julia, who prided herself on being most intelligent, who had taken the longest to spot—and admit—its existence.

It took only a few minutes, once back at the inn, for Julia to finish packing her trunk in preparation for fleeing France.

While Jamie went downstairs to inquire of the proprietor where they might hire a rig to port, Julia carelessly stuffed her belongings in their approximately proper places. Alexia sat on the bed, clutching a doll dressed in blue satin to her chest, and wordlessly watching Julia scurry about the room. Her dark eyes reflected a dull, emotionless shock, one that prevented Alexia from either objecting or approving of her new surroundings.

Julia saw a flicker of relief cross Alexia's features when Jamie finally returned to their room and absently stroked the little girl's hair. To Julia, he whispered, "I am afraid that we have a minor complication, m'lady."

Gesturing for Jamie to move away from Alexia, Julia beckoned him into a corner and hopefully out of her hearing range to ask, "What is it? What has happened?"

"I had a nice bit o'chat with the fellow who manages this domicile. In his broken English he told me an alert's been sounded to every Charlie—or whatever they're called here—in France, by a gentleman in Paris, who claims his daughter's been snatched by criminals, for the purpose of extorting ransom."

"No," Julia covered her mouth with one hand. "How? How could Henri have heard of it so quickly?"

"The household staff at Miriam's."

Julia shook her head. "They are very loyal to her."

"You will forgive me for saying so, m'lady, but, based on my rather extensive personal experience with the service class, I would hazard to guess that the only loyalty Miriam's staff harbors is towards the soul that doles out their weekly salary. And that, unless I am mistaken, would be Monsieur, not Madame, de Mornay."

"Someone must have sent a messenger to Henri in Paris."

Jamie said, "We'd best be going then. And quickly."

Walking the distance from the inn to the livery stable two streets away, Julia imagined she could feel the eyes of every passerby pasted upon her, upon Jamie, and, most importantly, upon the eerily silent Alexia. If one child had been reported missing, surely then, every couple with a little girl would instantly fall under some sort of suspicion. Especially when they were strangers to the area, and looking for transportation out of the country.

Loosening her cape, Julia wrapped one end of the reddish brown garment about Alexia's shoulders, as if protecting her from the chill, but, in reality, struggling to keep her face hidden. Alexia acquiesced without a peep, as she had acquiesced to everything else since being forced to leave home. And her unnatural solemnity, to Julia, seemed to scream louder than any other piece of evidence, that all was not right with the three of them.

At the livery stable, Julia had barely gotten a chance to open her mouth and request a rig, when the establishment owner's eyes slid to Alexia. He smiled at the little girl, and asked a few rather innocuous questions on how she were enjoying her holiday. But, unfortunately for them, Miriam's frightened daughter merely stared back blankly, and shook her head from side to side.

Desperately, Julia hoped that he might merely think Alexia dull-witted and stop his nosy-poking to return to the subject at hand. But, instead, the man peered queerly

at Alexia and then at Julia and Jamie, taking a step back
and placing both hands on his hips, as he studied the illicit
threesome from a different angle.

Eyes narrowing into slits, he asked Julia, "Strangers to
this part of the country, are you?"

"Yes." Julia pulled Alexia closer, wishing she could
somehow make them both invisible. "Yes, we are."

The man wagged his finger at the little girl, and clicked
his tongue. "Have I not previously seen you about, mademoiselle?"

"No," Julia stubbornly insisted, while Alexia continued
staring straight ahead in deafening silence.

Unwilling to wait and see what sort of conclusion he
drew from their most peculiar family portrait, and realizing
that, at the very least, should the law ask him questions,
Alexia's unnatural behavior had insured his remembering
and identifying them, Julia grabbed Alexia by one arm,
swiftly yanking her out of the stable and onto the street,
without barely a glance back to check if Jamie understood
to follow.

She realized that he had when Julia felt a pair of masculine hands scoop Alexia out of her grasp, so that the
three might move faster, followed by a tug on her own
shoulder, and a hiss to duck into the alley rather than attempt to escape in plain view of everyone on the sidewalk.
She could hear the livery stable's owner shouting after
them, as well as the startled exclamations of the men and
women they were forced to push aside while running.
Julia's bonnet flew off her head, and she left it to lie on
the street. Julia's skirt tangled about her legs, and, propriety aside, she hiked it up a few inches above her ankle, no
longer able to force herself into caring what other people
might think.

Following Jamie, Julia turned the corner and into a back
alley, no longer running on paved road, but rather on
sewage-drenched cobblestone. The hem of her gown grew
gray and damp. Pebbles flew up, scratching her calves,
tearing her stockings.

The distance between her and Jamie stretched greater, as
Julia felt the stabbing pain in her left side that suggested

she may have run a bit too much. She could barely breathe, needing to gasp and cough. Spent, Julia leaned against an alley wall, doubled over in pain, and rested her head on her arms. She had not even the strength to call out for Jamie to stop.

Willing her head to cease its spinning, and her stomach to unclench, Julia barely heard the echo of Jamie's footsteps as he doubled back through the alley, setting Alexia on the ground, and standing beside her, demanding, "Have you completely lost all of your senses, Julia?"

Considering how she felt, chest constricting, heart pounding, legs, arms and side throbbing in painful unison, Julia could only wish for his sarcastic question to come true. Instead, she shook her head weakly.

He continued, "I swear, I think you have gone mad. What was the meaning of running off in such a pell-mell manner? If the gentleman did not judge us guilty previously, I assure you, he most certainly does now. Running away always implies guilt."

"I was frightened," Julia choked out.

"Needlessly. We were doing nothing wrong, save hiring a rig. And there is of yet no law against such behavior in France."

"If you . . . if you," Julia slowly forced herself to rise and inhale, "if you truly believed that running were the worst course of action to take, then why did you follow me?"

"I would have looked rather the fool letting you bolt off like a madwoman, whilst I continued carrying on our business transaction as if nothing were amiss. Secondly, I may be dressed like a gentleman, but I still possess the instincts of an East End boy. When I see someone running, I run. There is usually adequate opportunity later to inquire what it is that we are running from."

"But why did you not simply stay and attempt to explain my most peculiar behavior?"

"Mainly because the only words of French I feel confident in uttering are *maman, merci, noblesse oblige,* and *oui.* However, no matter what order you arrange them in, that hardly qualifies for even one side of a coherent conversation."

Feeling the blood gradually returning to her brain, Julia felt confident enough to actually look around and note her surroundings. She hadn't a clue to where they were, save a back alley, nor any concept of how to get to the nearest docks.

"Jamie," Julia struggled to keep her voice from breaking. "Tell me, what do we do now?"

16

66"W"ell, what exactly did you have in mind as a plan
of action, when you fled from the stables?"

She shook her head. "I beg of you. Don't mock me. Not
now."

Was that politeness that Jamie actually heard in Julia's
voice? It were so unfamiliar, he couldn't feel certain.

Julia looked up at him hopefully, her face strangely devoid of the contempt and insolence she usually offered.

Unfortunately, nothing could wipe from Jamie's mind
the memory of her harsh words last night, *What do you
think you are doing?*

Every man had his limits, and Jamie had, at long last,
reached his. He was tired of making overtures, tired of
reaching out in friendship, only to have his good intentions
so brutally slapped away. If Julia insisted on treating him
like a barely housebroken savage, then a savage he would
be. No more gestures, no more efforts, no more baring his
chest for her to stick the knife in.

Jamie told Julia, "This was your escapade. I was not
even supposed to ask any questions. My job was to listen
and obey. Very well. I am listening. What do we do now?"

She straightened up, smoothing down her windblown
hair with both hands, and inhaling deeply, letting the air
waft out in one even breath. Never having previously seen
Julia so out of her element, standing ankle-deep in the

165

grayish dishwater housewives tossed onto the street, skirt dragging behind her, curls twisting completely from out of the restrictive hair pins, Jamie, for an instant, felt as if it were only now that he were seeing the real Julia. Not to imply that back alley filth was more true to her character, but rather that the fine *ton* clothes and immobile hair styles were equally as ill-fitting. Julia truly belonged neither there nor here. Like him, she was doomed to go through life forever trapped someplace in between.

Julia said, "Well, clearly, the first thing we need is to hire another rig, and head towards port."

"Do you truly believe that there is a person in this tiny town who has yet to hear the tale of us? Think, Julia. We are barely five miles from Miriam's home, and we have been spotted running away with a child. Not to mention that it is quite conceivable that a few of the good citizens might even know our Mademoiselle Alexia here by sight. Surely, Miriam came into town once in a while. We cannot risk showing our faces there again. Especially in light of our guilty behavior."

"All right then. We shall have to find some other way to get to port. France is a large country. News of Alexia's disappearance may be in Paris and here, but it could not possibly have reached every corner. Not this swiftly. All we need is to make our way to Le Havre, and hire a boat across the Channel there."

"Well and good," Jamie said, "but how are we to escape, unnoticed, from Nogent-le-Rotrou, especially in the absence of a horse and carriage?"

"We can walk."

"Oh, that will prove most inconspicuous, m'lady."

"I suppose that you possess a better plan?"

"One does spring instantly to mind, yes."

Either too desperate or too tired to argue, Julia demanded, "Well, out with it then."

"We may . . . borrow . . . a horse and carriage." Jamie snuck a sideways peek at Julia, gaging her reaction.

"Borrow?"

"Steal."

She wrinkled her brow, biting down on a fingernail. "I don't know, Jamie."

"Would you feel more comfortable thinking of it as a fair trade? In exchange for us commissioning a single horse and carriage from the good people of this town, they may keep all the items in our trunks still at the inn. I suspect that we won't be going back for them," he said.

"Our clothes," Julia gasped. "I'd forgotten."

"So, it's decided, then." Jamie reassuringly patted Alexia's hand. All during their conversation, the child had stayed pressed against the wall, staring mesmerized at a quartet of rats eating through the garbage. He said, "Wait for me here. I'll be back in a few hours, hopefully properly mounted."

"You are going now to steal a horse?" Julia grabbed Jamie's arm. "In broad daylight?"

"If I wait for nightfall, I may end up coming back leading a large dog on a rope."

"Jamie," Julia reminded, "you cannot go out into town alone. You do not speak any French."

"I am not meaning to engage the animal in conversation."

"What if you are caught?"

"I will run," Jamie said. "I will run very fast."

"No," Julia insisted. "This all is my fault. I should be the one to take the risk. I should go."

Jamie sighed and rolled his eyes. "My dear, dear, Mrs. Lowell. While such sentiments are indeed most noble, may I remind you of a single fact."

"And what may that be?"

"I, Mrs. Lowell, was already thieving horses, whilst you were still in the cradle."

Jamie finally convinced Julia to stay behind by insisting that her fluent French might be needed more in case she and Alexia were spotted.

Walking back towards town, Jamie took care to avoid looking conspicuous. Knowing that the stable owner had probably already told anyone who would listen about the well-dressed couple and child who fled his establishment in a panic, Jamie first removed his coat, wrinkling it into a ball, and stuffing it under his arm. He pulled the ends of his pantaloons out of his boots, letting them drape over the top, then rubbed dirt onto his shoes.

Jamie walked through the streets with his head down, eyes averted. No one paid him very much notice, and he liked it that way. It felt strangely comfortable. After a month of being Jeremy Lowell, finally, he was Jamie again.

His search for a horse that just happened to be roaming free brought Jamie to a smattering of farms on the outskirts of town. At the second house he passed, a horse and wagon stood hitched to the front post, seemingly unattended. Jamie got as far as actually resting his hand on the bridle before he happened to glance inside the window, and spotted a woman with three small children, rushing about the kitchen attempting to peel babies off her leg and simultaneously prepare dinner. If this horse and wagon were her only means of transportation for going into town, then Jamie's snatching it would effectively strand the family. And he could think of no worse fate for any creature than to be stuck inside of a single-room house with three restless toddlers.

Vowing to either rob someone slightly better off or at least to stop glancing into strangers' windows, Jamie kept on walking. A mile and a half down the road, he stopped in front of a barn, noting that the structure stood a good out-of-sight distance from the main house. Jamie looked both ways to ensure he weren't being watched, then crept towards the door.

Inside, he tripped over a hen scurrying across the hay covered floor. It squawked in protest and hopped up, nearly taking a penned-up baby goat's eyes out with its claws. Three horses paced their stalls. One, an old mare with a back so sagging that its stomach all but brushed the ground, eyed Jamie with interest, raising her head and trying to butt him with her nose. The second pony looked no older than a few weeks. Its skinny legs still buckled under the body weight, and every step resembled a drunk trying to walk home through a storm. Horse number three was a gelding. Looking into its eyes, Jamie imagined he could spot the animal's displeasure at the course of events that had made him such a creature. He snapped and bit at Jamie, and, snarling, kicked the stall door with one powerful hoof.

Julia's four-chestnut team back home, Jamie decided, had very little to worry about from this lot.

He stood, lips pursed, hands behind his back, trying to make a decision over which animal to appropriate. The too old, the too young, or the too mean? His enthusiasm was hardly spilling over for any one of them.

So focused was Jamie on his task that he did not hear the barn door opening behind him until it proved too late and the farmer whose land he was trespassing on stood blocking the light, shouting at Jamie.

Jamie spun about, instinctively opening his mouth to begin haggling, when he remembered that his legendary verbal tricks would be of no help here. The only thing left for him to draw on, was his other legendary skill. His ability to, as he explained it for Julia, run very, very fast.

Unfortunately, there was only one way out of the barn, and it was through the single door. Swallowing his neck into his shoulders, Jamie bent from the waist, charging at full speed towards the farmer. In a perfect world, the man would have been frightened enough of being rushed by a madman to kindly step aside. In this world however, the gentleman continued to stand rooted in his doorway, still screaming French obscenities at Jamie. He may not have been fluent in French, but he understood curses in any language.

Slamming his head and shoulders full force into the man's chest, Jamie managed to knock the farmer off balance. As he fell to the ground, Jamie easily leapt over the squirming figure, escaping into the sunshine and heading towards whichever road would take him as far away as possible.

A bullet spat past Jamie's ear, and he ducked instinctively, all the while wondering where the farmer had gotten his hands so quickly on a rifle. Not that it truly mattered. The fact that his pursuer now possessed a weapon, was certainly much more important than where he'd gotten it.

Although confident in his ability to outrun most anyone in a fair fight, even Jamie did not think so highly of his talents that he believed himself capable of moving faster than a bullet. His head swiveled from side to side, searching for a tree or some other natural obstruction that he might take cover under, but the road leading away from the farm was frustratingly free of any shelter. For the next half a mile, Jamie would be the sole target for the farmer to shoot at. And, if the old man decided to climb into the gig he'd arrived in, and chase him, then Jamie would not have a single prayer left.

The gig.

Its image struck Jamie with the same impact that the previously fired bullet had nicked his ear.

Did he dare do it?

Did he dare *not* do it?

Did he really have any other option in the matter?

Falling to the ground and rolling, Jamie unexpectedly changed directions, running no longer towards the road, but away from it, and back towards the homicidal farmer. Back towards the gig standing by the side of the barn.

Noting the two beautiful animals saddled to its carriage, Jamie now understood that the horses inside were but the bottom of the barrel for this man. Well, as long as he had decided to rob the fellow, he might as well steal his very best.

Puzzled by Jamie's sudden change of direction, the farmer hesitated. Which gave Jamie enough time to literally leap up into his gig, a task made more difficult by the fact that it were the latest model—the one where all four wheels were as high as Jamie's head, and the perched seat nearly twice his height. Jamie clambered up like a monkey, yanking the reins off the brake, and slapped the horses with such force that they rose on their back legs and whinnied, before tearing like the wind down the road.

"This is your definition of an inconspicuous carriage?" Julia asked the moment she spotted Jamie inside a gig that would have turned heads at Windsor Castle. Driving through a back alley, it all but hollered for unwanted attention.

"No." Jamie said, "This is my definition of a I-had-no-other-options carriage."

A half-mile from port, all three climbed out of the gig, so as not to arrive in too conspicuous a carriage. Jamie slapped the lead horse on the rump, sending it running.

He told Julia, "This way, someone may find it and return the team to their original owner."

"But what if the person who does find it simply decides to keep the rig and horses for himself?"

"Then," Jamie pointed out with a logic it had taken him years to perfect, "he will be the thief, and not us."

At the docks, the hustle of men running about carrying boxes crammed with tea, coal, and rice, and the bustle of well-to-do passengers, accompanied by maids, abigails, footmen, and valets distastefully pushing through the crowds en route to their own ships, made it relatively simple for Jamie, Julia, and Alexia to lose themselves in the mass of bodies.

Jamie asked Julia, "Which of these ferries did you book us passage on for England?"

"The *Lady Margaret,*" she answered, then hesitated. "Jamie?"

"What is it?" He had to step on the tips of his toes to see over the crowd, and search for the *Lady Margaret.*

"Will you promise not to shout?"

He absolutely hated it when women prefaced their remarks with such a question. Jamie turned very slowly, crouching so that he and Julia might be at eye level. "And would you care to tell me, Mrs. Lowell, why I might have been inclined to do so?"

She pulled a lock of hair loose from behind her ear, and thoughtfully pulled on it. "I did book us passage on the *Lady Margaret.* And I had the tickets in my hand. And then I packed them in my trunk. And then I left the trunk at the inn while we went to hire a carriage. And then . . . well, you were there."

She took a step back.

"And why did you not tell me so before, m'lady?"

"You had other concerns. Like stealing us a horse and carriage, for one thing."

"All right," he forced himself to speak very slowly, because Jamie knew that, if he sped up, it would all explode out his chest in a violent torrent of words. "But tell me this. What was the point of my stealing a carriage and horses, if we had no place to go?" Despite his attempts at civility, the last trio of words Jamie shouted loud enough to turn a few French heads in their direction.

"But we did, Jamie. We did have someplace to go. Regardless of whether I still held the tickets or not, the only way for us to leave France is by water. We had to come to the docks."

"Do you propose that we climb into that box of grapes over there, and mail ourselves to England?"

"Do you think we could?"

"You are acting the idiot."

"I know." She let her fingers brush his arm. "I am sorry, Jamie. I suppose I should have planned it all better. But, as you insist on reminding me, I've never done this sort of thing before."

He felt himself deflating like a hot air balloon at too high an altitude. No matter how pleasant it might feel, screaming and cursing at Julia was not going to improve their circumstances in the slightest.

He asked her, "Do you think there is still time to purchase tickets for a ferry that leaves tonight?"

"There might be," Julia said. "Except that . . ."

"What?" He threw his arms up in the air. "What now?"

"All the money I had, I put in my reticule."

Jamie indicated Julia's obviously empty hands. "And which reticule might that be, m'lady?"

"The reticule that I dropped on my way out of the livery stable."

"Ah. Of course. I'm surprised I even had to ask."

17

For a moment, Julia truly believed that Jamie might give in to his impulses and strangle her. And she would not blame him for attempting it. Surely, after all Jamie went through to secure them safe passage to port, the last thing he needed to hear was that they possessed no manner of continuing further. Julia knew she should have told him earlier about their lack of both tickets and money, but she was too frightened.

Too frightened of making Jamie angry. Or rather, of making him angrier than he already was. Considering her behavior over the past few days—considering her behavior over the past few months—what was to prevent Jamie from disgustedly washing his hands of the entire matter, and of her?

Knowing that he would be perfectly within his rights to do so, Julia wasn't about to give him either the provocation or the opportunity to leave.

And not because Julia felt frightened of continuing her journey without him. That may have been true in the past, but, if Jamie had given her anything, it was the confidence to believe that, in a pinch, Julia could con with the best of them. She wasn't afraid of Jamie's leaving because she feared being helpless and stranded. Julia did not want Jamie to leave because, quite simply, she would miss him.

But now was hardly the time to admit such sentiments.

Standing amidst the chaos of a dozen multipurpose sailing vessels preparing to depart before sunset, Julia looked up at Jamie and prayed that he might suppress the urge to kill her. His back to the sinking sun, Jamie's hair glowed an almost indescribably beautiful shade of red, with golden and auburn highlights. Stripped of the aristocrat's coat, he now resembled more the man she had first met than the puppet Julia had attempted to transform him into. Back in his element for the first time in weeks, Jamie looked happier than Julia had ever previously seen him.

Except when it came to dealing with her. For Julia, Jamie's mirror-blue eyes clouded over until not a single positive sentiment remained to peek through the anger.

Yet, to Jamie's credit, in the interest of not frightening Alexia, he kept his tone level as he hissed to Julia, "You should have told me earlier."

"Yes. I know I should have. But I thought that, maybe, I might be able to think of a way out of our predicament during the course of the journey."

"And have you?"

"No. Not yet."

"It is very difficult to get about without money, Mrs. Lowell. I know. I've done it. It is not pleasant."

All around them, people pushed and shoved their way through the crowds and towards the water. One footman, carrying a lady's trunk large enough to comfortably fit all the crown jewels and then some, nearly collided with a French sailor pulling a net full of freshly caught herring. Juggling his precariously swaying trunk, the footman paused long enough to soundly curse not only the sailor, but his parents, grandparents, and any other ancestors either living or dead.

Grabbing Jamie's arm, Julia asked excitedly, "Did you hear that? The servant, he spoke English. And if the footman speaks English, then perhaps the couple he works for, the one boarding that vessel over there, perhaps they are English as well."

Julia pointed to the left, and towards a yacht bobbing among the surf beside an anchored freighter. The grandeur of the furniture on deck, and the presence of at least three smartly dressed servants, suggested that this vessel was, more likely than not, of the pleasure cruise, rather than service, variety.

"There is our transportation home," Julia told Jamie.

"Do you propose that we stow away in the cargo hold?"

"No, Mr. Lowell. I propose that we acquire ourselves an invitation to go sailing."

She would show him.

Julia would show Jamie he wasn't the only one capable of playing a part when in pursuit of a goal. All she needed to do was strike up a conversation with the English couple on board the yacht, and, in a manner both subtle and simultaneously forceful, somehow manage to plant in their heads the idea to invite Julia and her entourage on board.

It was a simple plan, and, although Julia suspected that Jamie might be the better scoundrel for the job, she was nevertheless determined to carry it out herself. As a matter of principle.

Leaving Jamie with Alexia, Julia fixed up her hair the best she could, administering pins into whichever curl happened to feel loose, without the aid of a mirror. Her clothes, she realized were another story. They were beyond hope, especially the hem of Julia's dress. Over the past twenty-four hours, its colors had changed from white to gray to dark gray to undeniably filthy. Her shoes were covered with dried sewage that left streaks upon the previously gleaming leather. She looked less like the niece of Collin Highsmith, duke of Alamain, and more like some wench he would never dare hire even to sweep his fireplace. Would the English couple even believe her claim?

Julia hesitated. Never before had she needed to prove her status to anyone, and she hadn't given much thought to the accoutrements that went into creating a credible picture. People accepted that Julia were of the class that she was, because of the many trappings that went with it. The fine clothes, the servants, the manner of carrying herself as if everyone else had best scurry out of the way. Stripped of these identifying marks, Julia was dependent completely on what lay within for her survival.

She supposed it would have to suffice. Jamie had taught Julia enough about best making do with whatever assets you possessed at the moment. In fact, if Julia recalled correctly, another of Jamie's lessons had covered the turning of what on the surface seemed like a disadvantage, into an advantage.

Certainly that was exactly the track he'd taken when they were spotted kissing at the ball. And with the marquis of Martyn.

And with her.

If he could do it, well then, so could she. Julia would show Jamie she knew how to turn a potential disaster into victory.

Disposing of her plan of only a moment earlier, Julia bent over, shaking all the pins out of her hair in an attempt to look more disheveled. She rubbed some of the mud from her shoes off with two fingers, then, distastefully, rubbed it on her face.

Then, Julia turned and ran towards the yacht.

Screaming.

It was a half an hour before Julia returned for Jamie and Alexia. Both sat on an empty crate, Jamie patiently teaching the child a most intricate version of cat's cradle. Seeing the rope in his hands, Julia hesitated, remembering Jamie's magic tricks of a few days past. If Jamie recalled the evening as well, he gave no visible indication.

Instead, when he looked up and saw Julia, Jamie's eyes grew large and he asked, "What in blazes happened to you? You look like you've been dragged for an acre by a colt in need of breaking."

"Close," she said. "My husband, child, and I were robbed on our way to port by a passel of French thieves who made off with our every belonging, franc, and ferry ticket."

"You don't say, m'lady?"

Julia knew she hadn't married a fool. It didn't take more than those words for Jamie to understand exactly what she was trying to say to him.

"And then, pray tell, what happened?"

"Our child went into shock, and has yet to say a word, while I fell into such a panic that I was reduced to running along the water's edge, calling desperately for someone who spoke English to pray help me. I, you see, do not speak a word of French."

"I see. Not a word."

"And it wasn't easy. I daresay I must have run blind and hysterical past their blasted yacht at least three times before the master and mistress noticed me, and inquired what the matter was."

On board the pompously dubbed *Ship Perfection*, everyone proved very sympathetic to poor Julia and Jamie's plight.

Maids and footmen were dispatched to draw them baths and launder their clothes, and, once Jamie and Julia cleaned up, the yacht's proprietor treated both to an extensive discourse on the French people's inadequate police force, and on the general inferiority of all things French to all things English. Jamie, in particular, felt hard pressed to contain his merriment when the gentleman spent a good five and twenty minutes explaining how, back home in London, no criminal ever went unpunished for his crimes.

By the time the topic of how terribly fortunate Julia and Jamie had been to find a single civilized English couple among all those dreadful French types at the docks was stated and confirmed and discussed to death for possibly the fifth time that evening, Julia could barely keep her eyes open.

She prepared to excuse herself at the same instant that Jamie rose from his chair and suggested that they call it a night, seeing as how the yacht was due to dock in England early the next morning.

After another round of profuse thanks for their gracious life-saving hospitality, Jamie and Julia bade their hosts a grateful good-night, and escaped below deck.

As they walked toward the cabin, Julia teasingly asked Jamie, "What did you think of my performance?"

He shrugged, almost as if he knew how much his ap-

proval of her mattered to Julia, and was deliberately with-
holding it.

She pressed on, explaining, "I turned a disadvantage
into an advantage. I knew I looked too ragged to be taken
for a lady, so I made myself appear worse, and passed off
as a lady in distress."

He didn't reply, and, instead, indicated their cabin door.
"You told our benefactors that we were married, did you
not?"

"I did."

"Then how do you propose to explain our needing to
slumber in separate rooms?"

There was no logical way to explain it, and Jamie knew
that as well as Julia. They would simply have to make the
best of their circumstances. Unfortunately, Julia's feelings
lay in such a tangle at the present moment that she could
no longer decide just what "the best" might be.

Alexia already lay sleeping on a cot beside the larger
bed. She clutched her doll tightly, and periodically whim-
pered in her sleep. One side of the pillow was wet with
tears.

Kneeling briefly beside the little girl, and straightening
her blankets, Julia whispered, "She is suffering so much.
I am beginning to wonder whether we did the right thing."

"It is what Miriam wanted."

"I know. My mother died when I was about her age. I
still miss her," Julia confessed.

Behind her, Jamie stripped blankets off the bed. She
heard the rhythmic snap of the sheets, she felt the cooling
breeze they stirred up caress the damp warmth of her back,
making her shiver, as she wondered what Jamie's next
move might be. She remembered the gentle way he'd carried her upstairs to the inn, and the way his hands had felt
as he reached to remove her shoes. The memory of it
made Julia wonder longingly what it might be like to lie
beside him, to feel the heat of those hands all over her
body.

She turned to Jamie, ready to tell him . . .

Ready to tell him what? Julia had not the faintest idea
what she wanted to say. It didn't matter that her head and

heart were so filled with emotions that she felt ready to burst at any moment. No words were forthcoming.

Thinking that maybe actions should speak louder than any meaningless sounds, Julia rose to approach Jamie, hoping that, by the time she reached him, she would be able to at least show him all those things she hadn't the language to say.

Back turned to her, Jamie continued neatly folding the bedspread, halving and quartering it with needle precision. Swallowing her pride and her modesty and every other virtue Salome had once deemed indispensable, Julia gathered instead her courage and, tentatively, rested her palm on Jamie's shoulder.

He stopped folding, but did not turn around.

"Jamie?" Julia's voice sounded strange even to her own ears. The remains of her question dried and crumbled like a rose pressed inside a dance card. But Julia already knew that it weren't her question that was important, but Jamie's answer.

He straightened up. The muscles in back of his neck stood tense and hard, forming the slightest of hollows pointing up towards his hair line.

She heard him inhale, licking both lips and swallowing hard, and coughing to clear his throat before speaking.

Julia's entire body tensed, so poised to hear how he might answer that, at the first sound of Jamie's voice, Julia shuddered, as if a gunshot had unexpectedly torn through the silence.

Jamie pretended not to notice. Voice neutral, he thrust the pillow and blanket he was holding into Julia's arms and announced, "You and Alexia can share the bed. I'll take the cot."

It seemed to Julia that Jamie fell asleep the instant that his head hit the pillow. He lay on the cot, one arm under his ear, the other wrapping the blanket around his shoulders. His calm, even breathing filled the room.

Hoping that it might put her to sleep as well, Julia attempted to match her breathing motions to his, but that only succeeded in making her more aware of his presence than ever.

Which was hardly what Julia had in mind.

She told herself that her inability to drift away stemmed from Alexia's tossing and turning in the bed beside her. But such lies no longer convinced Julia in the least. The reason she could not sleep was because she still felt the harsh sting of Jamie's pointed rejection when he shoved the bed linens between them, then retired without so much as a courteous good-night.

A few weeks back, Julia might have felt comfortable with attributing such a slight to bad manners on his part. But now that she knew just how much of a gentleman Jamie could be when he put his mind to it, she was forced to think of his actions as nothing less than a deliberate insult.

Surely he could not still be angry with Julia about her behavior at the inn? Maybe he was angry with her for neglecting to tell him about the missing tickets. Or for her lying to him. Or for her patronizing him. Or for her calling him uncivilized.

Julia sighed so hard that her bangs fluttered above her forehead. He certainly did possess quite a tidy little list of grievances against her, didn't he?

Then how to explain Jamie's continuing to assist Julia in her scheme? If he really, truly despised her, then Jamie would have fled at the earliest opportunity.

Wouldn't he?

Clearly the fact that he were still here meant something. Didn't it?

The only thing it meant was that Jamie were a man of his word. Or, in more base terms, he was a man determined to fulfill his duties to the end, if only to collect on the money promised to him.

Conceding that, tonight at least, sleep was most definitely out of the question for her, Julia stealthily rose from her bed, and crept to crouch beside Jamie. She watched the taut muscles in his back contract with each breath, and the way he ever so slightly puffed his cheeks upon exhaling.

To Julia, the act of observing someone while he slept

had always seemed dreadfully intimate, if only because the poor targets had no idea that they were being watched. Yet, it gave her the same thrill as eavesdropping. Jamie's eyelashes cast dancing shadows upon his cheeks. The image reminded Julia of Gavin, and the way he'd looked the night of the ball, walking in her garden. And it reminded her that, all during the course of their journey, she still had yet to think of Lord Neff even once.

Tentatively, Julia reached out her hand to touch Jamie's hair, gently patting the slight wave at the very base of his neck, and marveling at how fine and thick it was. When he didn't respond to the intrusion, Julia grew braver, softly brushing her fingers along his jawbone. She felt the faint stubble of tomorrow's beard. Because of Julia's follies, Jamie hadn't shaved in over a day. It felt rather pleasant. Almost as if the tiny red and gold whiskers snatching at her fingertips were an invitation for Julia to continue with her explorations.

Jamie stirred, sleepily slapping at his face with one hand. Julia barely had the chance to snatch her arm away. Her heart beat in double-time. What if Jamie had caught her? How would Julia have explained her behavior then?

Jamie rolled over onto his other side, facing Julia, but he did not open his eyes. She knew that she should hustle back towards the bed, pull the covers over her head, and pretend to be sleeping in case he suddenly awakened. But Julia felt loathe to do so. He looked so sweet when asleep. So innocent. Almost like the boy Jamie must have been at one time, before life took its first bite out of his soul.

Knowing that what she was doing reached the supreme heights of giddiness, but yet unable to stop herself, Julia leaned forward until her face were almost touching Jamie's, and, quickly, lest she change her mind, kissed him ever so lightly on the forehead.

She then flew back toward her bed and under the blankets, as if the devil himself were in broiling pursuit.

Despite her conviction that she would never be able to fall asleep with Jamie so delectably close by, exhaustion at last caught the better of Julia, and she did doze off. Only to awaken to the sounds of Alexia's terrified, muffled screams.

She had barely rubbed the sleep out of her eyes and turned towards the child, when Jamie was by the bed, sweeping Alexia into his embrace and soothingly rocking her in his arms.

He wore a nightshirt loaned to him by their host, and its smaller size stretched to once again emphasize Jamie's solid, muscular chest. Pink sleep marks danced up one side of his face, giving Jamie the sweetness of a newborn baby.

Jamie sat on the edge of the bed, barely a foot away from Julia. She could feel the heat emanating from his body, and inhale the unfamiliar, masculine, nighttime smell. Julia's heart made a sensational leap into the pit of her stomach at the thought of Jamie's sitting so close by her while she wore no more than a silk dressing gown.

Jamie kissed the top of Alexia's head, then began to sing some silly, nursery rhyme that Julia did not recognize, but one that had Alexia giggling within minutes.

When it appeared that the child had calmed down a bit, Jamie started Alexia on making a list of all the new things they'd seen that she could write to her mother about once they got on shore.

As effective as counting sheep, the activity put Alexia to sleep within fifteen minutes.

Reluctant to wake her, Jamie shook his head at Julia's suggestion that it was probably safe for him to return to his bed now, and only leaned against the headboard, settling Alexia more comfortably into his lap. He winced as the board's carvings, dug into the skin of his back.

Wanting to help, Julia pulled his blanket off the cot and carefully slipped it around Jamie's shoulders, hoping to ease some of the discomfort. He smiled gratefully.

Buoyed by his friendly reaction, Julia awkwardly crawled on top of the covers and into the bed beside him, resting one hand soothingly upon Alexia's head, and letting the other fall against Jamie's arm. He didn't pull away or comment.

For close to an hour, they sat shoulder to shoulder, neither moving nor speaking.

Then, moving so slowly as to make her movements nearly imperceptible, Julia reached for Jamie's free hand, sliding it gently into her own.

He turned to look at her, eyes glowing in the darkness, reminding Julia of that night on the balcony, when she had thought him to possess some sort of magical power over her.

It were the same now. Julia could neither recognize the expression in his eyes, nor pull away from it. Julia's actions were no longer under her control, and she could truly, freely say that she would have had it no other way.

Silently, Jamie raised their intertwined hands to his lips, softly kissing each of Julia's fingertips in turn.

She shivered, exhaling in a series of brief nervous gasps as if calming after a crying jag.

"Good-night, Mrs. Lowell," Jamie said softly, moving his arm so as to encompass Julia as well as Alexia in his embrace, and gesturing for her to lay her head on his shoulder.

Where they stayed for the rest of the night, and well into the next morning.

18

Compared to what went before it, the remainder of their journey towards home proved disappointingly uneventful.

Julia and Jamie bade their hosts good-bye at the docks, and, once again, showered them with thanks. Although both stopped short of an invitation for a reciprocal visit. Considering how tentative their marital state was, neither Jamie nor Julia wished to risk the awkwardness of having to explain why the seemingly loving couple were no longer together.

Still penniless, but at least now on home soil, Jamie and Julia worked together to convince a livery stable owner to rent them a carriage with no money in advance. They promised that he and the driver would receive twice their standard fee once Julia returned home, and the combination of greed and Julia's imperious accent helped win the fellow over to their way of thinking.

On their ride to the house, Alexia, sitting comfortably between Jamie and Julia, grew more animated, surveying the English countryside with genuine interest, and asking questions about the homes and sights they passed on their way.

She even asked if she might call Mr. Lowell, Uncle Jamie.

"Well," he looked at Julia, feeling as sincerely curious as Alexia. "May she?"

Julia did not know how to respond to his question. To stall, she said, "Actually, Mr. Lowell is more your cousin, your cousin by marriage, then he is your uncle, Alexia."

"Does that matter very much? Maman instructed me to call you Aunt Julia. Because you are older."

"I am hardly that old."

"You're old enough," Jamie said.

He winked at Alexia, who giggled. She bounced in her seat and looked at Julia, still waiting for an answer to her question.

Slowly, Julia replied, "I suppose you may, if you wish, call him Uncle Jamie. It is only that . . ."

"Only that what?"

"It is only that I—I am not certain how long Mr. Lowell, how long he plans to be . . . with us."

Julia looked up and her eyes met Jamie's. He could feel her searching his face for a sign.

A sign of what?

Did she want him to contradict her? Did she want him to declare his intentions? Did she want him to beg for permission to stay? And, if Julia wanted him to stay, why did she not simply say so? If Julia wanted him to stay, why did she act as if she weren't certain whether or not Jamie would?

He forced his features to remain placid. Jamie crossed his arms and stared back at her defiantly. Between them, Alexia could only look from one to the other in confusion.

The child asked, "Are you going somewhere away, Mr. Lowell?"

"I don't know. Am I?" Jamie asked Julia.

The directness of his question startled her. She averted her gaze and pulled Alexia closer, using the girl as a shield between the pair of them. "That—that, I believe is up to you, Jamie."

And they were back to where they'd started from.

* * *

Salome came racing out of the house the moment she spotted Julia, Jamie, and Alexia from the upstairs window.

Unable to wait even for her granddaughter to climb out of the carriage, Salome swept Alexia into a hug while the child still stood on the top step, crying and talking so quickly Jamie could barely decipher the older woman's words.

Alexia flung both arms around her grandmother's neck, jabbering away equally as quickly. And, without a backward glance, both of them disappeared into the house, leaving Julia and Jamie standing alone on the front steps, looking after Moses as he settled their account with the livery.

Julia and Jamie exchanged glances, newly shy in each other's presence now that Alexia were no longer around to chaperon them.

Jamie coughed into his fist, looking down over his fingers at Julia. She busied herself with picking at the ivy growing around the banister, plucking a stray leaf here and there, rubbing it between her thumb and forefinger, than dropping it to the ground.

Jamie said, "Well, then."

"Yes." She could not look in his eyes. Julia knew that if she looked in his eyes all would be lost.

And, naturally, she could not look at his hands, for only a glimpse of the tanned, slightly calloused palms and fingers was enough to make Julia giddy, recalling how they'd felt against her arms when the two of them danced, and her face when he'd kissed her, and the fever that seized her body in response.

So that left only Jamie's shoes, which, in themselves, did not fill Julia's head with images to make her swoon. But it did make for a rather awkward conversation. Him addressing the top of Julia's averted head, and her addressing his footwear.

"I must look a fright. I'll run and change." Julia brushed past Jamie, still unwilling to tear her eyes from the ground, and ducked inside the house before he could move to prevent her.

Later that evening, while Jamie waited for Julia to change frocks and clean up a bit, he asked Moses, "Did you come to work for Julia's family after her father married her mother?"

"Yes, sir, that I did."

"What sort of work did you do before?"

The older man sighed, pausing in his task of collecting Jamie's dirty garments for the laundry, and, with a pained expression, confessed, "I swept floors at a men's club in London."

"Gor." Jamie tried to imagine the stately and dignified Moses wielding a broom and dust pan. "Why, you're not so different from me then after all, are you?"

"Please, sir, that difference is the only solace I have."

Jamie burst out laughing. Who might have guessed that beneath that most proper exterior lurked such a sly sense of humor?

"Did Julia's mother employ her entire family here?"

"As many as she could. Sarah said that she could not bear to be living so well while the rest of us languished in poverty." Moses reflected. "She was a most extraordinary woman. But then, she had to be. As you may have guessed, not that many of my relatives ended up as wives of peers. She could be very enchanting, and very convincing. It were she who talked Master Lloyd into providing Miriam with the dowry that enabled her to wed that French fellow. Although, in retrospect, I suppose that bit of generosity was hardly for the best."

"So," Jamie leaned forward eagerly, "let me understand this correctly. Everyone in this house is pretending to be someone that they're not. I am not a marquis, you are not a butler, and Julia is not a proper young lady of the *ton*."

"I beg to differ, sir. I may not have been trained as a butler, but I have performed the duties of one for over twenty years, so, consequently, I am one. And as for Miss Julia, as long as no one discovers otherwise, she is a fine young lady of the *ton* in every sense of the word."

"But not on the inside. On the inside, she is living as much of a lie as I, or you. She is playing a game."

"A hundred years ago, sir, both Miss Julia and her parents might have been burned alive for playing such a game."

"But we are living in a much more civilized time, Moses."

"Oh, really? Tell me, Mr. Lowell, what you think would happen to Julia if the truth were ever to come out about her parentage?"

"What would happen?" Jamie shrugged. "I don't know. She wouldn't be burned alive, that much I'm certain of."

"No. She would not be. But she would be socially ostracized. Unwelcome by the same people she once believed to be her friends. An imposter like you, Mr. Lowell, possesses more options in this nation than a half-breed of any sort. Look at how wickedly those who are part Indian are treated. Once the truth about Julia becomes common knowledge, she will end up isolated here in the country, without even a London season to look forward to. Julia's life will shrink to what is contained between these four walls."

"But what about the Jews of London? Surely, Julia could find companionship among them?"

"Do I need to explain to a gentleman of your sort the paradox of living in two worlds? You may be a part of both, but you will never belong to either. Julia's life and upbringing would be alien to those of her own race. The same way, I suspect, that someone of your intelligence and talent never quite fit in with the rest of the riffraff in the East End."

Jamie couldn't be sure, but there might have been a compliment directed at him somewhere inside of Moses's speech.

"That is most difficult," he conceded. "I guess that Julia and I are even more alike than I suspected."

"Of course, sir," Moses agreed, then added, without a trace of the irony Jamie might have expected, "That is precisely why you have so fallen in love with her."

"One moment, Mr. Lowell," Salome's voice caught up with Jamie as he were exiting his bedroom. He turned around reluctantly. Three months of living in this household had succeeded in making Jamie most wary when it came to a summons from Mrs. Weiss.

She hurried down the hall after him, her gray and white taffeta dress rustling along the floor. "Please. I should like a word with you, if I may."

Her tone was gentle, which intrigued him enough to actually slow down and allow Salome to catch up with him.

They paused in the hallway, beside an ornate monopodium mahogany table inlaid with ebony and silver. Jamie casually leaned against it, one arm propped along the edge, and looked down at Salome expectantly.

"I wish . . ." Salome uncharacteristically looked down at her hands, rubbing her right thumbnail along her left palm. The rest of the words came out in a hurried rush, almost as if she feared losing her nerve. "I wish to thank you. For what you did. Julia tells me she would have been quite lost without you."

Jamie knew that it were the duty of a gentleman to respond to such a heartfelt, albeit forced, show of gratitude with a modest assertion that she must think nothing of it. But, as Salome had spent months pointing out, he was most certainly not a gentleman.

When no response from Jamie proved forthcoming, Salome added, "And I should like to apologize to you as well."

Again, no answer. Jamie remained where he was, looking down at Salome with a face successfully devoid of all expression.

Yet, she appeared determined to finish her piece, drawing confidence with every word uttered.

"They say, Mr. Lowell, that we hate in others that trait which we most fear in ourselves. From the moment you entered this house, you reminded me of my own precarious position, of my own deception. You forced me to remember how close all of us perpetually are to discovery." Salome sighed, smiling wistfully, "When my sister, Sarah, married Julia's father, she insisted on bringing me into their household. I was a widow by then, and Miriam barely seven. Eventually, she made a fine companion for Julia. But Sarah were determined that we would never be treated like servants or poor relations by her husband's peers. The *ton* loved Sarah from the first day. Not only because she was beautiful. This city is filled with beautiful women. But because she was good. Truly good. She glowed with it. She drew people to her, like some priceless work of art. And she always made certain that I were included in her circle. She never bought a new gown without seeing that I were outfitted in something equally as lovely. She never accepted an invitation, unless there was also one in the post for me. I was so terrified in the beginning. I hardly opened my mouth to say a word. Funny how, in the end, that worked out to my advantage."

"I beg your pardon?"

"Everyone in London is so busy talking, they have no time to listen. I was petrified of saying the wrong thing, so I kept my mouth shut. I listened when the rest of them spoke. It branded me very popular. It even carried me through after Sarah passed away."

Jamie said, "And then I came along, threatening to spoil it."

"I apologize for my rudeness, Mr. Lowell. You did nothing to provoke or deserve it."

Jamie smiled, genuinely, for what was probably the first time ever in Salome's presence. He reached for her hand, grasping firmly, and enthusiastically shaking it. "Apology accepted."

"Thank you, Mr. Lowell."

He continued, "And now, seeing as I am in the presence of a charlatan with decades more experience than my humble self, perchance you would care to share a few pointers?"

Hair washed and combed, clean dress, a few hours rest, and Julia entered the parlor positively beaming. All the tension and worry that monopolized her features in France seemed to have been scrubbed away along with the dirt. Seeing her looking so very beautiful only served to remind Jamie of how close he'd come last night to breaking his vow of making Julia come to him.

She smiled and took a seat on the windowsill. Jamie continued standing where he was, leaning casually against the bookshelf, leafing through a tome on the life and times of Leonardo da Vinci.

Julia began, "I want to thank you. Jamie. I don't know what I would have done without you."

Well, at least Salome had not lied about that bit of it.

Remembering her ease in acquiring them a boat ride home, he sincerely corrected, "You would have thought of something."

"Yes. I suppose. But I am glad that I did not have to." Julia pulled a lock of hair out from behind one ear and began twirling it around her fingers. "I want to thank you, from the bottom of my heart. You were most kind to Miriam, and to Alexia, and to myself. I—I wish to give you something. As an expression of my gratitude. I hope that you will accept it in the manner that I—in the correct manner."

He closed the book and replaced it on the shelf. His hands shook so hard, that Jamie could barely fit the work back into its narrow space. This, he knew, was the moment. The one he had been pushing and waiting for, for weeks. The one that would decide matters one way or the other.

Julia said, "I—I am giving you your freedom, Jamie."

"I beg your pardon?"

"I am letting you free. Right now. Earlier than the time we originally arrange—contracted for."

"I see." Jamie could hear himself stalling for time as he struggled to comprehend the full meaning of what she was saying.

"Yes. Good. I am glad."

The anger that flooded up from the depths of his soul struck Jamie against the rear of his skull like a smith's hammer, yet he struggled to keep it from floating visibly onto his features.

Like a drowning man sinking deeper and deeper into a life-sucking undertow, Jamie frantically flailed, searching for any way to pull himself out. His common sense urged him to slip easily and comfortably into the behavior pattern he knew best. Now was the time to crank up every bit of heavily practiced charm he'd ever acquired, and let Julia have it all with such force that the lady might never know what hit her.

Only, to his horror, Jamie found himself unable to

squeeze free so much as a drop. And he did not need a public school education to explain why.

All of Jamie's famous charms, all of his tricks and carefully chosen phrases, were false and rehearsed and so frequently misused that the words themselves had long ago ceased to have any meaning. And, consequently, none of them were in any way fit for Julia.

Julia deserved honesty, not stock platitudes. Unfortunately, Jamie had used up seemingly every flowery word in the English language to pledge emotions that he did not feel. And now, when it came time to truly express himself, there was not a single untainted, genuine syllable left for him to offer.

So, instead, with a great deal more calm than he actually felt, Jamie clasped on to the one tangible thing he could still hang his hat on. He inquired, "And what about my money?"

"Money?" Julia looked as if that were the last thing she'd expected Jamie to inquire about. "Oh, your money, of course. I'll still pay you the full amount. A bargain is a bargain, after all."

Jamie could feel himself nodding, but he no longer knew for certain exactly why. Here they were, coolly discussing his fee as if Jamie were no more than the fellow coming to walk the horses or chop wood for the fireplace.

What about her behavior last night? What about their kiss at the ball, and the earlier one in this very parlor? Was she going to continue to insist that none of it had ever taken place?

"You want me to go?"

"Today, if you like," Julia said. She looked away, biting her lip and, softly, qualified, "That is, if you want to go."

He cleared his throat. "Is it up to me then?"

"Certainly. Who else would your decision to leave or stay be made by, Jamie?"

"Well, there are other factors to consider."

"Indeed."

She was not helping him by uttering such vague generalities. Jamie attempted the lackadaisical approach, remarking, "Well, this truly is the finest home I ever had the privilege of staying in."

"Thank you." Julia's tone was that of a polite young lady making conversation with a stranger.

He wanted to scream. He wanted to grab Julia by the shoulders and shake her, hard, until she once and for all spat out what it was that she wanted from him, what it was that she felt for him, and how it was that she expected him to just disappear and never see her again, when, for the past month, Julia Highsmith had been all Jamie could drink, live, and think of.

But, gentleman that he had become, Jamie did no such thing. His pride would not allow it. He could not, and would not, lower himself to groveling before Julia in the same manner that a few women of his past acquaintance had done. If she wanted him to leave, then he would leave. And he would not grant her the satisfaction of knowing how much it affected him.

But he would damn well make sure that his final exit wreaked as much havoc with his bride as it did with him.

Crossing the room in three brief strides so that he might tower over her one last time, Jamie demanded, "And what is it that *you* want, Julia? Do you wish that I should go, or that I should stay? I am your legal husband, after all. You have the right to at least express an opinion one way or the other."

She scrunched deeper into the windowsill, back nearly pressing against the glass. "I—I may be your legal wife, Jamie, but you owe me nothing save what we initially agreed on."

Again, with the rhetoric.

"Just answer my question. Do you want me to stay and continue being your husband, or do you want me to go?"

The minute he uttered those words, Jamie sensed that he'd gone a step too far. It was that extra phrase, "be your husband," that tipped the scales against him.

Funny, Jamie was usually such a good card player, and here he was showing his trump much too early. He knew it, and Julia knew it. And Miss Highsmith was not the sort of lady to let a mistake by her opponent go unnoted.

"As I have explained to you previously, Jamie, you are only my husband in the legal, not the moral, sense. I told you that I did not mean those vows which we recited in the church. So, as far as I am concerned, we are not married."

"Well, then, would you wish for me to be your husband in the moral sense, as well?"

At least his question made her blush and turn away. Too bad that, with Jamie standing so close by, there was nowhere that Julia could turn without having to look at him.

Now it was Julia's turn to seize upon the tangible in lieu of trying to make sense of her more obscure emotions. "We can't very well throw ourselves a second ceremony, could we, Jamie? What would people say? It would look most odd."

"You're right," Jamie conceded. "A second church wedding would seem terribly peculiar."

"Well, there you have it then."

"But, considering your rather tangled heritage, it does not necessarily need to be a church, now, does it?"

Her eyes grew side, as she grasped his meaning. "A synagogue?"

"There must be some advantages to two Gods watching over you."

"No, Jamie. No, absolutely not. What if someone were to see me going inside? I can't risk it. How would I explain myself?"

He sighed in disgust and shook his head, running one hand through his hair and briefly resting it there. "Very well then. We could stand here all day, me finding loopholes, and you searching for excuses to reject them. But, philosophy and semantics aside, you still have not answered my question. Please, Julia, tell me. Should I go upstairs, pack my things, collect my wages, bid you and this lovely household good-bye, and then walk out that door for good? Or should I stay? Permanently."

She mulled over his words, at last quietly asking, "What would it take for you to stay, Jamie?"

He answered, "Nothing very complicated. I will stay, Julia, if you will ask me to."

19

How very simple.

And, at the same time, how very complicated.

All she had to do to get Jamie to stay was to ask him. No games, no tricks, no bribes. She just had to ask him.

Only she couldn't do it.

He was waiting for Julia to reply. Standing in the doorway, one hand on his hip, the other already on the knob, Jamie was waiting for Julia to decide his fate. But what he did not know, though, was that it were her fate she was deciding as well.

For a young woman so willing to risk life and limb traipsing across Europe with no money and a stolen child, Julia felt strangely frightened of risking something a tad more difficult to mend—her heart. And so she merely stood there, saying nothing, until, with an indifferent shrug of his shoulders, Jamie Lowell opened the door, stepped into the foyer, turned, and waved one hand over his shoulder, without even looking back.

"Be seeing you, miss."

It did not take Jamie very long to pack up his things.

He refused Julia's offer to take all the clothing she had bought him, explaining, "I really haven't any use for buffcoats and tall-crowned hats. You best keep them for the next fellow you make an arrangement with."

He requested his money in cash, and Julia moved as if in a dream, from his bed chamber to the vault in the cellar, and back again. She handed over the bills, letting her palm briefly brush against Jamie's, and straining to imprint the sensation of his touch upon her skin. She asked whether he would like to take one of the horses from her stable, but Jamie shook his head no, explaining that he planned to follow their arrangement to the letter. The day in Newgate, Julia had stipulated that when she grew weary of him, Jamie was to disappear from England and feign being dead. Well, he was holding up his part of the bargain, and catching the first ship heading for the Americas.

"I should do well there, don't you think? Bit of money in my pocket, fancy manners, winning smile." Jamie flashed his smile for Julia's appreciation.

"I'm sure you'll do well in whatever you decide, Jamie."

"Thanks, luv." Julia wondered if it were for her benefit, or whether, now that their charade were over, Jamie simply felt more comfortable slipping back into his lower-class accent. He slapped a simple gray cap atop his head and announced, "Got to be off, now, I do. Wouldn't wish to wear out my welcome."

He was wearing the same pair of slacks and the white shirt that he'd donned the first day Julia peeked at him through the crack in the door. The only difference was that now he no longer seemed nearly as starved or as frightened or as angry. And now, she were in love with him.

Jamie hugged Alexia good-bye, trying to assuage some of the panic in her eyes by assuring the child that both Julia and Salome would still be at home to take care of her. She stared at him, heartbroken, then begged him to stay.

No one in the room would ever understand just how badly Julia wished that she could get over this paralyzing fear of hers, and do exactly the same thing.

Because Alexia was weeping, Julia momentarily turned her back on Jamie to try and console the little girl. She wiped Alexia's eyes with her handkerchief, and offered a torrent of hopefully soothing words in French, none of which even came near to offering the same comfort as Jamie's brief speech to Alexia had back home.

She was so consumed with attempting to calm Alexia that by the time Julia turned around again Jamie was gone.

Neither one felt much like eating the luncheon Cook had prepared. Julia, Alexia, and Salome sat at the table, listlessly picking at their meat pastries, and waiting for the other to offer a solution for their common grief.

Finally, Alexia asked, "What if Papa tries to come to England and to take me away with him? What shall we do then?"

So focused was Julia on missing Jamie that she actually felt relieved, having another difficult problem to worry about.

She assured Alexia, "Do not fret, dear. I have a close friend who is an expert in the law. I shall go see him this afternoon. He will tell us what we need to do next."

Julia carefully timed her visit to Gavin's home so that she incurred the least likelihood of encountering Lady Emma. The last thing she needed that afternoon was the added irritation of hearing Emma's insults, even if they were delivered in tones as sweet as boiled maple sugar. And she certainly did not wish to face the sticky situation of having her ladyship inquiring after Jamie.

Fortunately, Julia's coming an hour after luncheon, insured that Emma would be out visiting one of the many acquaintances she'd worked so hard to cultivate since her marriage to Gavin.

A butler escorted Julia to Lord Neff's study, cautioning that he were very busy, but also more than happy to see an old friend.

Julia entered the book-paneled room with trepidation. She and Gavin really had not spoken since their argument over the propriety of Jamie's waltz at the ball. At her wedding, all they'd exchanged were a few pleasantries. She wondered if he were still cross with her. And then, much to Julia's combined surprised and relief, she realized that, quite honestly, Julia no longer cared what Gavin, or anyone else for that matter, thought of her. It was rather hard to get all in a tither over public opinion, after having spent the previous day and night stealing children and horses.

That, Julia supposed, was another gift she had Jamie to thank for. He'd taught her not to pay much notice to what other people thought, as long as she got what she wanted. And, by extension, he'd shown her that there was no excuse for Julia to feel damned over who she was.

Gavin looked up from his desk and smiled when she came in, laying down his pen and pushing away the stacks of papers he'd been working on. After a few minutes of insignificant dialogue about the weather, local gossip, and the upcoming London season—a few minutes during which, although most likely for different reasons, neither mentioned their respective spouses—Gavin politely inquired why exactly it was that Julia had sought out his council. After all, Gavin was not Julia's regular barrister. Besides, he thought all issues regarding the transfer of her father's estate from Collin to Julia had been settled.

"They have been," she said. "Thank you for asking. I am afraid that I have come to speak with you on another matter entirely. A more personal, sensitive matter."

Briefly, Julia told Gavin about Miriam, about Alexia, and about Henri's desire to banish his child to a convent. For an instant, Julia wondered if she might be able to complete her story without getting into the specific details of why Miriam feared so severely Alexia's being forced into a nunnery.

But, when Gavin mentioned, off-handedly, that, truly, he saw no harm in Henri's wishes—after all, Alexia were his child, to do with as her father liked—that Julia knew she would have to share with him the true reason for Miriam's desperation.

Squeezing both fists so tightly that the stubs of what were once Julia's nails cut through her palms, she was about to hang her head and, mumbling, confess to everything. And then Julia remembered Jamie. Jamie and the way he'd always managed to discuss even the most unsavory details of his past, with head held high.

"After all," Jamie had explained to Julia, "if I behave as

if I believe that my actions deserve condemnation, then why should anyone else think differently?"

Heeding his advice, Julia reconsidered her posture. Instead of sinking, curled up, into Gavin's chair, she straightened like a soldier, shoulders squared, head held high, and, looking Gavin straight in the eye, proudly announced, "The reason my cousin requested that my aunt Salome bring up her daughter, rather than see Alexia's father send her off to a convent, is because she feared her husband treating Alexia as cruelly as he had Miriam, and for the same reason. You see, that which my cousin told her husband, that which she had hidden from him for ten years, was the fact that Miriam and her child are both of the Hebraic faith. They are Jews." Julia pointedly added, "As am I."

Gavin's eyelashes sprang upwards until they lay nearly parallel with his brows and his jaw dropped slightly. Then, unexpectedly, Gavin began to laugh. It was the laugh of someone finally getting the joke, and chortling in appreciation at having been momentarily fooled.

The laughing stopped when, thanks to Julia's solemn facial expression, Gavin realized that she were not fooling.

He swallowed hard, raising both arms as if to beseech Julia, "Surely, you cannot be serious. Why, your father, and his father, and his father before him, they've all been peers for generations."

"It is my mother's family who were the Jews." Julia added. "That is why I refused to marry you."

"Oh." Gavin awkwardly replaced his hands atop the desk, linking his fingers. "Oh." He cleared his throat, momentarily looking away from Julia and up at the mantel above his fireplace. A stack of social invitations lay neatly organized by date of reception. Finally, he asked, "But surely, might it not have been better for all concerned for your cousin to have kept such inflammatory information to herself?"

"Miriam loved her husband. She did not relish the idea of deceiving him. And she believed it when he claimed to love her in return. Foolishly, she assumed it to mean that he would continue loving her, regardless. After all, Miriam remained the same woman after her confession as she had always been. Only the assumptions had changed, not the person."

"Do you truly believe that, Julia?"

He asked her the question she had been wrestling with since Collin maliciously punctured her previously settled existence.

A few months ago, she might have been unable to answer either way. But no longer. Not after Jamie.

"Yes, Gavin," Julia's voice carried not a seedling of doubt. "I do. I believe that who you truly are cannot alter simply due to some external circumstance, or another's change of perception."

"I see." Gavin appeared so serious, Julia half expected him to begin taking notes on their exchange. He continued nodding his head up and down. For a moment, Julia imagined she could almost see Gavin pulling further and further away from her, until he was nothing but a speck along the background of his office chair.

Salome and Moses had warned Julia to expect such a reaction from strangers, but from her oldest, dearest friend? She refused to believe Gavin capable of such narrowmindedness. And yet, perhaps that wasn't entirely true. After all, if Julia had not feared exactly this response from Gavin, why then had she taken such pains to hide the truth from him all these past months?

Considering who he was and where they were, Gavin, truly, could not have been expected to react in any other manner.

"I am sorry, Gavin."

"So am I, Julia. Good-bye."

Doubting he would understand that she were not apologizing for her existence, but for the awkward situation that she'd put him in, Julia turned and walked out of his house. She had no business dragging yet another innocent party into her family problems. Especially not when the reasons behind those problems caused such a tongue-tying unease.

But here, again, Julia had fallen into the erroneous trap

of assuming that every man might prove as understanding, and as kind as Jamie Lowell.

Once back in her own home, Julia knew that she should be feeling horrified by what had transpired. After all, Gavin's behavior screamed an indication of how everyone else would react when they found out the truth. Julia was not foolish enough to believe that he might keep such explosive information to himself. Even if Gavin found that a barrister/client relationship forbade him from running through the countryside, shouting the news, then, surely, Emma would be more than happy to perform the honors.

At the end of a fortnight, everyone who was anyone would know of Julia's deception. And she supposed she should be feeling terror-stricken at the prospect. But she wasn't.

The only thing Julia felt was giddy with freedom.

Because she knew that now neither Gavin nor anyone else with a penchant for looking down their noses would ever be able to hold anything over Julia's head again. She had confronted her biggest fear, and, in the aftermath, the Earth still continued to spin, the ground did not open up and swallow her, and England had not yet crumbled into the sea. Julia had faced the thing she feared most, and nothing horrible happened.

She was free.

And that left only one more terror for her to conquer.

Flushed with feeling that she could do anything at this moment, Julia hollered for Isaac to hurry and fetch her carriage. Julia was going after Jamie.

And she was going to ask him to stay.

Easier said than done.

It was one thing to fly out of her house, shouting battle cries, and urging for Isaac to make her horses gallop faster. It were quite another to seek out a single man, one as adept at keeping a low profile as Jamie, in a country the size of England.

Julia recalled him mentioning something about America. Well, the only way to reach America was by ship. And the nearest port was Bristol.

* * *

Standing on the wooden planks of a seaside dock for the second time in two days, Julia noted that she was no longer nearly as affected by the smell of rotting fish. In fact, it stirred up all sorts of pleasant memories.

Looking about, Julia searched for the vessel she needed. If luck were with her, she might spot one on the hull of which was written in large letters, "This is the boat to America." But, somehow, Julia doubted the probability of such convenient fortune.

Instead, she settled for moving from sailor to sailor, inquiring whether they'd seen any man fitting Jamie's description. The answers Julia received were most colorful in nature. She made a mental note to write them down and inquire of Jamie as to their meaning, although Julia doubted the bulk of them would be quite appropriate at Almack's.

Of course, after Gavin got through spreading the news, Julia doubted she would be receiving many vouchers for the Wednesday night gatherings. It was just as well. Their tea was tepid, their lemonade sour, and the cakes stale.

"You are a bloody fool." The voice came from above, but it was a sound Julia would have recognized anywhere.

Shielding her eyes from the sun, she peered towards the sky. Halfway up, Jamie stood on one step, holding on tightly to a second rung of a rope ladder that dangled from the deck of his ship down to the water.

Julia shouted, "I am the fool? You are climbing up one side of a boat when there is a perfectly decent gangplank available, and I am the bloody fool?"

"What are you doing here, Julia?"

"Expanding my vocabulary." She indicated the ladder. "What are you doing?"

"Combatting boredom," he said. "Ship does not leave until sundown, and I have nowheres else to go."

"You can afford a hotel. What with all the money I gave—"

Julia never got a chance to finish her sentence, as Jamie unexpectedly let go of the rope, and changing direction in mid-air, dove down towards the water. He surfaced a few moments later, shimmying up a wooden pole and onto the dock, and clamping a hand over Julia's mouth.

"Have you lost your senses? Do you wish for me to have my throat cut in the middle of the night, is that why you came?"

She pushed him away, feeling the slimy droplets of algae-infested water dripping down her cheeks and neck. "If you had purchased a ticket on a decent vessel, one that caters to people with some means, instead of this floating rat boardinghouse, you would not need to worry about such things."

"I have no intention of squandering my earnings. I worked most hard for them. Didn't I, Julia?"

She refused to let him bait her. Instead, Julia said, "I came down here to look for you, Jamie."

"The vocabulary extension was just a fringe benefit?"

"I came down because I realized that there was something I forgot to ask you before you left."

"And what may that be, m'lady?"

"I forgot to ask you if you would please, for me, consider ..." She gathered all her courage. "If you would consider staying."

There. She'd done it. Julia had done exactly what Jamie demanded. Now he had no more excuses.

"Why?"

"I beg your pardon?"

"Why this sudden change of heart?"

"Because ... Jamie ... I love you." This was exactly what Julia had so feared. The only reason Jamie wanted her to ask was so that he could reject her.

"I don't believe you," he said simply. "Something must have happened to make you change your mind."

"Well, yes, something." She told him of her afternoon encounter with Gavin.

"Ah." Jamie nodded his head, beginning to understand. "So you think, now that your future in the *ton* is thoroughly ruined, you might as well settle for me, since, clearly, no one better is likely to come along now."

"No, Jamie. It isn't like that all."

"That's right. Because you are laboring under a mistaken assumption. Gavin will tell no one what you confessed. It would make him look too much the fool. Everyone knows how he loved you. He wouldn't embarrass himself in such a manner. And he certainly will not tell Emma, and give her the ammunition to taunt him with." Jamie, patronizing, patted her hand. "So you need not worry, Julia. Your reputation is safe. You do not need me, after all."

"But, I do. I do need you." Julia all but jumped up and down on the dock to emphasize her point. "What can I say to make you believe me, Jamie?"

20

I love you, Jamie. I want you to stay with me."

"I do not wish to be any woman's second choice, Julia. I am not a consolation prize."

"You do not understand."

"No. I understand too well. This morning, you failed to make up your mind whether or not you wanted me to stay. You had a choice—me or Gavin."

"Not you or Gavin. I do not want Gavin."

"All right then, me or someone of Gavin Neff's ilk. Is that better?" Jamie continued, "And you chose him— them. It is not my fault that when you confessed your secrets, the pompous prig could only cough and sputter in reply. You are afraid. You think that he would tell all to your society chums among the *ton*, and that they would turn their backs on you. You panicked. Suddenly, the prospect of living out the rest of your days alone and ostracized did not seem nearly as appealing. So," Jamie said, "you decided to fall back on the one person you'd made do with before. You came after me. Only I am tired of hanging about your table, begging for scraps. I will not be a replacement. Not for any man. Not for any woman. Not even for you."

"You think that I came to you because Gavin turned me away?"

"What else could I think, Julia? What else could all

your combined actions over the last months possibly lead
me to think?"

"I know," she said. "I have treated you dreadfully,
Jamie. I realized as much while we were still in France."

"Then why did you not say anything? What is more,
why did you continue behaving in such a manner?"

"Because . . ." Julia looked away. The wind whipping at
her hair made Julia's curls dance wildly behind her head.
Strands blew into her mouth, but she wiped them away, indifferent, and continued talking. "I was scared, Jamie."

"Scared? Of me? What was there for Miss Julia
Highsmith to fear from a piece of trash like me?"

"You are not trash, Jamie. You are a kind, caring, brilliant, gentle man. And that, I am sorry to say, is why I
feared you so."

"Ah." Jamie nodded thoughtfully. "Kind, caring, brilliant, gentle. And what rotten character traits those are."

In spite of herself, Julia's lips twisted into the faintest of
smiles. She confessed, "It sounds foolish, I know. But, often, I suspected that I might have been happier if you were
a lout and a boor. At least then, I would not have been so
sorely tempted to fall in love with you."

"Would that really have been so terrible?"

"For me, yes, it would have. Falling in love would be
the most dangerous thing that could ever happen to me.
Because then I might be seduced into revealing all. And
such a revelation might prove the death of me."

He'd never thought about it in that way. Julia did speak
some sense. A slipped word to the wrong individual, and
life as she knew it could very easily be brought to a
screeching halt. Like him, Julia lived in constant fear of
discovery. But, unlike him, should she receive a life sentence, there would never even be the possibility of a pa-
role. The ladies and gentlemen of the *ton* were an
unforgiving lot.

"But why in the world did you confess to Gavin, then?"

"Because of you."

"Me?"

"You were so sympathetic when I told you of Miriam
and Alexia's plight. Why, you even risked your life to help

them. Naive little fool that I am, I thought perhaps I have been wrong all these years. Maybe my mother's and Uncle Collin's and Salome's fears have poisoned my mind against other people. Maybe the prejudice out there is not as insidious as everyone claims. After all, you did not call me names, or accuse me of stealing holy wafers that are the body of Christ and slicing them with knives."

"I may only be an uneducated sot from the East End, Julia, but even I never believed the rumor that Jews have nothing better to do with their days than torture bits of cookie."

"I know. Unfortunately, I made the mistake of assuming that Gavin would be as generous an individual as you. I was wrong."

Jamie rubbed his hands together. Water still dripped from both shirt sleeves, and his pretending to be busy wringing them out, gave Jamie the time to think, and the excuse to avoid looking Julia in the eye.

Unable to bear his silence, Julia pressed on. "So, you see, it does not matter to me if Gavin keeps silent or not. The moment I confessed all to him, I felt as if a great weight had been lifted off my shoulders. I no longer had anything to hide, so I no longer had anything to fear. I was free. Free to live my life as I wished, unencumbered by the presumptions of others. Free to go after you without the paralyzing fear of rejection, because, finally, I believed myself strong enough to be vulnerable. You gave that to me, Jamie. You, not Gavin. All he did was allow me the chance to put your theories to the test."

"Then why did you not stop me from leaving this morning?"

"Because I was a silly, frightened fool."

"And now?"

"Now I am still a silly, frightened fool. Only this morning, I was afraid that you might accept my offer. And now I am afraid that you might reject it."

"What if you change your mind?"

Julia repeated dumbly, "Change my mind?"

"Yes. Listen to yourself, Julia. You just said this morning you felt one way, this afternoon you feel another. God

only knows what this evening might bring. Consistency
has never been your strongest character trait." Jamie mimicked Julia's voice, "No, Mr. Lowell, I will not dance the
waltz with you. Yes, Mr. Lowell, I will dance the waltz
with you."

Julia's eyes grew large with indignation. "Surely, you
will not judge my current statements on the basis of such
. . . frivolity. How can you believe me to be so fickle and
capricious a creature?"

Jamie shrugged, "Convince me otherwise, Julia. Offer
me an example of consistency in your behavior."

The look on Julia's face indicated that, even in her wildest dreams, she had never dreamed he might prove so difficult. But Jamie felt he had to be. Julia's constant
rejection had worked him into such a state that Jamie now
categorically, absolutely, refused to go with her until he
felt thoroughly convinced that she would never turn her
back on him again. He was not asking such difficult questions merely to tease or taunt her. Those games had long
ago moved to a part of their past. The only reason Jamie
was asking Julia such difficult questions was because he,
for his own peace of mind, badly needed to hear her answers.

Julia waved her arms in the air, desperately searching
for an adequate example. "I—I—I held to our initial bargain, did I not? You received the money I promised. Every
farthing."

"Our contract was for the period of one year. You termi-
nated it at the end of three months."

She rolled her eyes. "I was being kind. Surely, you are
not going to hold my own kindness against me?"

He shook his head, and redefined, "You were changing
your mount mid-horse-race, again."

Julia looked ready to scream.

So that was exactly what she did. Throwing back her
head, Julia let out a howl of frustration so loud, a handful
of sailors turned to stare queerly. Julia ignored them.

Inwardly, Jamie smiled. At least Julia had told him the
truth about her no longer fearing what other people might
think.

She demanded, "How can I convince you of my sincerity, Jamie? How can I make you believe that I truly, truly mean it when I say that I want you to come back with me. To stay. For good."

She covered her face with her hands, inhaling deeply and racking her brain for the perfect bit of proof that might convince Jamie once and for all.

And, despite all of his resistance, inside of Jamie beat a heart that, with every knock against his chest, ached for some simple honest truths from Julia.

In point of fact, he even wondered who wanted it more, Julia to convince him, or Jamie to be convinced.

Finally, she dropped her hands to her sides. A peaceful smile illuminated Julia's face. Calmly, she told Jamie, "I know how I may convince you. But it requires your coming with me. I wish to show you something."

"My ship departs tonight. I have already paid for passage."

"Give me a single afternoon, Jamie. If you still wish to leave the country at the end of that afternoon, I will personally purchase you a replacement ticket. First class, so that you need not fear getting your throat cut. What have you to lose?"

Isaac smiled broadly when he saw Julia returning to the carriage with Jamie in tow. Yet, his expression darkened ever so slightly when Julia whispered their next destination into his ear.

"Isaac," Jamie reached up, in a horrible breech of standard protocol, to shake the footman's hand. "How wonderful to see you again. How long has it been? Three, four hours?"

He did not know where Julia was planning to take him, except that the roads they moved along on were all decorated with signs hammered onto posts that pointed to London.

Jamie and Julia sat facing each other inside the carriage, neither saying a word. Jamie, still wet, and now also cold from his spontaneous swimming exhibition, blew on his hands, trying to stay warm. Silently, Julia reached across, wrapping both her palms around his fingers and rubbing gently.

God, but how he wanted to believe her. He yearned to believe her. But, still, there were those nagging doubts.

Jamie did not—could not—believe that Julia sincerely loved him. What, after all, was there to love?

On the one hand, hundreds of women had already fallen for Jamie's charms in the past. But that had been different. They fell not for the true man, but for the fiction he'd created. Their love for him was based on an illusion he'd personally created.

But Julia knew the real Jamie Lowell. She knew him better than any other woman ever had. And she proclaimed to love him anyway. That was what Jamie could not understand.

He did not recognize the part of London that Julia ordered Isaac to drive through, and Jamie grew even more confused as they approached a large wooden gate that seemed to stretch for blocks in either direction. Through the gate bustled what, to Jamie, resembled an entirely walled-in city.

And then he recognized why this were an area of the capitol Jamie had never been to.

He turned to Julia, whispering, "This is the Jewish ghetto."

She nodded. "No need to hush your voice, Jamie. They know where they live."

Slowly, Isaac maneuvered his carriage through the gate, trotting the horses at a lesser than average pace, so as to avoid the holes in the road, and the crowd of people milling about in too small a space. Inside, boys and men, all to the last wearing small hats that, to Jamie, resembled Catholic cardinal caps, pushed and shoved through the crowds. Some pulled barrows heaped with fruits and vegetables, some carts with rags.

Others, from the sagging bags of coins tied to their belts, Jamie recognized as the money lenders who plied their trade in the shadows of fine gentlemen's gambling clubs. And they did not look nearly as sinister in the day as they did in the night.

Isaac continued maneuvering their carriage through the tight and crowded streets, hissing in a language Jamie could not understand for those who got too close to keep their distance. He stopped at the door of a two-story building in the center of the ghetto, the upper level of which was dominated by a large, six-point star, carved from wood and mounted on the western wall.

Julia beckoned for Jamie to follow her inside. He climbed reluctantly out of the carriage, looking down at the mess he'd made of his clothes, and wishing that he had chosen to keep some of the more proper coats and shirts Julia bought for him.

Indoors, the sole illumination for the synagogue came from its nine windows. Obviously, gas lights had yet to make their appearance in this part of town. Twelve pews, in two rows of six, stretched from the front door to the altar. If it weren't for the desk tops jutting from the backs of the benches—and the lack of a large cross at the head— Jamie might have thought he were in a rather poor, unadorned, country church.

Julia explained about the desks. "The synagogue is also used as a school for boys during the week."

"Oh," Jamie said. "Well, now that I understand that, all I need to know is why we are here."

"Sit down and wait," Julia indicated the front pew. "And you might want to cover your head while we are here."

As Julia disappeared through a back door by the altar, Jamie searched high and low for a little hat like he had seen other men wear outside. But there were none to spare.

He picked up one of the prayer books lying in a box in the corner, but could not recognize a single letter. Not only that, but the text seemed to run from right to left, instead of left to right, like in normal volumes.

"Jamie," Julia kept her voice low, although they were the only ones there. She emerged from the back room, leading by the hand an elderly man with a long white beard and stooped shoulders, who shuffled his feet one ahead of the other in his walk towards Jamie.

"This is Rabbi Mennahem Mendelson," Julia said. "He will be performing our wedding ceremony."

Jamie did not know what to say.

A lump rose in his throat as the full significance of Julia's actions became clear. She was taking a terrible risk, going into the ghetto in daylight. Anyone could see her either entering or departing, and raise all sorts of awkward questions. And yet Julia was willing to take such a chance, so that she could prove to Jamie the truth of her words.

The rabbi explained to Jamie, "I will be performing the ceremony in the holy language of the Jews. All that I require of you, my son, is a confirmation. After I have finished reciting the prayers, you must give your consent to this marriage by answering with a single word. The word amen."

"Amen?" Jamie asked in surprise. "But, I—people say that in church. How can that be the language of the Jews?"

The rabbi and Julia exchanged smiles.

He said, "It is a combination of two of our words, Mr. Lowell. Ani, which means I. And me'ameen, which means believe. Ani me'ameen. I believe."

He beckoned Jamie and Julia towards the altar, underneath a piece of cloth stretched between four posts. Both silently took their places. The rabbi produced a small, well-worn, leather covered book from out of one pocket, and solemnly began to read, or, rather, to chant, out loud.

"Do you believe me now?" Julia whispered in counterpoint to the ceremony. "Do you believe me, Jamie, when I say that I love you? When I say that I want you to stay with me for good? No matter what happens with me in the ton, no matter what Gavin does or does not do. Do you believe me when I say that I do not take the vows I make in this wedding ceremony lightly, and that I intend to be a good wife to you in every sense of the word?"

The rabbi was coming to the end of his prayer. He turned, expectantly, to Jamie and gestured that it were his turn to speak.

It was now or never.

So Jamie Lowell, the fictitious marquis of Martyn, took a deep breath, and, turning from the rabbi to Julia, he took her hand in his, and softly said, "Amen."

EPILOGUE

"They don't like the English very much in America, do they?" Julia leaned against the ship's rail, tilting her head to prevent the warm summer wind from playfully tossing her hair back in her face, and looked out at the water, noting how their vessel's narrowed tip seemed to slice every wave neatly in two.

"Especially titled English." Jamie wrapped both his arms about Julia's waist, pressing her back to his chest, and lightly kissing the top of her head. "I believe they hang them. But perhaps that was only during their revolution."

"In the interest of not reliving our first meeting, I suppose you shall have to stop playing the marquis, and become simply Mr. Jamie Lowell again."

"Thank goodness," he turned her around so that Julia might face him. She raised one hand to shield her eyes from the sun. "I was growing rather weary of being bowed to. Made me think the poor chaps had dropped something."

Julia laughed and rested both her arms against Jamie's chest, smoothing down the buttons of his shirt. "I am glad that we could stay long enough to witness Aunt Salome's wedding. Just think of it, Jamie. She and the marquis even beat our record for speedy marriage. Only my aunt could

214

arrange an entire wedding ceremony and celebration breakfast in a single fortnight."

"Tell me something." Jamie cradled Julia's hands between his, rubbing her fingers with his thumbs and bringing first one palm, then the other to his lips. "Why can no one woman in your family simply get married like a regular person?"

"Whatever do you mean?"

"What is this fascination you seem to possess with striking marital deals? Did you know that Salome had agreed to wed the marquis in exchange for my temporarily borrowing his title?"

"Not a word, Jamie, I swear it."

He clicked his tongue against his teeth, playfully chastising, "There I am, dueling for my life, and she had already arranged for it all beforehand."

"It was the only way that the marquis would agree to go along with us. He never did gracefully accept Salome's turning down his proposal all those years ago." Shivering slightly, Julia slipped Jamie's arms about her shoulders, pressing her cheek against his chest, and sighing contentedly. "I am so glad that Salome found someone to take care of her and Alexia. And if I ever worried about Henri de Mornay returning to cause trouble, well, the marquis of Martyn is most certainly a match for any man, wouldn't you say?"

"Walking stick and all." Jamie mimed ducking one of the old man's notoriously wild swings. "Although, considering that letter Henri sent, damning us all to hell, I doubt that he shall be taking much of a future interest in Alexia."

"Thank God for that. Miriam can finally rest in peace."

Jamie took a step back, pensively studying Julia at arm's length, and, repeated the same question he'd been parroting ever since they'd climbed aboard. "You are certain then, that this is what you want? Leaving England and your family and your life?"

"I was the one who suggested it, after all."

"I hope it isn't Gavin that's driving you away, because all you need do is say the word, and I can arrange a chat with Lord Neff to insure his never so much as thinking of opening his mouth to disgrace you and Salome. I can be very persuasive when I want to be, you know that, luv."

"Oh, that I do indeed." She laughed gaily, remembering both the instances he'd proven as much, and Jamie's delicious attempt to teach her the tricks of the trade. "But, truly, this is what I want. I am so tired of pretending, and I know that you are as well. If it weren't for Salome's marriage, I would have felt perfectly content to confess everything to the *ton*. But I will not embarrass the marquis of Martyn in such a manner." Julia swore, "I want us to start a new life. No history, no lies, no bargains. Just you and I, Jamie."

He still looked unconvinced, head cocked to one side, lips crinkling and sliding toward the left of his face. Julia wondered how she might assure Jamie of her sincerity in swearing that, truly, as long as he were beside her, she did not care where they lived, or if she ever saw London again.

"I could have gone on pretending. I do not want you giving up the life you love, for me," Jamie insisted.

"But it is you that I love, Jamie. More than everything else put together."

His eyes lit up at her oft-repeated declaration, filling Julia with pleasure at the thought of being able to make him so happy. But, just as quickly as the merriment bloomed within his features, it faded away, leaving only guilt and failure.

Awkwardly, Jamie struggled to second her emotion, finally needing to explain, "I am ever so sorry, Julia. But I have sworn false sentiments to so many women in my time, that now I cannot chance on a single untainted word worthy of my feelings for you. I want to tell the world how much you mean to me. Yet, I am afraid that the right word simply does not exist in the English language."

Undaunted, she assured, "Then we shall make it up ourselves."

He smiled at her determination.

"Or ..." Jamie playfully tapped one finger against Julia's lips, then touched it to his own mouth. "Perhaps it might be best if we simply act the feeling out for all to guess at."

"A game of charades?" Julia laughed and reached for him. "Why, Mr. Lowell, what a splendid idea."

And, by the time her arms finally slipped around Jamie's neck, the act he'd already imagined so many times felt sweetly and wonderfully familiar.

Avon Regency Romance

SWEET FANCY
by Sally Martin   77398-8/$3.99 US/$4.99 Can

LUCKY IN LOVE
by Rebecca Robbins   77485-2/$3.99 US/$4.99 Can

A SCANDALOUS COURTSHIP
by Barbara Reeves   72151-1/$3.99 US/$4.99 Can

THE DUTIFUL DUKE
by Joan Overfield   77400-3/$3.99 US/$4.99 Can

TOURNAMENT OF HEARTS
by Cathleen Clare   77432-1/$3.99 US/$4.99 Can

DEIRDRE AND DON JUAN
by Jo Beverley   77281-7/$3.99 US/$4.99 Can

THE UNMATCHABLE MISS MIRABELLA
by Gillian Grey   77399-6/$3.99 US/$4.99 Can

FAIR SCHEMER
by Sally Martin   77397-X/$3.99 US/$4.99 Can

THE MUCH MALIGNED LORD
by Barbara Reeves   77332-5/$3.99 US/$4.99 Can

THE MISCHIEVOUS MAID
by Rebecca Robbins   77336-8/$3.99 US/$4.99Can

...oy... this book,
*take advantage
of this special offer.*
Subscribe now and get a

FREE
Historical
Romance

No Obligation (a $4.50 value)

Each month the editors of True Value select the four *very best* novels from America's leading publishers of romantic fiction. Preview them in your home *Free* for 10 days. With the first four books you receive, we'll send you a FREE book as our introductory gift. No Obligation!

   If for any reason you decide not to keep them, just return them and owe nothing. If you like them as much as we think you will, you'll pay just $4.00 each and save $.50 each off the cover price. (Your savings are *guaranteed* to be at least $2.00 each month.) There is NO postage and handling – or other hidden charges. There are no minimum number of books to buy and you may cancel at any time.

**Send in
the Coupon
Below**

To get your FREE historical romance fill out the coupon below and mail it today. As soon as we receive it we'll send you your FREE Book along with your first month's selections.

Mail To: **True Value Home Subscription Services, Inc., P.O. Box 5235
120 Brighton Road, Clifton, New Jersey 07015-5235**

YES! I want to start previewing the very best historical romances being published today. Send me my FREE book along with the first month's selections. I understand that I may look them over FREE for 10 days. If I'm not absolutely delighted I may return them and owe nothing. Otherwise I will pay the low price of just $4.00 each: a total $16.00 (at least an $18.00 value) and save at least $2.00. Then each month I will receive four brand new novels to preview as soon as they are published for the same low price. I can always return a shipment and I may cancel this subscription at any time with no obligation to buy even a single book. In any event the FREE book is mine to keep regardless.

Name		
Street Address		Apt. No.
City	State	Zip
Telephone		
Signature		Terms and prices subject to change. Orders subject to acceptance by True Value Home Subscription Services, Inc.
(if under 18 parent or guardian must sign)		**77811-4**